CHASING GHOSTS

M.K. Hardy

Published by
NineStar Press
PO Box 91792
Albuquerque, New Mexico, 87199
www.ninestarpress.com

Warning: This book contains sexually explicit content, which is only suitable for mature readers, and references to alcohol addiction.

Print ISBN # 978-1-947139-56-5
Cover by Natasha Snow
Edited by Elizabeth Coldwell

Nic is a successful ghost writer, making a decent living churning out best-selling autobiographies of celebrities and other notable figures. She's also a recovering alcoholic—three years sober and still tempted, every day, to open the bottle again.

Luckily she has distractions—this time in the form of Isobel DeWitt, an award-winning and well-loved actor in her prime, who has decided to release a tell-all autobiography. Nic finds her likeable, charming and fascinating...but also impossible to crack. Every draft sounds like just another magazine piece full of perfectly crafted sound bytes, but there's no soul.

Undeterred, Nic continues to dig into the actor's history in search of the clue that will unlock it all and finds it in the form of one Melody Graham, a reclusive playwright and, if rumours are to be believed, Isobel's erstwhile lover. Nic chances everything to reach out to her and unbelievably she responds, sharing stories about her time with the tempestuous actress and helping Nic get further and further into Isobel's head. The problem now is figuring out where Isobel Dewitt starts and Nic ends...

Chapter One

"HI, MY NAME is Nicola, and I'm an alcoholic."

Not much of a way to begin a story, is it? But as James, my agent, always says, "truth is what makes the story." On the other hand, my sponsor Mary likes to tell me to "be honest with yourself and screw the rest of them." Either way, you can't get any more truthful than that, can you?

"It's been two years since my last drink."

I was sitting in a dingy church hall on a flimsy folding chair, surrounded by people who looked as if they've been chewed up and spat out by Fate like disused pieces of chewing gum on the pavement. Some of them couldn't even bring their eyes up to meet the gazes of their fellow addicts. Instead, they focused on the streaked wooden floor, following the whorls and gouges with their bloodshot eyes. I didn't recognize all the faces; for every regular there was a newcomer, who more likely than not would come for one, maybe two weeks before disappearing off the map in a haze of empty vodka bottles, never to be seen again. Sometimes on my weaker days, it made me angry to see them, knowing by looking at them that they wouldn't be back next week, and hating them for being weak enough to succumb. Just like I wanted to.

You're supposed to share your story at these meetings, but that wasn't really why we were here, was it? You don't want to hear my story. Nobody does. There's a reason my name never shows up on the front jacket—why if you read between the lines of each tell-all memoir you won't find me mentioned there. It's because I'm very good at my job, you see. I can draw out even the most reluctant person, put their words, their life down on paper so that the masses can't help but want to read it, and the supposed author can't help but rake in the cash. So I hope you don't mind if I just give you the bare highlights of my own life—my name might be all over this, but it still really isn't my story.

The smattering of half-hearted applause at my testimony had stopped now, and I was talking again. I was sharing my experiences of the past week—the times I'd wanted to drink, the times I'd been glad of the clarity I now had... You don't need the details.

The truth was I could do without the clarity. Clarity, if you ask me, is overrated. I wasn't sober because it made me clear-headed or better able to deal with my day-to-day life—honestly, I was a high-functioning drunk. That's the thing about a Calling—you don't have to be sober to be able to do your job. I could write just as well—maybe better—when I was drunk. I met my deadlines, I made meetings when I had to, my cat never went hungry, and I was never the type to get into fights or wake up in a gutter because, like all good alcoholics, I drank alone, at home.

No, to be brutally honest, I got on the wagon because when I hit thirty I was starting to develop a slight gut, and that's not attractive on anyone. And believe me, some days I wish I had just switched to gin and slimline, but here I am now and so here I stay. Never let it be said I don't see a story through till the bitter end.

After the meeting finished, the group disbanded, drifting away from each other like autumn leaves pushed by a capricious breeze. There was a table set up with orange juice, tea, and biscuits; some of the newcomers lingered there, hoping to meet kindred spirits who would reassure them that everything's okay and it'll just get easier with time. The regulars knew better.

Me, I picked up my sleek black laptop bag and hoisted it over my shoulder, exchanging curt nods with a few people before heading for the door. I wasn't in full Bitch Mode, which on a normal day meant I might stop and exchange pleasantries, but I'd got a meeting to get to across town and not a lot of time. Chances were I'd probably be late. Why didn't I just skip the meeting, go to a later one, you ask. To which I reply: you've never been an addict, have you?

I grabbed a taxi as soon as I could, promising the driver a generous tip if he could get me to my destination by four o'clock. That's the other thing about having a Calling—you can make plenty of money doing it. I have even more now that it doesn't all go on booze and mixers, but it mainly just sits in my bank account or occasionally serves to entice cab drivers to get me where I'm going on time.

Don't get me wrong. I'm not saying that what I do is necessarily what I saw myself doing when I majored in Creative Writing at college (you don't really care where, do you?). My starry-eyed teenaged self thought I was going to be the next Kerouac, or the next Tartt, or at worst the next Stephen King. I think my younger self would probably want to knife me in my sleep if she saw me trampling all over her dreams of renown and accolade, making a tidy little profit without my name ever appearing on a single dust jacket.

It's still writing, though. It scratches that eternal itch. And I'll tell you what, it's satisfying, in its own way—getting into someone's head, finding their voice, putting their life into their own words when they can't make that transfer from mind to page for themselves. I'm like a conduit—weirdly, I feel connected to them. It's an addictive sensation in its own right, and I am, after all, an addict.

Some people go from vice to vice, trying to find something that fills in that emptiness. I knew a guy in the early nineties who, after nearly killing himself on a five-year bender, sobered up almost overnight only to begin falling into bed with a different person each evening. What alcohol couldn't accomplish, AIDS did. When you look at it like that, my way doesn't seem so bad, does it?

We got to the hotel at five past four—even though we were technically late, I still gave the driver his promised tip. It wasn't as if he had any control over London traffic, after all. I slid out of the cab, barely looking around to check my surroundings before heading inside. I have a lot of meetings at hotels, so I'm well acquainted with them—the plush beige carpets, the myriad mirrors, the waxy, sunlight-starved pot plants. These initial meetings are always in the bar, so perhaps it's unsurprising that I ended up the way I did. Liquor is a natural lubricant; it gets peoples' tongues wagging. Even now, hours before dinner time, the bar was half full, cluttered with businessmen soothing their jetlag with a pint of ale, nervous tourists tittering over a glass of merlot.

I caught sight of myself in the mirror behind the bar. It's a rule, in writing—you have to tell the reader who they're looking at. Never mind the picture on the cover, they want to be reminded of the sparkling blue eyes, the crisp white smile, the smooth, even tan. And you won't be seeing my picture, so I suppose I ought to lubricate my own descriptive skills with a bit of introspection. Not that I'm going to tell you what you want to hear.

See, unsurprisingly I guess, I'm about as ordinary-looking as it gets. I'm about average height, maybe a little over but not enough to be tall.

I'm average weight—maybe a bit extra on the hips and thighs from time to time; it comes and goes. My eyes and hair are a mid-brown that's neither particularly drab nor particularly inspiring—my hair pretty much lives in a perpetually slightly dishevelled ponytail. I'm the kind of pale that you only get by staying indoors most of the time, summer or winter, and only holidaying to northern European cities that don't require you to wear sunscreen or mosquito repellent. My wardrobe is mostly brown, black, and navy. I don't wear rings and my ears aren't pierced. I'm basically the definition of a cipher.

I didn't start out that way—I am told by reliable though biased sources that I was a very pretty little girl. And I went through all the normal teenage rebellion phases—heavy eyeliner, dyed hair, outrageous clothes (though who could live through the eighties and *not* claim fashion victimhood?). But somehow, I ended up like this: a plain Jane, nondescript and unmemorable. Maybe it's the exterior reflecting the interior, since my job is more or less all that defines me these days. Or maybe it's just that spending so long in a drunken, intensely personal, and yet wholly impersonal haze erased all desire for self-expression. But if that's the case, why am I writing this? I honestly don't know. You tell me.

The woman I was there to meet wasn't hard to find. Unlike me, she was well-known enough to create a bubble of impermeability around her, one which no tipsy tourist or errant waiter was likely to overstep. And even if they didn't know who she was, she was striking in a way that caused people to stop and stare rather than come too close. And as used to celebrity as I am, I'll admit I hesitated for a moment before breaching that no man's land and approaching her table.

"Ms. Dewitt? Nicola Booth. Sorry I'm late."

"Oh, are you?" she said politely, in that tone where it was obvious she'd noticed and was pretending not to—which I hate, by the way.

"Yep," I said, tamping down the urge to roll my eyes as I took a seat opposite her at the table. *Lord, save me from the well-meaning ones— give me a stone-cold bitch any day. They're so much more fun.* "Anyway, I've just got a few questions before we get started. I assume your agent told you what I'll be doing?"

"Well, I know what a ghostwriter does, of course, but I'm sure you all have your own methods..."

"Sure." I sat back in my chair, nodding. "A lot of writers like to pore through articles, past interviews, watch appearances on Jay Leno, that sort of thing. Really bumps up the research fee."

She raised an eyebrow—just the one. You know how in books everyone can do that? I'll tell you what, not everyone can do that. "And you?" she said in this arch tone and I'm not sure whether it's getting my back up or turning me on.

Not wanting to give her the satisfaction of watching me jump through any of her little hoops, I turned, motioning for the single waiter who's loitering by the bar. He hurried over, more for her sake than mine, I knew, and I ordered a mineral water with lemon before looking back to Ms. Isobel Dewitt with all her arched eyebrow and perfect lips.

"I like to talk."

"To talk."

"Mm. I mean, yes. To talk. You're supposed to be telling your life story, right? So the best way to do that is to... talk about it. To me. I'll record it, take notes, ask questions...and then I'll whisk it all away and transform it into a bestselling account of your life." Maybe it sounds conceited, but trust me, it's true. I have never failed to turn out a book that exceeded the publisher's expectations, and I've even helped a few minor celebrities to climb the social ladder to better recognition.

The great Isobel Dewitt pursed her perfect lips and tossed her perfect hair and relaxed back in her chair with a nod. "All right. So when do we start?"

Well. This is it, then. "We can start right now," I told her, leaning over to pull my recorder out of my bag, then set it on the table between us. No time like the present. "Let's talk about what you want out of this book."

Chapter Two

Usually after an afternoon with a client, I would put the Dictaphone away for a couple of days, work on something else, go back to it with a fresh ear, as it were. That evening when I got in, though, I found myself pulling the recorder out and clicking it on. The first thing I heard was a warm, throaty chuckle.

"God, I don't know. You'd have to ask my agent that..."

Just that laugh, that voice, were enough to make me squirm in my seat, as I had right there in the hotel bar. It was no surprise she had "captured the hearts of millions"—the woman was basically sex on legs. There was a pause on the recording as I sipped my water, letting the sensation pass before I pressed on.

"C'mon, you can tell me. I'm not going to write anything you don't want published, remember? You have the last say in all of this."

The corners of Dewitt's mouth had twisted up, just a little more on one side than the other. "There are no secrets of my life I wouldn't have published."

"That'll make for a good book, then." Secretly I'd been disappointed—sure, it made my job easier, but I didn't always like an easy job.

"Oh, I don't know. People will read anything, right? Isn't that the principle?"

"So you don't think your life is worth reading about?"

God, even on the tape that chuckle of hers sent a shiver down her spine.

"Well, I was there, it kinda spoils the end." That accent of hers should've been annoying—the Americanized English of a Brit who's spent too long living in the States, and yet...

"We'll try to keep them in suspense as long as we can, hm?" I'd sipped my water again, surveying the other woman across the table. She was sitting there as cool and collected as could be, oblivious to the stares she was getting from everyone—men, women...everyone. I hated her a little bit for that, even as I was basking in it.

"Whatever you need. Do you want to start at the beginning, or just ask a question and go from there?"

"Let's just see where it takes us, shall we?"

AND GOD, WHERE it took us. One thing was for sure, Isobel Dewitt was a fascinating woman. Violin virtuoso by the age of fourteen, she'd toured Europe performing for several years before settling down at Cambridge University at seventeen to pursue English Literature and Philosophy, where she gained a first class degree. She then went on to model for several years for Storm Models before parlaying this into her first acting job, a turn as a down-on-her-luck waitress, which earned her recognition and several more film offers from production companies in both the States and the UK.

The next five years or so were a whirlwind of films both popular and critically acclaimed, awards, praise from all quarters, and in her early thirties, she'd decided to take another turn in her career to try her hand at directing.

"Of course you did." I couldn't keep every trace of sarcasm from my tone, no matter how hard I tried.

"I did! I completely failed. It was an utter mess." Dewitt talked with her hands, and they'd been all over now, describing the catastrophe that was her first directorial effort. "The only reason it wasn't completely panned was my reputation, and the cast."

"Oh, come on, it was a solid film," I found myself arguing. "Just because it wasn't the same runaway success as everything else in your perfect life..." I'll admit, I was prodding. Can't make an omelette, and so on.

"Oh, I know. It couldn't have come at a better time. I was almost out of control, and it brought me screeching to a halt," Dewitt said with a rueful smile and a shake of her head. "It made me stop and think about what I was doing, and—as wanky as this sounds—it made me think of what I wanted to *do* with myself and my directing."

"And that was when *Hearth and Home* happened."

"Yes. I don't know exactly how that happened, either—it was mostly pure luck. I mean, Melody Graham was a friend of mine from way back at Cambridge, and when I heard she had a script out, I begged her to be able to read it. And it was, of course, amazing. I knew I had to direct it."

I paused the tape—well, I say tape, but of course, I use a digital recorder now just like everyone else on the planet—and ran it back a few seconds.

"Melody Graham was a friend of mine from way back at Cambridge, and when I heard she had a script out, I begged her..."

Was it wishful thinking on my part, the slight warmth I heard creeping into Dewitt's voice there? In this day and age, of course, admission to same-sex collegiate affairs—for women, at least—was hardly front-page news any more. And in honesty, although that sort of thing's of interest to some, it's not the kind of book I write. Unless, of course, there was more to it than that. I chose to let it go.

"...begged her to be able to read it. And it was, of course, amazing. I knew I had to direct it."

There was the sound of me clearing my throat, then, "It was an interesting choice for you. You'd only made one period piece and that was *Front Line*, and there you were making a film about the Highland Clearances. Did it have some personal resonance for you, or...?"

"Something like that, yes," Dewitt replied thoughtfully. "There were branches of my family affected by the clearances, and beyond that, it's such a shock to me that more people don't know about them. I mean, you have thousands of families being displaced from their homes, forced to emigrate from the land of their birth. And all for the sake of money. I thought that *Hearth and Home* might bring some attention to this, and I'd be lying if I said I wasn't trying to draw attention to similar current practices around the world today."

"So you have some Scottish ancestry?"

God, what an inane question.

From there, the conversation devolved into a combing-over of Dewitt's ancestry; something that would probably get a page or two in the finished book but lasted a good twenty minutes, during which I finished my mineral water and ordered another. Dewitt was an animated speaker, bright and bubbly and thoroughly engaging. It wasn't hard to see why she was such a media darling, even as she entered her late thirties, a time when most women were being dropped in favour of younger, less "age-ravaged" specimens.

"But really, my connection was to the emotional truth of the story rather than the historical," she said as we turned back to the film.

"Well, that's...admirable." God, she was so *good*. Interesting without being pedantic, witty without being annoying, righteous without being saccharine. "The critics seemed to agree—you were nominated for Best Director and were a shoo-in to win in '99."

"Oh, I don't know..." I remember that Dewitt shrugged then, and even her shrug was this smooth, graceful gesture. "I wasn't surprised not to win."

"A lot of people were surprised for you, then. There was quite a backlash against John Davidson—did you two ever clash over that?"

Ever the pragmatist, it seems, Dewitt shook her head like the very idea confused her slightly. "He's a very talented director. And you know how the Oscars work anyway; he'd been robbed in '97."

Okay, let's get this straight: I'm not a dirt-digger. That's not my job, and it's not something I particularly enjoy. Celebrities are under enough scrutiny as it is, and the last person they need trying to trash them is their ghostwriter. That being said, there was nothing I wanted more right at that instant than to find *something* damning about Isobel Dewitt. Well, except a drink.

"I suppose you're right. And so after that, you did a series of films..."

I clicked the Dictaphone off, pulled out the memory card and stuck it into my laptop to transfer the recording across. The rest of our meeting had been more of the same—endlessly interesting from an intellectual point of view, and yet at the same time entirely impersonal. Of course, that was normal for a first meeting—you couldn't expect to delve into a person's private life before spending some time together, so I don't know why it surprised and frustrated me so much. I think maybe because at the time, she made everything *feel* so personal, so intimate. The way she talked about her own life—she pulled you into it with her, making you feel as though you'd been there, or at least as though she wished you had been.

In other words, she was a born storyteller. I was beginning to wonder what on earth she needed a ghost for.

Still, it was good for me—her agent and mine had agreed on a tidy fee, and the schedule was relaxed enough that I wasn't going to have to rush this one through. No, I'd have plenty of time to get to the bottom of Ms. Dewitt.

Now, however, was not the time. I needed to let things sit, percolate. I had another meeting scheduled with Dewitt in two days; I'd review my notes at some point before but needed something to take my mind off of things until then. Which meant of course that I had to come up with something to do with my time that wasn't writing. These days, that could be a bit of a struggle.

Eventually, I threw on my coat and went out café crawling.

Chapter Three

"CAFÉ CRAWLING" IS my version of "pub crawling." Except that I don't go to bars, I don't really "hop" so much as sit in one drinking tea, and I'm not trying to pick anyone up or get drunk, which is basically the only reason people actually go pub crawling. Other than that, it's just the same.

I drink a lot of caffeine nowadays. It's a stimulant, supposedly, but I don't feel it any more. It's not like I need it to wake up or to keep going during the day—it just doesn't affect me any more. Which is good, otherwise I'd probably be able to walk through walls, or up them, or something.

I had a few coffee houses on rotation to keep things fresh, and that evening I was visiting J+A—a tiny hidden gem of a place with good natural lighting and comfortable seating, as well as a massive wooden table that I'd never sat at. After all, as when I used to go to bars, I was almost always alone.

The light was just beginning to fade as I sat down, and one of the waiters was making his way around with tea lights—which I hate, by the way, because they provide next to no light and I always end up reaching over them and accidentally burning myself, even sober. He caught my eye and smiled, and I gave him a friendly nod as I fished my book out of my bag.

As is probably unsurprising, I spend a lot of time reading. Not fiction, though; I don't know why, but ever since I quit drinking I have almost a pathological aversion to reading anything that isn't absolutely, positively, 100 percent non-fiction. I tend to veer between historical accounts of battles or trade routes or religious sects and how-to books, which is great for making really dry dinner conversation. Right then, I was halfway through "The Divorced Dad's Handbook," which I had picked up for fifty pence at a charity shop two days before. It's a surprisingly interesting read. You'd think it would get me funny looks, but for people to look at me funny, they'd have to look at me at all, and, well, like I said before, I'm not much to look at.

Okay, so this evening was very boring, so rather than tell you about my coffee and reading extravaganza, let me tell you about my process. It's not quite as simple as I make it sound when I sum it up for clients. It's true I don't do what a lot of ghostwriters do and pull from past interviews and articles—it might be effective, but frankly, I think it's lazy and boring. I *do* read all the past material, obviously, since I need to know everything I can about the person I'm writing about. But I don't write from them.

Ultimately, every single word that I record on my Dictaphone gets transcribed and pored over—I immerse myself in my client's words, in their voice, until I almost feel as though I *become* them on some level. And it's not until then that I type a single word of my own.

See, it's not enough to be a good writer; I mean, obviously, you have to be able to turn a phrase, and translate between "casual chat over coffee" into "witty, scintillating prose". But there's more to it than that. You have to be able to draw people out, and even more so, you have to know what questions are going to lead to interesting, relevant stories.

On top of all that, of course, I have to make sure that nothing of my voice creeps in. These books aren't by Nicola Booth. It's vital that my writing takes on the right personality, and the only way I can do that is to immerse myself in it.

I know I'm really belabouring the whole immersion thing, but go with me. It's important.

So it won't be surprising if I tell you that the plan for the next day was an Isobel Dewitt film marathon. What better way to start immersing myself than watching as many samples from the Dewitt oeuvre as I could get my hands on? And for that, I planned to enlist the company of my best and only friend.

It takes a very good friend to stick with someone through many years of binge drinking and drunken mishaps, and an even better friend to stick with someone through two years of bitter sobriety. Julie was that good a friend for me.

She was *also* a huge film buff, and was always on hand when I was ghosting for someone in film to help me devour and get a handle on their work. And she worked freelance, so I could usually persuade her to take a day off for me, especially if I promised takeaway and first pick of seating on the most comfortable sofa known to man.

SHE HAD PROMISED to get to mine as early as she could, but as I had a lot of movies to get through, I didn't feel like waiting for her to show up before beginning. After an exciting breakfast of yogurt and some grapes, I retired to the sofa and pressed Play on Dewitt's first film, *Victoria Street*, which I had actually never seen before.

She wasn't in a lead role—the film itself was a sort of series of loose character sketches rather than a solid narrative, all taking place over the course of a single day on the eponymous street. Dewitt was the waitress in a café frequented by the lead characters as they went about their lives, the viewer piecing her story slowly together as they caught brief, scattered glances across the day.

Despite my hard-won cynicism, I enjoyed the film; it was well-shot and scripted, and the performances were solid. I could see how Dewitt had earned her acclaim too. Despite being in a minor role, she seemed to steal the scene whenever she was featured, even with a minimum of dialogue on her plate. I mean, sure, I was watching her with a closer scrutiny than most people would've, but I'm sure everybody else felt just as relieved as I did when Sophie, her character, threw off her apron at the end of the film and ran out into the lamp-lit street, looking impossibly lithe and gorgeous after a ten-hour shift. In some ways, she was the only character in the film who actually got to escape at the end, making her portrayal, although not in any way pivotal to the plot, a linchpin for the mood, providing a vital counterpoint that only highlighted the vicious circles the rest of the cast had found themselves trapped in.

It was just as the film was finishing that Julie arrived, using her spare key to let herself in. Leaning my head back, I arched an eyebrow (yes, all right, I can do it too) at her over the back of the sofa, watching as she disengaged various plastic bags and purses from her person like a fungus shedding spores.

"Hope you remembered the kitchen sink."

"Thought you had one of those," came the cheery response. Julie shrugged off her coat and then picked up a couple of plastic bags again. She took them through into the kitchen.

My flat is small. I mean, it's not like I need much space. It's a one-bedroom, with a decent-sized lounge so I have room for a home office, and that's about all there is to say about that. It's usually fanatically tidy—not because I much care about clutter but because I don't sleep too well and tidying is one of those activities that can be done at any time of day.

"You missed *Victoria Street*," I called to her then, propping my feet up on the coffee table in front of me. "I liked it."

"Hah, really? I thought it was wank," Julie called from the kitchen. I could hear her opening and closing drawers and cupboards looking for whatever she needed, even though she'd been in my kitchen a billion times and really ought to know where everything was by now.

"You think everything's wank." One of the many reasons we get along so well. "You have to admit Dewitt was good, at least."

"She was just the central fantasy," Julie argued, coming over to lean in the kitchen door (well, just turning around, really, it's not a big kitchen), and looking across the lounge towards me, one of those four-packs of dips in her grasp. "Escaping from work at the end the way none of the rest of the characters can escape from their lives—come *on*..."

"I meant her performance, you hypercritical cow. This isn't about critiquing the filmmaking, we're here to watch *her*. Hey, is that guacamole?"

"Hm? Oh, no, this isn't, but I did get some—Sainsbury's finest. So what's next?"

"Well, if we're going chronologically, *Call Me in the Morning*. If we're going thematically, *Humble Pie*."

Julie made a face. "You know that there's really only one Isobel Dewitt film that you of all people need to see, right? You have seen *She Talks in Her Sleep*?"

"I didn't really see a lot of films in the nineties, Jules. You know that." Nor do I now, for that matter. Some people find it amusing. I just don't understand the appeal of paying ten quid to sit in a dark room that smells like popcorn and the bottoms of people's shoes with a bunch of strangers. Doing research for my books is one of the few times I actually turn my television on.

"Well, you've got it, right? To watch now, I mean?" Julie looked mildly amused that I'd managed to miss this particular film for some reason, and it was irritating me slightly, making me want to lie that I hadn't. I nodded grumpily in the direction of the pile of DVDs I'd picked up, which did indeed have the film in question in its number.

"We're still watching either *Call Me* or *Humble Pie* just now, though. So pick one."

"Okay, okay—let's be purists. We'll go with *Call Me in the Morning.* You get it set up. I'll get the snacks."

THE FILM WAS...well, it wasn't necessarily to my usual tastes, if I'm brutally honest. It was that sort of slightly indie rom-com fare that basically presses all the same predictable buttons as every other romantic comedy, but the girl's quirky and the guy's weedy and they have all the latest bands who can't play their instruments on the soundtrack. These films are ten-a-penny now, I guess, but in the nineties, as the sleeve tells me, this was fresh and original stuff.

Luckily Julie disliked it as well, and we passed the time making snarky comments and inhaling tortilla chips and guacamole. As soon as it finished, we put on the next film in line, which to Julie's dismay was not *She Talks in Her Sleep* but the period film *Front Line,* in which Dewitt played a glamorous heiress who becomes embroiled in a murder plot against her father-in-law. I liked the Second World War setting; Jules hated the stylized dialogue.

"Guess we'll have to agree to disagree," I said as I got up to use the loo between films. "Are we going to watch *any* films tonight that you don't hate?"

"Oh, I didn't hate it. I just thought that Dewitt was basically the only good thing *in* it. Besides, you know what's next..."

"Chicken jalfrezi and popadums?"

"Oh baby... I meant that the next film on the list is *She Talks.*"

"Gosh, I can't wait. Fine, order us some dinner, and then we'll watch this cinematic masterpiece or whatever it is. Use my card, okay?"

OKAY, SO HERE'S the thing. When someone talks something up to me, I dig in my heels. I really don't think I'm any different from anyone else in this regard—someone tells you you're going to *love* something and you sort of key yourself up to prove them wrong, right?

And there's very little I dislike more than being proven wrong myself. But, and I hate to admit it, I loved *She Talks in Her Sleep*.

Firstly, if you didn't know who Isobel Dewitt was, you wouldn't recognize her. Not that there's anything wrong with the way she looked in the first place, and not that physical transformation is the beginning or the end of acting, but with her hair shorn and having gained what looked like a good few extra pounds, mostly in muscle, between her last film and this one, her whole demeanour had changed. I thought perhaps, in her cheeky way, that this was what Julie had been referring to when she said this was the only film I needed to see, but as soon as Dewitt opened her first bottle of whisky, I realized what Julie had meant.

Now, I'm not saying that most portrayals of addiction in the media are particularly accurate, or that I enjoy watching them—in fact, I tend to avoid them, since they annoy the hell out of me. Maybe subconsciously that's why I hadn't seen this film before now. But, as we made our way through it over naan and pilau rice, I was blown away by the honest, raw portrayal of a woman battling demons I was all too familiar with.

Of course, unlike me, "Ellie" wasn't lucky enough to have a career where you can get away with such indiscretions. The world of women's boxing had become a hot topic with the success of *Million Dollar Baby*, but this film, the best part of a decade ago, had been much lower key.

Dewitt's performance was, as the box proclaimed, "a tour de force." She had really come into her own by this point, and with a solid script behind her, she delivered an absolutely knockout (hah!) performance that had me glued to the screen for the entire latter half of the film.

And sure, it didn't hurt that she was playing a lesbian. Which, in case it wasn't already clear, I am. Anyway, as the credits rolled Julie turned towards me with an expectant look on her face, which I ignored as I sipped my mineral water and perused the rest of the stack of DVDs.

Predictably, she exploded almost immediately. *"Well?"*

"Well what?" I could barely keep the smile from my voice, but I managed to remain stony-faced as she rounded on me.

"Oh come *on*—of all the films in all the world that should resonate with you..."

"Hey, I've lived it, who says I want to watch it all over again?" Well, it was my principle about these types of films *most* of the time...

"Yeah, I could tell how *not* completely hooked in you were there."

I slumped down and chucked a tortilla chip in Julie's direction. "How come you never told me that Isobel Dewitt dyked it up?"

"Honestly? I thought you already knew. It's a well-known film among the lesbian audience," Julie said with a shrug.

"Jesus..." I shook my head.

Honestly? It worried me. I try to make a point of not taking on clients I have an actual opinion on—whether I like them or hate them. Before I started researching Isobel Dewitt, I had very little opinion either way— she seemed like she probably wasn't an idiot and that was about as far as it went. Since meeting her, watching her films... I was becoming a fan. And that was a bad thing.

See, the thing about being a ghostwriter is that you have to be unbiased—not just against negative things, but against being too positive. You have to lose your own voice, and if the book sounds too adoring, too self-congratulatory...well, nobody wants to read that. So I'll admit that I was kind of hoping the next film would be awful.

The next film was *Humble Pie*, where Dewitt returned to a role similar in some respects to the first she'd played—another harried waitress, although this time as the lead. And, just like the last few films we had watched, it was good. Not exactly my cup of tea, but I could still tell that it was decent enough.

Speaking of which, we moved on from juice and water to tea and biscuits, lounging on separate sides of the sofa as the movie played on. I was beginning to get sleepy, mainly because I had only had about four hours the night before. It looked like we wouldn't be moving on to Dewitt's directorial efforts tonight, which was just as well, since if I became any more of a fangirl, I'd have to call my agent tomorrow and recuse myself from the project.

"So, what do you think?" Julie asked as the credits rolled on the last film of the night. "She's stunning, right?"

"Yeah, no doubt about it. She's got talent," I agreed.

Julie gave me a long look. Then she began to smirk and, oh my God does that piss me off when she does that mind-reading thing.

"What? *What*? Oh, just drop it, Jules..." Rolling my eyes, I heaved myself off the sofa. I gathered up stray crisp wrappers and napkins from the table. "Honestly."

"You know, I'm sure I have some ancient nineties copies of *FHM* and *Loaded* lying around in the attic somewhere with poster specials in them if you want me to take a look for you..."

"I'll tell you where you can look." For all of her strengths—and trust me, I love her like a sister—Julie occasionally becomes fixated on my terminal singlehood and on driving me completely and utterly insane with annoyance. "She's an actress. She's *supposed* to be attractive."

"Oh, absolutely."

I'll draw a veil over the rest of the teasing. Rest assured there was much throwing of tortilla chips and a certain amount of name-calling.

Eventually Julie packed up and left, and in spite of my better judgement, I caved and settled back on the sofa with Dewitt's first film as a director. I'll admit I drifted in and out—it wasn't the best film in the world, and I was exhausted. The actual production was good—solid performances, a decent script, and some really quite innovative cinematography. But the plot was lacklustre and it was clearly a somewhat hasty adaptation from the book on which it was based.

Not entirely Dewitt's fault, to be sure, but all the same, I could understand where the criticism had come from. I really wanted to rewatch *Home and Hearth*, but this wasn't the time. As tired as I was, sleep was still elusive, so I settled for listening to my first day's interview once more, closing my eyes and letting the sound of Isobel Dewitt's cultured voice and throaty chuckle wash over me.

"God, I don't know. I suppose I wasn't camera-shy; people seemed to want to take my picture; I like working with artists, and so it seemed like a natural thing to do..."

"And did that 'natural' inclination carry over to the acting process? Don't worry, we'll talk more about this later, but give me a flavour—would you consider yourself more of the British or American school?"

That warm laugh again. "Hah, good question. The Dewitt school? Is that too pretentious? If I'm honest, I think probably the American—I do tend to lose myself in the part somewhat..."

"Interesting. And have there been any parts that were especially challenging for you?"

There was a long silence on the recording as she pondered this. Lying in bed, staring at the ceiling in the dark after a day immersed in Isobel Dewitt, I filled that silence with all sorts of answers. The one that I knew was coming, though, was more elusive.

"I'm not sure. I suppose we'll find out when we get into the nitty-gritty, eh?"

"Let's hope so."

Chapter Four

THE SIDE EFFECT of not sleeping terribly well at night is that I tend to lie in bed all morning—unless I have a meeting.

If I *do* have a meeting, well, then I don't get a lie-in—and I have to say it tends to affect my mood just a little bit. I'm not the most pleasant person at the best of times—I'll admit it—but my behaviour goes down the politeness scale just a few notches.

This meant I was uncharacteristically chipper that morning as Isobel Dewitt let me into her hotel suite.

"Good morning, Ms. Dewitt. You look...well."

"I thought we'd start from the beginning again. Except in a bit more detail this time," I told her, glancing up and giving her a reassuring smile. "Time to start fleshing things out."

"Okay... I, er, made some notes, actually, after last time," Isobel offered. "I was thinking about what we'd spoken about, my career shifts and the choices I made, and I don't know if it will help you, but I thought that if you might find a timeline useful, at all..."

"You made notes?" Okay, seriously, you won't have a hard time believing *that* was a first. Usually I'm lucky if the people I'm interviewing remember they *had* a childhood. "Uh, yeah, sure, that'd be great."

"I don't want to interfere with your process," Isobel explained as she stood, moving over to what I noticed now was a rather charmingly cluttered writing desk, presumably to fetch said notes. "I mean, obviously, I'm not a writer or I wouldn't be hiring you, but I just thought, shit, give me a minute...ah!" She waved what looked to be a few sheets of computer printed A4, decorated with highlighter and handwritten notes, before turning to lean back against the desk and continue. "I thought that, well, anything I could do to keep the story straight, let you worry about the telling. Y'know?" As her voice lifted on the 'y'know?' the tiniest hint of an American twang crept into her otherwise crisp enunciation.

"Right, well... thanks." She'd said she wasn't a writer, but I was pretty sure when I got hold of those notes, they'd be well-organized and well-stated. Was this my easiest job ever? It was too early to tell, but I was betting on yes. "I'm sure they'll be very useful."

"I hope so—I'm afraid I typed them all up and then kept thinking of more things," Isobel said apologetically as she handed them over before taking her seat again. "I highlighted stuff that you'll maybe want to focus on—I mean, that is, from my point of view, it seems either interesting or significant. You may not agree, but I figured it'd give us a starting point."

"Mm." I was already halfway down the page at this point—I'm a fast reader—skimming through the highlighted sections, noting that she had picked out a few things I had wanted to touch on myself. "Well, let's do that, then. Tell me about your mother. I can see from this that she was an entertainer during the war. That's interesting."

"Mhm—she was actually only twelve in '39, but she was in a singing group with her older sisters—sort of a younger British Andrews Sisters, I suppose. They never went to the front line to entertain the troops, of course, not at that age, but it meant she was in London during the Blitz when most kids were off in the country."

"Mm. That must've made an impact on her, at such a young age. And you—would you say your urge to perform came from her?" It wasn't the rarest thing in the world for parents in "the biz" to push their children into it as well. It could lead to resentment in the long run; I wondered if there was any sentiment like that between Dewitt and her family.

But Isobel was already shaking her head, even before I'd finished asking the question. "She was long past all that by the time I was born. To me, she was always just...my mum with the lovely singing voice."

"That's lovely." Completely and utterly boring, but certain audiences would lap it up. I gave her a carefully practised smile, making a note of the phrase in my notebook. To my mild surprise, she clocked me immediately, her easy smile turning slightly to a smirk.

"Oh, I'm sorry. Not dramatic enough for you?" Her words might have been cutting but for her amused tone.

"What? Oh, no, no, no..." Looking up, I shook my head emphatically, giving her what I hoped was a wide-eyed innocent look. "I think it's very nice. Everybody likes a happy family." Just not as much as they like an *un*happy one.

"Mm, well, I wouldn't go that far, necessarily..."

"Oh?" I had perfected that one syllable; I could get people to spill deep, dark secrets with just that and a lift of my eyebrows.

A purse of those full, perfect lips. Was this woman going to bust me every time? "Another day. Ask me about uni or something."

OKAY, SO HERE'S the thing. I really don't know what I was doing there. Isobel Dewitt had already decided exactly what she wanted to say and how it was going to sound—she fed me sound bite after sound bite, perfectly crafted like lines from one of her films. I dutifully took them down, followed her down the avenues she wanted me to explore, let her guide me past things that "just weren't that interesting." And the weirdest part was that I didn't feel like she was being dishonest—maybe a bit of a spin doctor, but not overly manipulative.

It did leave me feeling spare—more like a transcriptionist than a ghost. I was determined that I would find a way to get past Dewitt's carefully sculpted picture of herself and into the real story, but for now, I was happy to bask in the warm, deliciously well-enunciated fiction.

Which is exactly what I did when I got home. Lying on the most comfortable sofa known to man, I closed my eyes and let Dewitt's voice wash over me, listening to amusing tales of her uni days, her forays into student productions, and the colourful characters that filled her past. She'd had a fairly typical university experience, I suppose—well, typical for a pretty rich girl, anyway. She had her share of traumas and heartbreak and chaos, but nothing terribly ruinous. The stories were predictable enough, but the way she told them was engaging and witty and inviting...

Okay, let's get one thing straight. I'm a lesbian, but back then you might as well have called me a celibate asexual entity for all the sex I'd had in the past two years. Ever since I dried out, my ability to pull women had dried up—not to mention the inclination. I just couldn't be bothered coming up with stuff to talk about, or dealing with dating...not to mention, avoiding bars made it difficult to meet people at the best of times. So I was sex-starved, and if I began to have impure thoughts while listening to Dewitt's recording, well, it was understandable. She had a good voice, and if I closed my eyes I could still see her lounging on her love seat, her skirt slit just high enough to show one smooth, perfectly toned thigh.

Needless to say, however, this was doing nothing for my ability to dispassionately process all of this information and start getting anything down on paper. Usually by the end of the second meeting, I'd have a reasonably good idea for a structure, for how the narrative would spin. Tonight would be spent typing up sections of recordings, shuffling them around, organising them. Instead, at the end of two long meetings, I had more good audio than I needed, and no idea where to begin. I might as well just be typing up Isobel's own notes for all the clue I had.

Frustrated, I reached out for a glass that wasn't there, stopping midway through the motion and flinching just slightly. Old habits die hard, and though I had put a bullet in mine, they were still in their death throes, spasming and kicking me in the gut at the most inopportune times. Time for tea and a fresh look at things.

First, I would go back to her notes. Pot of tea newly made and sitting on my desk, steaming away as it brewed, I picked up the sheaf of paper and began to read it a little more carefully. After our discussions today, I was beginning to think that her highlighted passages were not so much what she thought was most significant but what she would prefer me to see. Perhaps I ought to be homing in on some of the areas that *hadn't* been highlighted.

Some of them, I could see why. I mean, there's only so many stories about primary school that anyone wants to hear, especially in the autobiography of someone who had accomplished so much, and though I had no doubt that there were more anecdotes that could be teased out of her modelling years, there were only so many ways to say "I got paid for being completely gorgeous and walking down a catwalk a few times a night." We'd still include a few stories, since it was "exciting" and "glamorous" and all that bollocks, but I could understand why most of that was left blank.

But there were some more mysterious gaps. There was almost nothing about her second year at university, and in my experience, uni was a time of constant change and activity, if not necessarily positive. I resolved that we would start there the next time, whether or not Isobel Dewitt wanted us to. If she only wanted to tell the stories that she had picked and chosen specially, then she could write the damn book herself.

Chapter Five

THE NEXT DAY, I woke up late—as was my wont—packed up the laptop and headphones, and headed out for the café. Though it was approaching lunchtime, there was still seating available, and I managed to snag one of my favourite corner tables, spreading out my things in a proprietary way before heading up to get a pot of tea. Once I returned, I got stuck straight in, reviewing my notes and typing up a stream-of-consciousness first chapter while my tea steeped.

I was so engrossed by what I was doing (and by Isobel Dewitt's voice in my ears) that I almost missed the polite throat-clearing by the shadow that fell over my table. Glancing up, I saw a cute redhead covered in freckles and a paisley sundress standing in front of me.

"Excuse me," she said with a smile, obviously glad to have gotten my attention. "Is this seat taken?"

"Huh? Oh, no," I replied, my concentration momentarily broken like a watch that has stopped ticking. "Go ahead and take it away if you like."

It was surprising, not to mention slightly disconcerting, when rather than simply steal the seat, she just shot me another bright smile and sat in it where it was. I looked up and around, meerkat style, to see that, although the café was far from empty, it wasn't exactly packed, and there were certainly more comfortable seats free elsewhere.

"Sorry," I said then, more than a little confused by this point. "Can I help you? I don't know if you're supposed to be meeting someone here, but I can guarantee you it's not me."

The girl blinked, looking taken aback. "Oh, no, I'm not meeting anyone. Well, I mean—" She went on with another of those smiles, "except that we're meeting now, of course..."

I was beginning to think she was slow—I mean, talk about stating the obvious. "Uh-huh. I guess that's true."

The smile faded slightly. "Sorry, didn't mean to intrude," she said, rising to her feet once more. She then lifted her jacket up from where she'd put it over the back of her chair.

"It's a bit late for leaving now," I commented wryly, lifting my lukewarm teapot to refill my cup. "I won't be able to get back to writing until I've finished this, at least."

But it seemed the young woman's decision was made, apparently not just to find another seat but another café altogether, as she pulled her jacket on. "Well, I'll let you get back to your tea in peace," she said, her tone slightly clipped, the first hint of a slight Celtic accent creeping in, and she turned to go without waiting for a response. I watched her leave, wondering what on earth had possessed her to interrupt me like that. It was only much later, as I was packing up to go, that I realized that she might well have been hitting on me—as rare as it was, it *did* happen. Feeling almost embarrassed, I resolved never to let Julie find out about this—there'd be no end to the mockery if she did.

THE WHOLE THING put a strange tilt on the rest of the day for me—it's funny how little things can do that when you get stuck in your routine, used to your own company with no interruptions. Although I was still able to float away into my own little world at the sound of the lovely Isobel Dewitt's voice, I couldn't seem to keep my mind on the draft I was trying to get into.

Which meant that it was a bit shit. Loose, undirected, slightly rambling... I very nearly deleted the whole thing upon rereading it, but I knew it was stupid to throw away a whole day's work just because it sucked. I might still be able to salvage something from it eventually, though it didn't look promising. With my laptop slung over my shoulder, I headed home, intent on reheating leftovers and maybe watching another Dewitt film or three until I fell asleep.

I was thrown, then, to receive a text message while en route home, from a number I didn't recognize.

Screening tonight at the Victoria art house, 2030 if you'd like to attend. -Id

It took me longer than I'd like to admit to figure out who had sent the text; I don't get a lot of invitations out any more, and it wasn't like it was a usual thing for me to be invited places by the people I was ghosting for.

Much less an insanely talented, rich, well-respected person like Isobel Dewitt. But the proof was there on my crappy mobile—she had invited me to a film screening, and as much as the prospect would normally send me running in the other direction, I was actually tempted.

I texted the one person who'd understand my dilemma. Mary's response was quick, and simple, and annoying. Exactly what I'd expected.

1. Will there be booze there? 2. Will you be stressed?

The answers to my sponsor's questions were obvious—I mean, it was a film screening; obviously there'd be booze. And of course I'd be stressed; I'm good one-on-one, but not so much schmoozing in crowds. And it wasn't so much a question of whether I'd be tempted to drink, but whether I'd be strong enough to resist the temptation. And that wasn't a question I could easily answer.

"NAME, PLEASE."

"It's, um, Nicola Booth. I was invited by Ms. Dewitt, she sent me a text..."

The casually dressed man scanned down the list in front of him, lips pursed, and eventually nodded. "Up the stairs and to the right to the reception room," he said, nodding his head.

The foyer of the Victoria Art House was not quite what I'd expected—lovely vintage furnishings, but quite worn and distressed (and not in a cute way). Honestly, it didn't look like the sort of film screening Isobel Dewitt would attend at all.

I fit right in, however—I owned almost no formal clothing, so at the last minute, all I had been able to cobble together was a pair of grey trousers and a dark red top I pulled out of the back of my closet, which probably hadn't seen the light of day in two years. It wasn't *shabby* per se, but it certainly wasn't glamorous.

The reception room was just as simple and run-down as the hallway, and was already half full of people, mostly dressed as casually as I was, milling around and chatting with their glasses of champagne and nibbles. I made a beeline for one of the waiters, who was carrying food, and requested a mineral water straight off. It was surprisingly helpful to have a glass in your hand in a situation like this. Once that was taken care of, I took up residence next to the wall, surveying the crowd and wondering not for the first time why I had been invited.

Isobel apparently wasn't here yet, and there was no sign anywhere of posters or flyers to indicate what film I was even here to see. Idly, I mused that this could all be some elaborate joke—Dewitt certainly had enough pull to do something like that, but I wasn't flattering myself that I meant enough to her to warrant being messed around like that. Right before I gave up all hope and headed off, however, Isobel finally entered the room, accompanied by a handsome, clean-cut young man in a suit who I didn't recognize.

She was immediately swarmed by half the people in the room, and she received them warmly, exchanging greetings and easy smiles with them all. It was admirable, watching the way she sorted deftly through them until they all appeared to feel they had been given due attention; I certainly couldn't imagine ever being able to do that.

Eventually, people began to scatter again, moving back into their own little groups, and Isobel scanned the room—I assume to see whether she'd missed anyone, since when her eyes alighted on me, she nodded in greeting and began to make her way over.

Well, shit. I felt equal parts anticipation and dread roil in my stomach as Dewitt crossed the room. She looked fantastic: she was wearing a simple black cocktail dress and heels, but she walked with such absolute confidence that she could've been in a couture gown. Guess that was the benefit of being a former model—not only looking but feeling amazing in anything.

She extended a hand as she reached me. "Glad you could make it," she murmured. "I hope I haven't made you wait too long?"

"Well, you know, not really," I replied with a graceless shrug. "I, uh... I'm looking forward to the screening."

"Yeah, sorry about all the mystery—it's a low-key thing," Isobel said. "I met this amazing girl—woman—last year at Sundance, and we got talking, and, well, long story short, I ended up financing this picture for her. She's a really great director—really honest, you know? God, I sound like such a wanker..."

"No, no, it sounds interesting, really. I'm sure it's going to be great—you have wonderful taste." God, I was gushing already, and I hadn't even seen the damn film.

Isobel was smiling slightly when I finally dragged my gaze back up to hers. "Might want to wait to see it first," she said with that raised eyebrow.

"Right. Right. Good idea." Desperately I gulped at my water, nearly swallowing the lime wedge and hacking it back into the glass in the process.

"Oh, can I get you some champagne?" Isobel asked, stretching a hand out to gesture to one of the waiters.

This almost made me choke *again*, and for a moment, all I could do was shake my head emphatically, my eyes watering. "No, thank you," I managed to croak out eventually. "Really, that's okay. Please. Thank you."

"Wow, okay," Isobel said with a smile. "We do have a full bar if you'd like anything different."

"I'm good with water," I wheezed. "Really." This was probably destroying any respect Dewitt had for me, which couldn't have been very much to begin with.

She didn't look overly bothered, though, as she nodded and favoured me with another easy smile. "No problem. Well, we'll be going in any minute now, and—oh! That's Laura—Laura, come over here, would you?"

Okay, look. I'm not a big believer in Fate or karma and especially not God, and I know that this was just some big coincidence, but it felt strange right at that moment to turn and see the red-headed, freckled girl from the café crossing the room towards us.

Of course.

She betrayed no recognition as she arrived, though it wasn't surprising; I wasn't anything to look at next to Isobel Dewitt.

"This is Laura Maguire," Isobel said, taking Laura's hand as she arrived with us. "She's the director of *Staircases*. Laura, I want you to meet Nicola Booth."

"Hi," I said, giving her a polite smile as I clasped my glass. "I'm looking forward to seeing your film."

"Oh, well, thanks," Laura said with a grin. "Me too. I mean, well, properly. I mean—well. You know." She glanced at Isobel nervously, and the older woman lifted a hand to pat her reassuringly on the shoulder. Suddenly, I was very jealous.

At that moment, people began filtering towards the door; I assumed it was because there had been some unspoken signal that the film was about to begin. "Well, we should—" I murmured, at the same time that Laura said, "Oh! It looks like people are going to the theatre..."

THE FILM WAS a little...indie for my tastes, I suppose. It's not that I don't appreciate "Art House" films, and I could see the potential in Maguire's work. I could certainly understand why Isobel had funded her. But it was still raw and a bit messy, and I didn't think it necessitated the amount of gushing and praise that various people heaped upon it at the gathering after the film. Phrases like "the next Jason Reitman" were thrown about like confetti, and it was all I could do to stand there and keep from making faces at the gathered sycophants. Eventually, I just sort of drifted away from the main group, availing myself of some more mineral water and propping up a wall while I waited for a good moment to slip away.

It seemed I wasn't going to make a completely unnoticed exit, however; on one of her periodic perusals of the room, Dewitt spotted me and a few minutes later, after detaching herself from a group of several older besuited men, came towards me.

"So, did your expectations pan out?" was the first thing she asked me, accompanied by that single raised eyebrow she was so good at.

It was a carefully phrased question, deserving of a carefully phrased answer. I nodded—carefully. "I'd say so," I said with a slight smile. "It was very...honest."

"That's what I like best about her work. Not everything can be like that, but the ones that are..." Dewitt trailed off, then gave a philosophical shrug. "I hope you enjoyed it."

I nodded again—I had enjoyed it, for all its flaws. "I did. I think she's very deserving of your attention." *Even if I didn't find her deserving of mine...* My eyes found the young woman across the room—she was currently engaged in conversation with a few of the younger attendees of the screening. I assumed they were her own friends and colleagues.

"It's very important to me to support young female filmmakers," Dewitt was saying as I eyed up her protégée, noting that she had eschewed the paisley sundress for a more business-like dark green shirt and pinstriped skirt. "And Laura is very talented. I have a feeling she'll go far."

I think my response was a distracted hum as I watched the girl in question. My mind was straying back to that moment earlier today in the café, wondering whether she'd really been chatting me up. I wasn't sure what the hell I would begin to do about it if I decided she had been, but that's me.

"Well. I suppose we can discuss this all at our meeting tomorrow, mm?" Dewitt offered, sipping nonchalantly from a glass of champagne. "I just thought it might be beneficial if you saw not only my past but my present."

"And Laura Maguire is your present," I murmured. I didn't mean to insert any underlying suggestiveness or double entendre to my tone, but somehow what I heard myself say did contain a little.

Dewitt merely shrugged and glanced over at the younger woman, smiling fondly. "I suppose so."

I felt my eyebrows give an involuntary twitch, my mind running wild in spite of itself.

"Well, thank you again for coming, Ms. Booth. I'm afraid I must go and continue making the rounds."

I blinked, shaken from my reverie at the light touch to my shoulder as Isobel took her leave, and I managed a nod of acknowledgement in her direction before she left my side to find another group of simpering sycophants. For my own part, I figured I was done for the evening and slipped my jacket back on in preparation to head back outside.

It seemed a simple escape wasn't to be, however—my clear path to the door was suddenly interrupted by an increasingly familiar freckled face, though it wasn't quite so jovial this time.

Laura Maguire faced me, green eyes narrowed. "I know you."

"Well, I wouldn't go *that* far..." I hazarded with a game attempt at a jovial smile.

"You were in the café earlier," she said, continuing her statement of the obvious. "What are you doing here?"

My gaze shifted back towards the room at large, although I wasn't really sure why—it's not as though Isobel Dewitt was about to come to my rescue. I wasn't in the habit, however, of making myself known as a ghost for my clients—it wasn't really the done thing.

"I, er, blagged my way in, pretty much," I lied, waving a hand vaguely. "I met Ms. Dewitt at a press screening a few months ago, we got talking, and your name came up."

"Hm." I could tell she liked this even as I watched her tamp down her pride in favour of another accusatory look. "And what do you do?" The words, though innocent enough on their own, seem barbed and venomous the way she delivered them.

I fought against the urge to grit my teeth, instead smiling carefully. I had a feeling it wasn't terribly convincing. "I'm a writer," I said.

"A screenwriter?" she asked, attempting a Dewitt eyebrow arch and failing, making her face look cutely lopsided.

"Hah. No, I've never written a screenplay."

"Then what do you write?"

I hesitated. There was a decent possibility that Maguire knew Dewitt was working on a memoir, and if I told her my profession she was likely to put two and two together. I had no particular desire to reveal that Isobel wasn't writing her own book.

"Hard to say," I tried.

This obviously didn't fly with Laura Maguire, who looked at me as if I had said "dead baby recipes." "What does *that* mean?" she asked, her expression one of reluctant curiosity, as if she was being drawn into the conversation despite herself.

I hoped the hint of a smirk that I felt didn't show as I smiled in response. "Just that I don't really talk about my writing," I said.

"Is that what you were working on this morning in the café? Some secret project?"

I shrugged. "Sure," I said, in the tone of "Why not?" I knew I was getting to her now, and in spite of myself I quite liked that. I guess I'm not a very nice person sometimes.

She narrowed her eyes at me—I hadn't realized it before, but I really had no idea how old she was. Maybe it was the freckles and the sundress or just the cheery smile that had made me think she was barely out of university when I had seen her in the café, but now I wasn't sure. When she looked at me like that, I could see tiny wrinkles at the corners of her eyes, and her body in its work-like suit and shirt was full and curvy. In any case, she certainly was behaving immaturely—I wouldn't have been surprised if she put her hands on her hips and called Dewitt over to make me stop teasing her any second now.

"Well. Good luck with that," she said eventually, obviously at a loss for a better retort. "I'm sure you must have some talent or Isobel wouldn't have invited you."

"I don't think that's why she…" I shrugged. "Sure." I mean, why not, right? I was already lying, what difference did it make what she thought now?

"Hm. So, what did you think of the film?"

Now I was the one at a loss. "I, er…"

"So you didn't like it." Was I crazy, or was Laura Maguire actually smiling?

I cleared my throat. "I thought it showed a lot of potential," I offered eventually. This woman was incredibly disarming, and not in a good way.

"So do scribbles on a chalkboard. That's not the same as a sonnet."

I let myself smirk slightly. "A limerick's a start, though, right?"

"Oh, I see how it is." Maguire pursed her lips playfully. "A limerick. Not even a haiku or an acrostic. You really hated it, didn't you?"

"I didn't hate it."

"You'd just liken it to a cinematic *Girl from Nantucket*."

I sighed, closing my eyes and shaking my head, thinking that I should've known better than to get into this. "I think you're a very talented director."

"You've only seen one of my films—that doesn't seem like a lot to go on," Maguire countered. "But thanks, I guess."

"I guess you're welcome."

Another arch look from the redhead, which shouldn't have made me feel quite so uncomfortable, or weak in the knees. God, I needed to get out of there. "Well, I'd like to say it was nice to meet you-- what did you say your name was?"

"I… Nicola. Booth. Nice to meet you. Again." I smiled, although I had a feeling it looked more like a grimace.

"Mm. Maybe I'll see you at the café again soon."

"I'll…be sure to save you a seat."

With another smirk, Maguire finally released me, moving purposefully back into the welcoming crowd while I stood adrift. Realizing this might be my opportunity, I wasted no time in offloading my glass on a passing waiter and making a hasty exit, though not before I noticed Maguire and Dewitt in some sort of huddle, arms entwined as they laughed over some secret joke. I tried hard not to assume it was me.

Chapter Six

SURPRISINGLY, THOUGH, PERHAPS, the evening did break my block. When I got back to the flat, I steered automatically towards my desk, and it wasn't long before I was ripping to shreds the draft I'd written earlier in the day, twisting and turning it. And when I'd done with that chapter, I moved onto the next, and then the one after that, Isobel's voice flowing from my fingers onto the screen far more freely than they had. Perhaps it was just seeing her again, familiarizing myself once more with her voice and mannerisms, that let me slip back into her persona. Or perhaps it was meeting Laura Maguire and imagining being close to her, my arm linked with hers, our voices fitting together musically as we entertained a crowd of people.

Don't get me wrong—it wasn't like I was fantasizing about this woman I had only met once. Well, twice. At least, not exactly. In honesty, it was probably worse than that—certainly much more pathetic. Because in my mind's eye, as I stood there beside her, I wasn't me. I was her—Isobel Dewitt with her perfect voice and her perfect face and her perfect body in its perfect black dress. Which is, well, you know. Normal. For me.

After all, that's the real reason I keep doing this job. It's not because I couldn't probably write something original under my own name if I wanted to—my agent's been urging me to do so for years now, not for her good (there's way more money for her in my ghosting) but for mine. I do it—I love it—because it lets me leave myself behind completely. And hell, it's the only avenue I have left to do that. So these days, I need it more than ever.

By the time I thought to look at the clock, it was nearing six in the morning—not an unusual sight for me but unfortunate as I had a lunch meeting with Dewitt in a matter of hours. I considered rescheduling it, but I was on such a roll that I honestly didn't want to stop. Addictive personality, remember? Nobody ever claimed it was good for you.

It was around nine, after I'd been in bed for about an hour, maybe, sleeping lightly at best, that I got a text from Mary.

So did you go?
Yeah. Survived.

It was another couple of minutes and I'd slipped back into a doze when the next beeps happened.

Cuppa this morn? Elevenish maybe? Could tell me how the book's going.

It wasn't like I was going to get much more sleep this morning anyway. Apparently.

Sure. Meet you at Lantana?

Lantana was one of my favourite cafés, largely because it was a bit dingy and consequently usually near-empty. Mary was already there when I arrived, nursing a large mug of tea, as usual wrapped up in more scarves and jumpers than were remotely necessary for the temperature.

I dropped my bag and laptop next to the table and immediately went to order my own tea, not bothering with a greeting until I had returned. "Hey."

"Hey yourself," came the usual response. Mary looked tired, as usual—like me, she never got enough sleep—and also somewhat ill. *Un*like me, she was never free of a head-cold or chest-infection or some such. Nonetheless, she looked cheerful enough, and she pulled herself to her feet to hug me as I reached the table.

I returned the hug—I had long since gotten past trying to evade them—and we settled back at the table with our mugs. "Late night? Out partying like usual?" I joked.

"Hah, yeah, that's right. Partying with a chesty cough."

"I'm sure you got *all* the boys' numbers."

Mary's reply was a dry smirk. "Yeah. That's right. So! Tell me about your night."

I filled her in on the evening's events, leaving out very few details. Mary had seen me at my most pathetic, trembling and weak, and despite the fact that I made a fool of myself several times over, I didn't really mind her knowing. She listened intently, nodding at the right moments and smiling in mild amusement at others—I can spin a good story when I want to, y'know.

I ended with a quick reference to how well my writing had gone the night before, though that I didn't elaborate too much on. It wasn't that I didn't trust Mary—far from it—but I don't think she realized exactly how wrapped up I got in it sometimes, and I wanted to keep it that way.

"Sounds like an interesting evening. Do you think you're likely to run into her again?"

I was writing the woman's memoir, what did she think? "Well, we have a meeting in two hours, so..."

"With the director?"

"What? Oh, no, with Dewitt," I said, shaking my head. "More interviewing for the book."

"I meant the other girl—Laura."

"Oh, her? I don't know." Last night, I had been tempted by her offer of meeting again—something about being caught up in the moment, I guess—but now in the cold light of day, I could see what a bad idea that was. I was in no headspace to try to be social, and I could tell Laura Maguire was sharp enough to catch me if I attempted to keep up with my lies. "Probably not."

"Hm." Mary frowned into her mug. "You can't hide away forever, you know."

"Yes, yes I can. With what I put my liver through, I might only have another fifteen, twenty years left... I could easily spend that wrapped up in writing and living like a hermit."

"Oh, don't be ridiculous, you know perfectly well that's not true," Mary said with a wave of her hand. "There's nothing to be gained from shutting yourself off."

I made a face; I hated these conversations. "There's nothing to be gained from trying to force myself to be someone I'm not. Socializing makes me want to drink. And I'd rather be sober than happy."

"But if you never learn to socialize without drinking..."

"I've tried. Hey—don't look at me like that. I have!"

Mary raised her eyebrows. "Try harder. This is your sponsor talking, love."

"Fine. I'll try harder. But not with her."

"Well, you should do it for yourself."

I grinned, lifting my tea. "Trust me, I've been doing it for myself for a *long* time."

Mary opened her mouth but seemingly couldn't think of a comeback, as she closed it again with a slight smirk, looking shy. Mary had never quite got the hang of my lewd humour.

From there, we moved on to chatting about other things—Mary's research at the university, gossip about the few mutual acquaintances we had, a bit more about Isobel Dewitt and her amazing, beautiful, shiny life.

"She sounds insufferable."

"You'd think so, but really she's not. She's—" I paused, glancing down at my mug while I tried to gather my thoughts. "She's really not."

Mary's lips pulled into a smirk again. "Wow, you're really on a streak with this quiet unrequited simmering stuff all of a sudden, aren't you?"

"No," I replied, scowling in spite of myself. She just didn't get it. My interest in Dewitt wasn't unrequited romantic feelings—it was a necessary part of my job.

"Okay, okay, sorry. You know me. I'm not judging either way..."

"No, just meddling..." I happened to glance at the clock then and realized I didn't have very long to get to my lunch meeting. "Shit, sorry," I told Mary, gathering up my things hurriedly. "Gotta run."

"Ah, yes, your lunch date. Have a good time, petal."

"Mm-hmm, sure. I'll talk to you later—take care."

Chapter Seven

"SO WHERE SHALL we start today?" Isobel sipped at her tea—not a mug but a fine china cup since this establishment was very different from the one in which I'd spent my morning. "The next thing on the list is my postgraduate…"

I knew exactly where I wanted to start, and delved right in, deftly manoeuvring around the sound bites Dewitt had already given me and instead focusing on things she hadn't mentioned so much—her second year at uni being a key example. I know it might be hard to believe, but I can be quite dogged when I want (I'm using sarcasm here), and no matter what deflections she threw at me or amusing stories she offered in exchange I kept coming back to that, phrasing the question differently each time with cheerful determination.

Eventually, she sighed, rolling her eyes, her mild frustration such that she didn't even hide it any more. "Second year at uni was the first time I ever acted."

"Right. And what was the first production you were in?"

"*Twelfth Night*. I was Viola, if you can believe that." Isobel's lips flickered past a smile at the memory.

"I certainly can. Although a leading part your first foray into acting—that's a bit unusual, isn't it?"

"I do lots of unusual things."

"All the more fortunate for me," I said, both enjoying and regretting her obvious discomfort.

"Mm, well, I was terrible, if you must know. I think they mainly chose me because I looked quite boyish at that age."

"Now that I find hard to believe," I told her, smirking. I had seen pictures of her younger days, and while she had been slim and long-limbed, I wouldn't have called her *boyish*. Something about her full lips.

"Well, believe it," Isobel said with a wry grin. "There was a second-year boy who I looked a bit like; I think it was him they wanted, really."

"Well, in any case, that was your first play. Was that when you 'caught the bug,' so to speak?"

Isobel shrugged. "Actually, no, not really. I was in another couple of plays that year, but I didn't act again for years after that." I could tell I was still missing something, but I just couldn't put my finger on what. Surely, she wasn't scared of me hunting down some old VHS of her university am-dram production?

"Why not?" I pressed, glancing down at my notes momentarily. "What stopped you?"

"Oh, nothing, particularly. I just didn't really have the opportunity or the desire." Isobel smirked. "If I'm honest, I didn't even consider it as a career."

"Obviously something changed your mind." *Or someone...*

"Well, after I got bored with modelling, I began to reconsider."

"You chose acting out of boredom?"

Isobel smiled slightly. "God, that sounds incredibly arrogant, doesn't it?"

"We're probably going to have to find something different to put in your book," I murmured, tapping my fingers against the notebook.

"I thought you wanted the truth."

"Hey, I love the truth. The book-buying public, on the other hand... they like interesting stories. And not thinking one of their favourite actresses got started in her life's work because of a post-uni slump."

"Well, I'm sure you could find some modelling-related drama to pin it on," Isobel said, sitting back in her seat, relaxing now. "But in honesty, I really just got tired of walking around without talking."

"Mm. I'm sure we'll find some way of putting it nicely." Suddenly I was tired, the earlier enthusiasm I felt for ferreting out Dewitt's secrets draining away despite all the tea I had drunk. It seemed that Isobel perhaps picked up on this on some level, because she placed her cup down then and rested her hands on the table as though about to push to her feet.

"Shall we get some air, maybe? We're quite near the park here..."

Sure, why not? Sluggishly, I roused myself, slipping on my jacket while Isobel retrieved a beautiful rose-coloured cashmere shawl to wrap around her shoulders. Thus attired, we headed outside, my laptop case knocking against my thigh with every step. The day was crisp— uncharacteristically fresh and clear for London but cool with it, and I was surprised that Isobel didn't seem at all cold as we made our way along the road to the park.

She didn't seem overly inclined to talk, either, which was fine with me, if surprising. Isobel Dewitt didn't strike me as the type of person with a lot of time to kill, especially with someone as insignificant as me.

Eventually, her pace (which was quite brisk, what with her long legs and all) slowed, and I realized we had reached the destination that I didn't even know we were aiming for. We were just in a little copse—nothing special, just one of those faux-natural clumps of trees you get in the bigger parks. There was a bench there, scattered with the same fallen leaves that littered the path. She bent to sweep it clear, pleasingly unconcerned by the prospect of getting grime on her cream-coloured, no doubt expensively tailored shirt, and turned to take a seat, conspicuously occupying only half of the bench. Feeling more than a little bemused, I took the hint and sat, shifting my bag until it rested at my side.

"Well. This is nice," I said unnecessarily, and Isobel shot me a sidelong look.

Eventually, she spoke. "You're quite good at this sort of thing, aren't you?"

I considered making a throwaway comment, but I had the feeling a compliment from Isobel Dewitt was not to be treated so lightly. At least I thought it was a compliment.

I shrugged. "I've had a lot of practice."

"I'm sorry if I seem evasive," she said. "I'm used to telling the story myself, not having someone else eke it out of me."

"I understand it can be difficult. You've been doing extremely well, though," I said, mostly truthfully. "It's going to be a good book." This was true.

"Do you think?" Isobel turned to face me, resting her arm on the back of the bench. "How can you tell yet?"

"Well," I said after a moment's pause so that I didn't look like I was shooting my mouth off, "you're an interesting person who has led an interesting life. There's no way your story will be bad. And," I added after another discreet pause, "because I've already started writing it. And it's good."

"Is that usual? To have started drafting already?"

"It differs from book to book—but I suppose I don't usually start quite this early, no."

"I see."

"If you'd like a break from the interviews, I'm sure we can work something out," I offered then. I'm not really sure why—it wasn't as if my schedule would be helped by unnecessary breaks.

"Hm? Oh, no, no." Isobel shook her head. "Not at all. I didn't mean to suggest that I was having a hard time with the interviews, or... I suppose I'm just finding it hard to reveal so much without being in control of its output. How closely are you used to working with your clients? I know you've written for a couple of very literate people in the past—surely they wanted input?"

"Most of them trusted me to do my job," I replied, realizing belatedly that this sounded like a rebuke. "That being said, I'm flexible with how involved my subjects want to be with the whole process." Although I had never collaborated that much with any of them—most were too busy or didn't seem to care.

"Are you sure? I really don't want to get in the way..." Isobel made a face. "I feel like I'm being a control freak now."

"It's your story," I said as soothingly as possible. "It's understandable." Something in the pit of my stomach sunk—was I really relinquishing control so easily?

Isobel seemed to sense this, in that infuriating way that she always appeared to be one step ahead of even my own feelings, and she extended the arm that lay across the back of the bench to touch my shoulder lightly. "Am I being a total pain?" She had never sounded quite so English.

Maybe it was the touch that threw me, or the apology in her voice that made me smile ruefully and shake my head. "That's one of the last words I'd use to describe you."

Her expression softened slightly. "I think I just... I feel like if you really want to get to the bottom of me, as it were, to build up a complete picture, no holds barred... If I'm going to do that, I'd rather create that picture together. You know?"

"How do you want to do that?" I asked her, my smile slipping into a frown against my will. It wasn't that I didn't want her to be happy with the finished product, but the whole reason I did what I did was because most celebrities couldn't be bothered sitting down and typing up (or dictating, or whatever) their life stories, or they lacked the talent to do so. Isobel obviously had the motivation, and I'm sure with a good editor would be fine—so why keep me around at all?

As usual, she hadn't missed my irritation. However, maybe her skin was still thin from our earlier conversation, because for the first time she matched it with a little flash of her own.

"You know, I kept diaries from when I was fourteen through until just a few years ago—perhaps I should just pass those onto you and get on with my life uninterrupted," she said, a distinctly sharp edge to her tone that, with her physical stance unchanged, felt almost threatening.

Fighting not to recoil at her tone, I swallowed, taking my time to reply. "I don't want to read your diaries—not if you want to keep them private. I just...don't understand what you want from me," I said honestly. "This is what I do. I talk to people about their lives and I form it into a coherent story and I write it all down. If you want more control over what I'm doing then...well, fine, but I don't know what you want. Drafts of each chapter? To write everything yourself and then have me edit it for you? This is a first for me, Ms. Dewitt. And to tell you the truth, I'm a bit lost."

At this, at least, some comprehension seemed to dawn. Isobel deflated slightly, shoulders slumping back on the bench. She smiled ruefully, shaking her head. "In other words, if I want to keep such a tight lid on myself, I should write my own damn autobiography?" The question was clearly rhetorical—she'd got the message. "I'm sorry." She sighed, turning her eyes from mine to take in the scene around us. "I'm not used to being...poked and prodded—or rather I am, but I'm used to telling people to fuck off."

I think it was the first time I'd heard her swear.

"It's not easy being in the public eye." Not that I'd know personally, but I had met—interviewed—*been* enough famous people to know. "You know that nothing is going in this book that you don't want, right?" I tried for a gentler tone. "It's just that this...prodding helps me get to know you, so I can capture your voice and make things more believable. We want people to think it's really you speaking to them, not some pathetic imitation."

"I can trust you on that, can I?" Isobel said, raising her eyebrows. Was that a tiny spark of vulnerability I sensed?

"Do you really think I'd still have a job if I went around putting tabloid scoops in my books?" I asked, looking back at her seriously. "Sorry, but I like getting paid a lot more than I like exposing people's dirty laundry."

My companion nodded slowly, as though processing this thoroughly. She didn't say anything for some time, and I thought that might be the end of our conversation. I was actually considering just taking my leave, in fact, when she spoke again, in a careful tone, as though trying the words out in her mouth as she said them, tasting something unfamiliar.

"I acted in second year," she said, "because I fell in love with a director. I stopped because our relationship did. And I didn't act for years after because that's how long it took me to recover."

I couldn't claim to be completely shocked, and it probably showed in my expression. "I see," I said, nodding.

If my lack of reaction bothered Isobel at all, however, she didn't show it. Maybe she was still formulating her thoughts, because she spoke again, quietly this time, and I amused myself with the thought that she was "getting into the part" now. "It was a private thing, even at the time—properly secret, I mean, not one of those open secrets everyone knows about. We both had our reasons. I... well, I was a nervy, anxious kid, younger than everyone else, better travelled but so much less experienced with plain old *life*, you know? And..." Isobel paused now, and I watched her wrestle again before delivering the punchline that part of me somehow *knew* was coming. "And she was older, and seriously involved with someone else. Still is."

"I can see why you lied," I murmured, wishing I had switched on my recorder but knowing that would have destroyed what fragile trust she had in me now.

"I don't lie. I edit."

That was a good line, even if it was patently untrue. "Mm. Do you still love her?" I asked, testing my newfound boundaries.

"Of course," she said immediately. Then, "And no, not really. You know how it is. It was a long time ago—God, nearly twenty years—and I'm not the same person. I suppose the twee thing to say would be that I still love the memory." She glanced back at me, clearly looking to take a reading.

My expression was carefully blank, though it was as much because I had no young romances of my own as it was an effort to show I wasn't judging her. "Hm. See, *that* would sell books," I commented, raising my eyebrows just slightly to show I wasn't serious.

"That can't go in the book. For more reasons than one, and not least because of the other people it would hurt."

"I know. But thank you for telling me anyway."

"I've been very, very careful about my private life," Isobel went on matter-of-factly. "I've been particularly careful not to make it look like it's an effort—I've never been one of those celebrities people describe as 'fiercely private' or 'secretive.' That's been the hardest part, and the most important. People don't see what they're not looking for. I don't want that to change."

Then you probably shouldn't be publishing an autobiography. I resisted the urge to roll my eyes. Then it occurred to me that in some ways it was the perfect method of burying something completely. Publish a "tell-all" memoir that tells nothing. "As I said, you'll have final say over everything that goes in the book. I might put things in there that I think would make a good story, but if they're too revealing, then, well, I'll find a way to cut them out." At least having her cooperating with me would mean I'd get a fuller picture, even if I wouldn't be able to use it all.

What I hadn't banked on, of course, with all my newfound permission to push and prod at the edges of Isobel Dewitt's comfort zones, was that she would begin to push back.

Chapter Eight

I WAS JERKED out my first sound sleep in ages by the ringing of my mobile, which had inconveniently become located practically underneath my ear due to various twists and turns I had undertaken while slumbering. Checking the flashing digital clock, I became aware of the ungodly hour—nine in the morning—and the fact that it was an unknown number. I considered not answering it, but now that I was awake there was no hope of even dozing, so I groaned and picked it up.

"Hello?"

"Nicola Booth, you lied to me."

"What? Who is this?" I scowled, reaching for the glass of water I kept by the bed as I heard how hoarse my voice was.

"How many people do you lie to on a daily basis—is it that hard to tell?" There was something familiar in the accent, a hint of Irish indignation to the words.

"Ah, Ms. Maguire," I murmured. "How did you get this number?"

"Isobel gave it to me. She also told me that you're helping to write her autobiography."

"And she gave you my number."

"Yes, she did. Why did you lie to me?"

"Because I didn't know that she'd want her ghost busted." There was a pause, and I smirked when I realize what I'd said. Of course, now she'd probably think I was making fun of her.

If she was annoyed by that, she didn't say anything, merely moving briskly onward. "Well, you have been. So now that that's over with, will you have dinner with me?"

It was my turn to pause. What the hell was going on? "Pardon me?"

"It's a simple question. Will you have dinner with me? I'm busy tonight, but tomorrow works."

"Why?" The word was out of my mouth before I could stop it.

"Why what? Why did I ask you, or why should you say yes?" She almost sounded like she was enjoying herself now.

I pulled the phone away from my ear to frown at it. It was too early for this crap. Before I could think it through and stop myself, I had pressed the red button and thrown it back onto my bedside table.

That certainly shut her up; at least, she didn't call back. I lay in bed, looking up at the ceiling and pondering this completely random turn of events. Why would Isobel have told her about me? Why were they talking about me in the first place? And why did Laura Maguire want to ask me out to dinner, especially after finding out I had lied to her?

"SO LET ME get this straight." Julie rolled her shoulders back into the couch behind her. She lifted a handful of crisps to her mouth and chomped them down with gusto before going on. "This cute, talented girl asks you to dinner, even after you've blanked her once and lied to her after...and you hung up on her?"

"First of all, it was incredibly early!" I protested, scowling. "You know I don't deal well with stuff before noon."

"And second of all?"

"I don't want to go to dinner with her!"

Julie gave me a look—one of those half-tolerant, half-exasperated looks that she's so very good at. Actually, I sort of love those looks because they mean she's not taking me seriously. When Julie's taking me seriously, I know there's something to be serious about, and that's usually a bad thing.

"Then don't," she said, as though this was an obvious idea that I clearly hadn't thought of.

"I'm not going to," I told her, despite the fact I had been debating all day whether to call Laura back or not. Like it or not, I was drawn to her, intrigued by her, and curious about her involvement with Isobel Dewitt, which having dinner with her would probably allow me to ascertain.

"Well then," Julie said, in her then-why-are-we-talking-about-this tone.

"Mary was lecturing me about being social the other day," I continued, as if there hadn't been a vast pause in the conversation. "She said I ought to do it 'for myself,' since I'm obviously withering away without human contact nowadays." I rolled my eyes to show how ludicrous this was.

"So is she saying you *should* be going to dinner with this woman?" Julie smirked. "Does she know you hung up on her?"

"Well no, that was just this morning," I huffed. "But she thought I should ask her out, or something."

"Interesting."

I made a face at her. I loved Julie deeply, but she could be so exasperating sometimes. "I'm sure."

"Oh, I just mean—well, Mary's pretty astute. And usually when she says jump, you ask her how high."

"She's my sponsor," I said dryly. "That's kind of the point."

"And this is an exception why?"

"Because...I don't date. And I think she's wrong to tell me I should."

"Oh, I'm not disagreeing necessarily, I'm just wondering why that's where the line gets drawn. You listened to her when she told you not to surf the net in bed—that's sort of personal too, right?"

"That's different. That's a sleep-pattern thing." And it was. Except that Julie was sort of right. I *did* usually take Mary's advice on most things. I wasn't sure why I was so resistant in this case, except for the fact that...I was nervous. I hadn't dated for years, and to be honest, I wasn't quite sure how to do it without involving alcohol. It seemed easier just to live like a hermit, even if it did mean I was alone for the rest of my days.

"I think you should call her back." Julie said, sounding decisive now. She had that I've-decided-to-chase-this-one tone. "At least to check whether you've totally blown it."

"What? Why would I do that?"

"Because you don't really want to end your days alone, and you've got to start somewhere?"

"If I was that worried, I'd just get a cat," I joked, leaning forwards to reach for the bowl of crisps. "Besides, I've totally blown it. She didn't call back, did she?"

"I'd have called you back just to tell you where to stick it."

"And if you didn't?"

Julie shrugged. "You should call her."

"If you're so enamoured, why don't *you* call her?" I challenged.

"She's not my type. Besides, she clearly likes you."

"Whatever."

I'LL ADMIT, THOUGH, the idea was now firmly implanted in my head, and it was all I could do not to pick up the phone as soon as Julie left that evening—in honesty, I think the only thing that stopped me was the fact it was already after eleven. Part of me thought it would only be fair dues to wake her up as she had woken me up that morning, but if I was trying to be apologetic, then a rude awakening was probably a bad idea. Still unsure about the whole mess, I went to bed, though I knew it was too early for me to get to sleep.

So imagine my surprise when I woke up at ten a.m., feeling well-slept and thoroughly human. This was not a usual turn of events by any means, but I knew better than to look a gift horse in the mouth. After a quick breakfast, I settled down to work, nursing a pot of tea at my desk as I began putting together a rudimentary draft of Isobel Dewitt's uni years. It was going well enough, save for the fact that I kept glancing at my mobile every five minutes, and I finally admitted defeat a little after noon. I picked up my phone, and after a good long stare at her contact card on the screen, I hit Call.

It rang out. Not about to leave a message, I hung up as her voice mail started, fighting the urge to toss my phone across the room. A moment later, it rang again, vibrating in my hand where I still held it, and I pressed the green button and held it to my ear without even checking it, giving my usual greeting of "Nic Booth."

"What do you want?"

"Uh, yes. Hi. I was calling to apologize, actually."

There was a long pause on the other end, and for a moment, I thought Maguire had chosen to repay the previous day's slight with one of her own. Eventually, though, I heard a faint sigh, and, "Oh?"

"I was sort of horrible yesterday," I said, grimacing—why had I not rehearsed an apology ahead of time? This was not going to go well. "And I'm sorry."

"Right."

"Listen, I'm not trying to offer excuses or anything, but I don't sleep very well and when you called, I was exhausted, so I may have reacted badly..."

Another long silence. "I see."

I sighed; this was a disaster. I should've listened to my gut, instead of Mary and Julie, the hopeless romantics. "Listen, I'm sorry, okay? I know I blew whatever...chance I might've had, but I just wanted to apologize. Good luck with all your...directing stuff. Sorry to bother you."

"How do you feel about Japanese food?"

"What?"

"Japanese food." She was speaking slower now, as though I was some kind of idiot. "Do you like it?"

"Um, yeah. I like Japanese." Japanese is good because it isn't one of those cuisines that automatically comes with a glass of wine—sometimes there's sake, but that stuff's disgusting anyway.

"Good. Do you know Akari?"

"Uh...yeah." Okay, I was back to being confused again. Was she asking me out? Even after my piss-poor excuse for an apology? Clearly, there was something wrong with her.

"All right. You can buy me dinner there," she said. "Tonight. Eight o'clock?"

"Okay. Sure." There was a long pause, and I cleared my throat nervously. "I'll see you there, I guess."

"See you there."

And *then* she hung up.

Chapter Nine

THE PROBLEM WITH having a date at eight o'clock was that it left me with approximately seven hours to work myself into a state of panic. It's not flattering, but you are probably aware by now that my social skills are lacking, to say the least—mainly from years of disuse and an addict's paranoia about functioning in the real world without a crutch. So by the time I was taking a seat in Akari—early even for me—I was basically vibrating at the speed of light and at this point even sake looked good. *How* did Mary think dating was a good idea? And was this even a date? I didn't even know now.

I had an excruciating twenty-minute wait in which I nervously fiddled with the menu, the small tea lights on the table (nearly burning myself in the process), my chopsticks, and my mobile phone, which I kept staring at as if it could somehow put me out of my misery. I wondered if Laura hadn't asked me here to deliberately stand me up—I *had* been rather rude to her on the phone, and I still couldn't fathom the idea that she might actually want to have dinner with me.

By the time she arrived, looking like she'd stepped out of a movie herself in a dark green dress that made me feel even more underdressed than I had already in my plain old shirt and jeans, I was actually slightly surprised to see her. I'd convinced myself that she wasn't going to show and mentally prepared myself for leaving the place alone. As such, where I'm usually not a terribly clumsy person, I almost knocked my own chair over standing up to greet her on approach.

"Hey," I said, stunned for a moment at the fact that she smiled as soon as she spotted me. "Um, hi. You look...great."

"So do you," she said easily in a tone that left me completely clueless as to whether she meant it or was just returning the compliment. I strongly doubted that I looked great, anyway. At best, I looked presentable.

We sat down, and immediately the dreaded small talk began. "So, um...do you eat here a lot?"

"Oh please," Laura said, rolling her eyes. "Can we skip all that? We've already managed to offend and insult one another to get here, we may as well skip the polite bit altogether, don't you think?"

"Uh, right." Of course, I didn't know what that left us to talk about. If there was one thing I was worse at than small talk, it was actually talking to strangers. Or near-strangers, anyway.

"So tell me how you're getting on with Isobel's book."

"What? Oh, no, I really can't talk about that…"

Laura frowned—though it looked to be in honest confusion rather than irritation (after all, I knew what her "irritated" looked like). "It's what you're working on right now, right?"

"Well, yes." Obviously. "But it's still a work in progress, and besides— I signed plenty of confidentiality agreements before I started. I really can't share any information." Part of me was disappointed—was this why she had wanted to meet? To find out juicy details about Dewitt's life? I shouldn't have been surprised, and yet…

"Oh, I don't want to know about *her*—I want to know about *you*," Laura said—that "idiot" tone was back again. "How are you finding it— easy, difficult? How does it compare to your last work?"

"Oh," I said, pleasantly surprised. Then, "I don't know. It's…not been my easiest assignment, but I think it's coming along well enough. Hard to say at this stage, though."

"How do you go about it—are you just interviewing her a lot? Reading her interviews?"

"I, uh…mainly talk to her, ask her questions about her past. Once I have enough to go on, I write it all up, try and get it sounding coherent."

"So you record it all?"

"Um, yes." I looked down at the menu, giving a slight shrug. "In one form or another."

"Can you write shorthand?"

Glancing up, I furrowed my brow. "Yes. Why?"

Laura's lips curled into a slight smile. "I just think that's cool."

"You think shorthand is cool?" Okay, she was *definitely* crazy.

"It's like a secret code. Well, to me. And it's retro." Laura shrugged. "I think it's cool, yeah."

"Huh." Strangely, I felt my cheeks growing hot. "It's not that hard to learn, really." I picked up a chopstick and reached forwards to a clear spot on the table. "The system I use is based on the alphabet, instead of phonetics, so you can pick it up really quickly. See, this is *a*," I said, drawing it out on the clean tablecloth. "And this is a *b*..."

SO IT TURNED out Laura was whip-smart, easier going than she'd first appeared, and on top of that, once I managed to stop second-guessing everything she said, a good conversationalist.

We ordered a few sushi rolls between us, chatting about everything from shorthand to Laura's upcoming projects. Maybe it was just that I was spending so much time in Isobel Dewitt's head, but I found all her talk fascinating.

"Yeah, I don't know. I mean, I enjoy directing, but I feel as though it's not where I'm really meant to be, you know?" she was saying now.

"Going to pull a reverse Dewitt and show up in front of the camera in your next film?" I asked with an amused smirk.

"Oh, I don't think so," Laura said with a chuckle, shaking her head. "I don't know, maybe I'm not even meant to be in film at all."

"I think you'd be hasty to quit altogether...you've definitely got talent."

Laura smiled. "Thanks. And no, I don't plan to. I just tend towards existential crisis when I get drunk, you know?" She waved her wineglass to emphasize the point.

"Ah." Luckily she hadn't pressed earlier when I had turned down a drink, and things were going well enough that the urge to reach across the table and grab her glass was minimal. "Well, it happens to the best of us. Have you considered...I don't know, writing, or producing?"

"I wrote my first film as well as directing. It was terrible. And I have no organisational ability," Laura added, looking sheepish, "so I could never produce."

"Isn't that what assistants are for?"

Laura laughed but didn't say anything, just sipped at her wine. This meant that the task of conversation fell to me, but unlike earlier, the thought didn't send me into a spiral of panic.

"So, um, seen any good films lately?"

THE REST OF the meal passed—dare I say it—very well. Laura seemed to have changed her opinion of me from "raging arsehole" to "tolerable, verging on funny," and it meant that things were quite pleasant between us. I was on reasonably good form, particularly after Laura ordered a water after her second glass of wine, which calmed my nerves considerably. Tipsy people I can handle—even enjoy. Drunk people, I didn't even like when *I* was drinking.

When the bill came, I reached for my wallet. Whether or not this was a date, I still intended to make good on my promise, and Laura made no move to stop me, though she did shoot me a slight smirk, obviously remembering the events leading up to my agreeing to pay for us both.

Jackets on, we emerged into the crisp night-time air. I didn't know how Laura had gotten there, but I assumed (and hoped) that after two glasses of wine she wasn't planning on driving home.

"So are you going to call a cab, or do you need a lift?" I asked, trying to keep my tone light and helpful.

"Which way do you live?" she asked. "I was going to get a taxi, but if we're heading in the same direction..."

Though we weren't going in exactly the same direction, I ended up giving her a lift anyway—look at that, irony, Nic the designated driver. We chatted a bit more on the drive, and upon reaching her flat, I pulled to the kerb, engine idling as we said our goodbyes.

This, of course, was the moment of truth, when I found out whether or not this was, in fact, a date. My hands felt glued to the wheel.

"Thanks for dinner," Laura said, reaching to unhook her seatbelt. "I had a good time."

"I did too," I said, surprising myself. I really had had a nice evening, in the end, for all my nerves.

"Well, good. Maybe we could do it again sometime."

I nodded, even though I wasn't sure if this was an invitation for a second date or just an offer of "hanging out."

Laura smiled again, looking amused, and not for the first time, she reminded me a little of Isobel in some respects—those knowing little smiles. She leaned over, and for a moment, I did think that she was going to kiss me, but then she turned her head smoothly to the side, and her lips brushed lightly over my cheek.

"I'll see you soon, Nicola," she said, pulling back and opening the car door.

"Nic," I said, "call me...Nic." The door was already shut, and without a second glance, Laura was making her way up the front steps to her door.

Took your advice and had a date. Well, not sure it was, but still had good time. And no booze. Go me.

The response didn't come until the morning—I hadn't expected it to. Mary's usually in bed by ten o'clock of an evening.

Well done you. Need to meet up and talk about it, or...?
Would love to, but can't—workday today. Meeting tonight. Will call afterwards if I need to.

Chapter Ten

So THE "DATE"—or whatever it was—was done. I'd survived. I'd even enjoyed myself. Now, of course, the paranoia and obsessing began. As I usually did when I wanted distraction, I threw myself into work with a vengeance. Which had varying levels of success. On one hand, I tore through a couple more chapters that, while not perfect, probably didn't need to be burned to the ground. On the other, the deeper I sunk into "Isobel Dewitt headspace", the more I thought about Laura and our date-not-date, and that, obviously, didn't help at all.

I kept finding myself flashing back to that moment just as I left the screening, the two of them, heads so close they were almost touching, talking in lowered voices, chuckling at their private joke. In light of what I'd learned about Isobel's history, the moment seemed to take on another dimension. Was it in my head?

The next opportunity I had to find out was my scheduled interview with Dewitt, which found us once again at the hotel bar, just in time for the pre-dinner crowd. We had a secluded table in the corner, and I set up my recording equipment as usual as the waiter arrived with my mineral water and (unusually) a glass of wine for Isobel.

"So I heard you had dinner with Laura," Isobel said immediately upon us settling, doing that single eyebrow arch thing. "Did you enjoy yourselves?"

"I can't speak for her, obviously, but I had a nice time," I told her with a small neutral smile.

"She said you were—and I quote—'very urbane once you relaxed,'" Isobel replied with that unreadable smile of hers. I was becoming a connoisseur of Isobel Dewitt facial expressions, but I still understood only a fraction of them.

"Well, that was...nice of her." What the hell did she mean by that? And why was she giving me that look? "I guess I'm a bit rusty on the whole socializing front." I almost said "dating," but changed my mind at the last second.

"Well, Laura's a good place to start, at least. She's very non-judgemental once you get past her temper."

"Do you know from experience?" I ventured curiously, pursing my lips.

"Of her temper, or her non-judgement?"

"Either. Both."

Isobel smirked. "I suppose I do, then, yes."

"Interesting." We stared at each other for a few more seconds before I broke first, clearing my throat and shuffling my notes. "So, last time we had gotten up to *Home and Hearth*—shall we continue?"

"Sure."

And there I was again, listening, rapt, to Isobel talking about her career, anecdotes on set, what it was like to work with this person or that person—standard stuff but endlessly engaging nonetheless.

Don't get me wrong—it would get in the book. If I was enjoying this, then the average reader would eat it up. They loved getting a glimpse behind the scenes, and Isobel knew how to give just what they wanted, just enough to be interesting without being repetitive or bragging.

She also knew, of course, how to smooth over the cracks and miss things out without the average reader noticing. I noticed. Every missing piece. But the question was, should I say anything?

Eventually, though, I couldn't help myself. "What was it like working with Melody Graham again after all those years? It must have been a bit strange."

Isobel raised her eyebrows. She knew what I was driving at. "Absolutely, at first," she said smoothly. "We hadn't seen one another at anything other than parties for, oh, since uni, I suppose. But we got back into the swing of things in no time."

How much "in the swing," I wondered. Pursing my lips, I nodded slightly, looking expectantly at her.

Her response was a smirk. "Besides, it was different working on a film—it always is."

"How so?"

"Film's easier. But at the same time, more absorbing, subtler, more...intimate." Isobel shrugged. "It's different."

"Hm." Just then the waiter arrived with another glass of wine for Isobel, who looked curiously at me. It took me a moment to catch it, after which I vigorously shook my head. "No, no thanks."

She nodded silently, that eyebrow quirking just a shade. I knew that look—oh, it wasn't quite as appealing on most people, but it was the same look. It was the look of a tickling in the back of the mind, the beginning of the dawning.

I smiled through it, as I usually did (unless I scowled), looking back over my notes as the waiter departed, leaving my glass empty. Well, I'm sure it wasn't the first time Isobel Dewitt's table partner was ignored.

"Anyway," Isobel said with a smooth smile, "are you going to see Laura again?"

Once again, she had caught me out. "I, uh, don't know. Again, that's sort of up to her, I guess."

"Hm. Funny, she said the same thing to me. More or less."

"Wait, she said she would?" I don't know which prospect appealed to me more—the fact that Laura wanted to see me again, or the idea that she and Isobel had spent time discussing me.

"Ah, no. She said that she wasn't sure whether she'd see you again, and that that very much depended on you."

"Oh. Right. Well, I mean, I wouldn't mind seeing her again, but if she wants me to pass some tests or jump through hoops—"

"...Then that would make it all the more interesting, surely?" Isobel said with a slight smirk. "Isn't uncertainty and power struggling part of the fun sometimes?"

"I don't do well with power struggles," I told her, frowning. "Or uncertainty. I like knowing where I stand and what's expected of me."

"Then I suppose you'll be used to being up front yourself."

"I try." Hey, you saw me at a meeting. I'm no liar.

"Then you should do just fine." God, that smile. If I wasn't sitting down, I think my knees would've trembled. There's a reason we keep people this perfect safely on a screen.

"Um, right. Anyway. I think we've got enough for today. I don't want to keep you—you said you had an event this evening."

"That's right. Do you want to come?"

"Excuse me?"

"It's a dinner, but I'm quite sure I could get you onto the guest list."

"No, that's *really* okay, thanks." I smiled tightly and gathered up my things, suddenly eager to get home.

"Laura's going..."

"Well then. I hope you two have fun."

Isobel raised both eyebrows this time, and I could tell she wasn't amused, and suddenly I was annoyed with her all over again. Where the hell did she get off, trying to interfere like this? Whose interview was this anyway?

I packed up the rest of my things in silence, then stood to put on my jacket as the noise of the restaurant buzzed around us. Isobel sat back in her chair, eyeing me and, I swear, holding her wineglass up like a shield between us—which didn't help.

"I'll call your assistant to set up another interview in a few days," I told her, reverting to Polite Professional mode and hoping it would help me escape unscathed. "Thank you for today."

"The pleasure was absolutely mine."

Chapter Eleven

"SO THE THING is that I don't know if I'm ready to see someone, not yet. It's not that I'm scared I'll want to drink—I always want to drink, I'm used to that. But the idea of laying myself out like that, making myself vulnerable... I put so much effort into staying strong. I don't remember how to be weak."

The nervous-looking young man sat down, immediately clenching his hands onto his knees as though to keep them from knocking together. His little testimony was met with a smattering of applause and supportive murmurings.

You know, when you put it like that, it sounds ridiculous. "I don't remember how to be weak." Seriously? Okay, never mind that it was the exact same problem I was going through at that exact same moment, never mind that he was *right*...it was just so stupid. I was annoyed with him for bringing it up, for putting it into words like that, just like I was annoyed with myself for feeling that way. So, of course, the first thing I did when the meeting was over was pull out my mobile and dial Laura's number before I even left the hall, as if I was trying to prove something.

It rang for a long time again, but this time, she did pick up. I could hear conversation in the background, and I remembered—the dinner. "Hello?" she said, her voice a little giggly.

"Um, hi. Laura. It's Nic. I was...ah, calling to see if you wanted to get dinner again sometime," I said, forging bravely onward.

"Oh. Well, sure, why not," Laura said, sounding noncommittal at best. "How about the weekend?"

"Yeah, okay." I felt embarrassed at her lack of interest—I mean, didn't Isobel say she wanted to see me again? "Actually, no. I mean, if you're not that bothered, then I won't take up your time," I told her, bristling slightly.

"What?" The background noise was clearly too loud for this sort of conversation.

"You know what...never mind. If you want to go out again, call me back. If not...no hard feelings." Except there kind of would be. What was wrong with me? "'Kay? Have a good ...party."

"Right. See you later, Nic."

JESUS. WHAT WAS *wrong* with me? I was staring up at the Excel Docklands, having taken a taxi all the way out there from my flat, and I was wearing a dress. One that had been hastily (and gleefully) lent to me by Julie after a frantic phone call.

The doorman, to my considerable relief, just glanced down at his list when I mumbled my name and then waved me through. Good ol' Dewitt had put me on the list just in case I showed. The self-congratulatory moment from my successful read on her was too brief to properly dispel my low-level panic.

I stumbled through the lobby, unused to wearing shoes with heels (or at least doing it while sober) and very, very close to turning around and leaving. It was only adrenaline that kept me going—that, and the fact that Julie would know if I chickened out and mock me mercilessly if I did.

The dinner was finished apparently. The various guests, more of them familiar to me from newspapers and magazines than I was comfortable with, were now milling around, seated chatting in corners, standing in little groups. It took me some moments to find the woman I was looking for, and unsurprisingly, she was with another familiar face.

"Uh, hi. Fancy meeting you here," I quipped after a fashion, clutching my purse tightly in both hands and giving both Laura and Isobel a smile. "How was dinner?"

Isobel smiled at me. Laura, I caught out of my peripheral vision, looked over at Isobel with a curious expression before doing the same.

"Lovely," Laura said. "Quite excellent."

"Mm, good. It's, uh, a nice event."

"It is—it's a charity dinner for refugees. A very worthy cause," Isobel said.

"Oh, right." I bobbed my head, giving the room a quick scan before looking back at Laura. "Could I, uh, talk to you for a minute?"

Laura pursed her lips. Then she nodded. She didn't, however, make any move to leave Isobel's side.

Great. Just great. Taking a deep breath, I tried to focus on the redhead in front of me. "I know I was a bit short on the phone earlier. It's been a long time since I've done...this sort of thing."

I spotted Isobel, who was listening openly, raising an eyebrow. Laura raised both, just slightly. "This sort of thing?"

Shit. Now was the point where I made a complete and utter fool of myself. "Socializing?"

Laura looked me in the eye, steadily, for a long moment. Then—you know, I don't know if she was cutting me a break or trying to make things worse, because then, in front of everyone including Isobel Dewitt, she leaned in, took hold of my arm, and kissed me firmly and more enthusiastically than I'm usually given to in public. I was basically frozen to the spot, the feeling only returning to my limbs at the point where she broke contact and tipped her head to whisper in my ear.

"Now go home. You're so uncomfortable it's embarrassing. I'll see you at the weekend."

AFTER THAT WHOLE...debacle, there was very little chance that I would (a) get any sleep or (b) get any work done. Luckily, I was so thrilled that I didn't really care. I mean, I had to get over my intense embarrassment first, but once I did, I came to the realization that for the first time in years I had a date with a woman—not just a fling in a back room or a one-night stand.

Of course, that meant a lot was going to have to change. I started by spending most of the night awake cleaning the flat. Not that I remotely expected to take her there any time in the next, you know, century.

It also meant that I had to get on a more regular working schedule, which wasn't helped by the all-night cleaning. So maybe the regular schedule would have to start the day after tomorrow. I also made a "date" to talk to Mary about stuff—not that I thought she'd be much practical help, being practically celibate herself, but she knew how to talk me out of the endless mental spirals I got myself into sometimes.

Julie, on the other hand, I tried to avoid. But as usual, being some kind of psychic as far as I can tell, she seemed to know somehow and showed up, unannounced, around lunchtime the next day.

I was barely out of bed and still clutching my first mug of tea when she sailed in, an I-told-you-so grin on her face. "Away, damn gossipy harpy!" I groaned at her from the couch, but she didn't listen.

"So," she said, collapsing down onto the couch. "Tell me everything."

"I already *told* you everything. On the phone. Remember?"

"Tell me again with facial expressions and gestures, then."

I rolled my eyes—how was that for a facial expression? "I showed up at the dinner, made a fool of myself and then, voila—" I spread my hands. "She asked me out anyway."

"Just like that?"

"Well. Something like that, anyway."

"Well." Julie sounded rather satisfied. "Looks like my dress did the trick, eh? Maybe I should make you keep it..."

"No way. You're taking it away with you. I'm seeing her at the weekend. I'll go out and get a nice shirt or something before then." Seriously, we were talking about clothes?

"Hm. Maybe I should go with you."

"Jules, no. You know how much I hate shopping. I don't want to turn this into a big thing."

"You've been needing a new wardrobe for a while—come on, don't tell me your advance wouldn't allow for it..."

"Yes, but—"

"No buts. We'll go tomorrow, whenever you're free."

I sighed. There was no point arguing with her when she got this way. "Fine."

FROM THEN, SHE seemed okay with leaving me alone, and we actually spent a nice couple of hours playing cards before she had to go off on some date. It was only after she had departed that I realized she had left the dress, but I figured burying it in the closet would probably protect me from random acts of girlishness.

That accomplished, I began to look over the chapters I had written thus far, reading them with an eye to how a general reader might see it. My conclusion? It was good—certainly nothing wrong with the writing— but there was something missing. There was glamour and excitement, highs and lows, humour and sadness... But there was no romance. And that was a big problem.

It wasn't as though she hadn't had plenty of love affairs that had reached the attentions of the public—she'd even been engaged for a time to a fellow actor she'd met, classically, on set—but somehow, none of it had seemed interesting enough to put into words. I wondered whether this was because she didn't find those relationships interesting or worthy of note, or because *I* didn't.

Whatever the case, we would have to fix that. Readers wanted romance, and if they didn't get it, well... The publisher's bank accounts would be none too happy with the book, and by extension, me. So one way or another, the next time we met, Isobel and I were going to have to delve into her romantic life. The thought made me equal parts nervous and excited.

Perhaps it was this excitement, as well as my own recent success with women (or at least one particular woman) that spurred me to make another phone call I had been putting off. It was already evening by the time I worked up the courage, so I fortunately got the answering service.

"Um, hi, my name is Nicola Booth—I'm a writer, and I was hoping to be able to speak with Ms. Graham about a project I'm working on. If she was interested, I could meet with her almost any time—or call her. Either way, um, if you could just ask her and get back to me that would be great. Right. Oh, and tell her Isobel says hi." Quickly I left my number and then hung up the phone, my heart pounding. That had been very cheeky. I hoped to God it worked.

I heard nothing the next morning, and in the afternoon, of course, Julie was dragging me around horrible, crowded, overheated clothing shops, which frequently had next to no phone signal, leaving me consistently even more annoyed than I already would've been—which was "quite."

When I was finally released—after Julie had decided my wardrobe was now less of an embarrassment and I had approximately fifteen heavy bags to lug home—I immediately checked my phone. The voice mail icon stared up at me tauntingly, and I dialled the mailbox with shaky fingers.

You have...two...new messages. First new message. Message received...today...at... twelve...forty...p.m.

There was a slight sigh on the line. Then, *"Hey, just calling to check up on the weekend—call me."*

Press one to listen to the message again, press two to—

I pulled the phone away from my ear and pressed three.

Message deleted. Next new message. Message received...today...at...one...eighteen...p.m.

A short silence.

End of messages.

Even without a message, I *knew* Melody Graham had called me. How could she not? She was obviously curious but reluctant—the real question was not whether I could get her to speak with me, but rather whether I could get her to tell the truth...

Chapter Twelve

"ANYWAY, I SUPPOSE he wasn't the easiest director to work with, but all things considered, I think I had more fun on the set of that film than almost any other I've worked on."

"Hm. That's good." Nodding, I scribbled a few notes—we were floating about quite a bit now, and I wanted to make sure I kept the timeline straight. "Thanks."

"Was there anything else about that film you wanted to know?"

"No, I...think that's enough for now." I glanced up at her then, giving her a smile. I had been a bit distracted that day, I admit, but I thought things were going well enough.

Isobel's sharp gaze seemed to miss nothing. "Are you all right?"

"Yes, everything's fine."

"You seem a little...elsewhere."

"Oh, I...I'm sorry." Ducking my head, I focused on the notes in front of me, unable to meet Isobel's enquiring eyes. "If you'd like to cut the meeting short, that's fine with me."

"No, no, it's fine. Anything you want to talk about? I'm quite a good listener, you know..."

"I'm sure you are." In truth, I had been distracted by thoughts of my evening with Laura the night before—I guess I could actually call it a date now, especially as it had ended with a rather longer kiss than the one in front of everybody at the charity dinner.

"So go on. Want to tell me how last night went?"

I had a feeling playing coy wasn't going to work, but I tried anyway. "Last night?"

"With Laura."

"Oh. Um, it was nice." I gave her a bland look, following it up with a shrug. "We had a good time."

"A very good time, I heard," Isobel said with a smirk.

Damn it. Now she had me. "Well, if you've already heard it once, you don't need to hear about it again."

"I'd like to hear your side. I mean, if you'll tell me," Isobel said with that effortlessly charming smile.

"There, ah, isn't much to tell. We...had dinner again. Talked. That's all."

"What did you talk about?"

"Oh, well, you know..." I shrugged. "Films. Books. Art."

"Anything exciting in common?"

"We both like Cubism?" Okay, maybe not exciting, but certainly unusual. Most people preferred bland, staid Impressionism. Laura didn't.

"Really? Interesting." Isobel narrowed her eyes in thought as she observed me. "Funny, I expected you to be more a super-realism type."

"What, I can't like two styles of art?" I quipped, smirking.

"So you *do* like super-realism?"

"Not all of it. But some, yeah."

"Interesting. I have a couple, actually, at the house. Must show you them, sometime. Perhaps we should schedule our next meeting there."

"That would be great," I said eagerly, interested more in seeing Dewitt's home than the art itself. "You don't have anything by Daniel Quintero, do you?"

"God, I wish. No, but I think you'll like what I do have..."

I smiled in spite of myself, enjoying the fact that she was very obviously showing off to me. "I'm sure I will."

"So what you're *not* saying," Mary said, pursing her lips and adjusting her fingers around the mug, "is that you haven't a clue what's going on with either of these women. Am I right?"

I stared at her, considered protesting, then gave up before I even began. "Pretty much. I mean, don't get me wrong, it's certainly interesting, but...I'm lost here."

"How was the date? You didn't really say other than 'fine' on the phone..."

"Well, I don't know. I mean, it was fine, as far as I can tell. It's not like I have a huge backlog of this sort of experience to compare it to." Pursing my lips, I surveyed my tea as if I might be able to divine some answers from it. None were forthcoming. "We had Italian, we talked, I gave her a ride home again... She kissed me."

"Like at the party?"

"Sort of." In truth, it had been quite different from the party—the anticipation had been building all night, so when she leaned in to press her lips to mine in the car, I had only frozen for a moment before returning the kiss. It had been light and lingering. She had tasted just slightly of red wine. I didn't tell Mary this.

"Do you like her? I mean, well, obviously you like her," Mary said with a wry smile, "but what I mean is do you actually see it going anywhere? Do you have things in common?"

"We, um... I don't know. I mean yes," I corrected myself quickly. "We do, actually. And I do like her. She's entertaining, and interesting, and..." *Not Isobel Dewitt.* The thought popped up completely unbidden, arresting my train of thought for a moment. "She's really nice. I just don't know if she likes *me.*"

"Hm. Have you told her?" She didn't have to specify what. Honestly, I was surprised she hadn't asked before now.

"Not yet, no."

"I'm sure I don't have to say it, do I?"

"I'm going to tell her, Mary. There just hasn't been the right time." I knew it was a lame excuse, but I didn't care. Dealing with an addiction meant moving in the timeline that worked for you, not anybody else. "It hasn't been an issue, anyway." Well, except for the part where it was *always* an issue. Especially that kiss.

"You know that you should be honest with all the people in your life," Mary said with a sigh, sounding as though she was speaking from a pamphlet. Probably because she was. "Holding this stuff back is the way you end up drinking again."

"I know, I *know*, I just didn't think a second date was the right time to bring it up. I'll tell her."

"Okay." Mary still looked worried.

"Anyway. I'm supposed to go to Isobel's tomorrow night, for more interviewing."

"At her house?"

"Yeah. She has some art she wants to show me. And I figured it might help me get a better handle on who she is, use it in the book."

"I see. You've never seen her house before, then?"

"No, not yet. We've always met at a hotel in the centre of town. It's more convenient."

"So where's her house?"

"She's got a place out in Hampstead," I told her, sipping my increasingly lukewarm tea. "It sounds nice."

"Lovely. Well, you must let me know how you get on."

"Of course. You know you're always the first I tell about my oh-so-exciting life."

Mary smiled. "Always glad to listen."

Chapter Thirteen

AS IF MY week wasn't interesting enough—my date with Laura, my impending evening with Isobel—not long after leaving the café, I received a phone call from one of the last people on earth I expected to hear from.

"Hello?" I asked, having frowned at the blocked number on the mobile screen before picking up. "Nicola Booth."

"This is Melody Graham."

"Oh! Oh, um, hello. Thank you for calling me back."

"What do you want?"

"Well, I...was hoping to speak to you about a project I'm currently working on. I'm a writer."

"I see. And you know Isobel Dewitt?"

"Ah, yes. She's actually the subject of said project." I know I said I don't like exposing the people I'm working on, but I didn't know any other way to get Graham to talk to me. I still wasn't sure she would.

"You know, it's a good few years since we've even seen one another, other than at parties," the voice said.

"Well, yes, I know. But I'm sort of doing an...overview of her life. So that's all right."

"She hired a ghostwriter?" I heard a low chuckle.

"You're very quick." I could see why Dewitt liked her. "Yes, she did. I'm currently most of the way through a first draft, but it's not quite right yet. I was hoping to speak to some important people from her life to..."

"To dig up some dirt?"

"I don't do dirt, Ms. Graham." And besides, I already had enough of that if I wanted it. "I just want to make it the best book I can."

"And you think I can help."

"I think so, yes."

There was another pause. "I'm not sure what qualifies me. I've known her for a long time, but our relationship has been very patchy."

"I understand that, Ms. Graham. I wouldn't have contacted you if I didn't think there was something you could help me with."

"What is it you think I could help with?"

"I'd like to get a better idea of what Isobel was like when she was younger. In uni."

"I didn't know her that well at uni."

I sighed. I had hoped Graham would have been intrigued enough to want to give her own side of the story. Clearly, she was sticking to the nothing-happened tack, though. I considered giving up; I wasn't a muckraker, and I really didn't need Graham's testimony for the book.

Something made me push just a little harder, one last time. "That isn't what I heard, Ms. Graham. Isobel told me you were very close for a time."

"Ms. Booth." I knew immediately from her tone that I was about to be shut down altogether. "Whatever you've discerned, or been told, there's really nothing about my relationship to Isobel Dewitt that would be of use to you. I assure you."

Damn it. I should've known that wouldn't have worked. "I'm sorry. I didn't mean to imply—" Except that I did. "Actually, scratch that. I did. But you should know, Ms. Graham, I'm *not* doing this to try and dig up dirt on either of you. There's no way it would get past Isobel *or* my editor even if I did. I'm not interested in gossip, I just... I want to know more about her."

A silence—I thought she'd hung up for a moment. "I see."

"But I'm sorry to take up your time. I won't bother you again."

"Look, Ms. Booth..." She sighed. "I'm sorry. I'll see what I can do. I'll have my assistant call you."

"That...would be great. Thank you."

"All right. But Ms. Booth?"

"Yes, Ms. Graham?"

"No recorders."

"Of course."

OF COURSE. SO now I had two meetings with beautiful women to look forward to—well, three, if you counted my next date with Laura. I wasn't sure which I was most eager for.

In the midst of it all, I was still writing—a lot, actually. Even though I had gotten down several solid chapters and was at a point where I'd probably stop and step back for a while, I realized I didn't want to. Isobel was still a mystery to me, but that didn't stop me from delving in, losing myself in speculation about her life and how she felt about it—not what she told me, but how she *really* felt.

I still wasn't reading back over my words and hearing Isobel's voice, though. Looking back at everything I had written, I was seized with the overwhelming urge to delete it all and start from scratch—which probably would've given my agent a heart attack. Instead, I turned my attention towards prepping for my dates—meetings—whatever they were.

The first would be my next appointment with Isobel—at her house.

Chapter Fourteen

I SHOWED UP early—I wanted to be polite, but I also couldn't wait to see her house. And as I pulled up outside, I could already tell my anticipation was well founded. The house was gorgeous. The grounds were pristine, the exterior well-maintained and inviting. I didn't know a lot about architecture, but it certainly seemed to fit in with the other swanky houses I had passed on the way there.

Naturally, Isobel didn't answer the door herself, and I found myself waiting in a beautiful, perfectly appointed, completely impersonal, and currently deserted drawing room. She kept me waiting a good few minutes before entering—sweeping into the room wasn't too strong a description for it. She was wearing a pair of loose linen trousers and a simple vest, a long silver necklace dangling between her perfect breasts. Once again, I felt grubby and unglamorous in my jeans and collared shirt, standing to greet her.

"Nicola, hello. I'm so sorry to keep you waiting—I was on a call from the States and they just kept rambling *on* and *on*."

I grinned, hoping I didn't look as nervous as I felt. "Well. Shall we...?" I gestured vaguely. I couldn't really imagine sitting and talking to Isobel in this room—honestly, I couldn't really imagine *anyone* sitting and talking in this room.

"Here? Don't be silly." Isobel waved a hand, beckoning me to follow. "Let's go somewhere more comfortable, shall we?"

I'm sure my relief was palpable as she let me through towards the back of the house, down some stairs, and into what felt like a completely different abode. The house was built on a hill, it seemed, with the rear lower than the front, so that there was a whole basement area looking out at the well-kept back garden through wide patio doors (although I'm sure they're french windows or whatever in houses like these). The living space down here was comfortable, homey, a lot less expensive-looking (in fact, I could swear I recognized an IKEA couch), and frankly looked much more like the sort of place a person might actually live.

"Take a seat," she told me with another expressive flick of her wrist. "I'm sorry it's a bit of a mess." I could tell she was enjoying playing hostess with me, and that she didn't miss anything even as I swept my gaze around the room to find a comfortable spot to sit. I opted for the IKEA couch, forcing myself to relax back, pulling out my usual accoutrements—the pad, the pen, the Dictaphone.

"So. What do you want to talk about today?" Not that I was necessarily going to stick to that. But hey, might as well let her start in her comfort zone.

"What did we leave off on last time?" she asked, still pottering around the room, opening a window to let in the late-afternoon air. "I think we were discussing my work with Peter Anderson, weren't we?"

"Ah, right," I said with a slight smirk. "The *From Within* series—with all the experience and accolade you had as an actress at that point, what was it that attracted you to a movie spin-off from a video game?"

"A bit of fun?" she replied with a graceful shrug and a smile. "Not that serious projects aren't fun, but I suppose I wanted a chance to throw away the script and 'kick some butt.'"

"You certainly lent some gravitas to proceedings—what was it like working with that sort of crew?"

"Oh, they were lovely. They were really very professional."

"Would you ever do another?"

Isobel laughed. "I'm afraid I might be a bit past my prime with regard to that sort of role. If the right film came along, I might be interested in being involved in some other capacity, though."

As she laughed, I succumbed to an involuntary grin. It was hard not to laugh along. "There were all sorts of rumours surrounding *From Within: 2*, weren't there? Regarding the scene in the swimming pool, among others?"

"I'll tell you what I've told every other reporter: I have not ever used a body double in my life. And I did almost all of my own stunts."

"Which means of course that you *do* have the tattoo that you catch that sneak peek of on slow replay?" I felt small getting into this, but I figured I might as well find out whether there *was* a story of any kind there. I'd even checked the DVD for myself. "Is there a story behind that?"

She hesitated, fussing a bit more with the blinds before turning and taking a seat on a well-used armchair. She didn't settle back, merely perching on the edge and folding her slender hands on her knees.

"I suppose, though it's not a particularly exciting one. I actually got it after—or during, I guess—the wrap party for the first film. A few of us did, to commemorate the experience."

"Do they all match?"

"Mm, I don't know. They were all done by the same artist, but everyone had theirs a bit personalized—mine incorporated a rose, for my character's name."

"So who else has them?"

"Oh, let's see..." Isobel pursed her lips. "Mostly just the main cast— Peter said he was going to do it too, but he chickened out at the last minute. But I know Bradley did, though he was a horrible wimp about it, and Nicholas...oh, and Grace Martinez, though it certainly wasn't her first."

I smirked, thinking of Martinez in the film series—a typical role for her, really, the tough woman-in-a-man's job part, tattooed and heavily armed in a vest and combats combo that thoroughly cemented her status as a lesbian icon, though the woman herself had never given any indication either way and had only ever been seen in public with men. Which reminded me, of course...

"Martinez said at the time that she found you hard to work with, although she also said that the two of you had got along very well. What do you think she meant?"

She wasn't so distracted as to dismiss the question, nor was she about to dish whatever dirt there might be. "You'd have to ask her for a definitive answer," she told me, narrowing her eyes just slightly as she regarded me over the low coffee table. "I think perhaps it was just that we came from different places—she was far more used to action roles than I was, and even though I tried very hard, all the stunts and activity didn't come naturally to me. We did become quite close off-set, though, as I'm sure you heard." This last statement seemed almost pointed, though she broke her gaze away and glanced out of the windows again as soon as she had said it.

I considered prodding further, but on balance, I realized it probably wasn't the best place or time. Instead, I shifted gear slightly. "I think this would probably be a good place to throw in some on-set anecdotes— people always like to hear about the sets of action movies."

As soon as I gave her the opening, she slipped back into "publicity Isobel" mode, gladly supplying me with plenty of funny anecdotes and stories from the filming of both movies—some of which I had heard before, some of which were completely new to me. It was good material, if somewhat mundane, and time flew by as she regaled me with tales until we were suddenly interrupted by the same young man who had answered the door earlier.

"Ms. Dewitt? Dinner is ready."

"Ah, thank you, James." Turning a benevolent smile at me, Isobel raised her eyebrows. "Hungry?"

"Oh, um..." I glanced down at my watch—it was after seven, a perfectly reasonable time to have dinner, of course, but I hadn't expected to be eating here and had assumed I'd just be sent home when my client got hungry. "Sure," I said with an easy enough smile once I'd recovered. Then, "Thanks."

"Of course. Leave the recorder, though, will you? I prefer to relax over meals," she chided gently.

"Oh, of course." I smiled wryly—I honestly wasn't sure whether I would've brought the recorder or not.

We followed James upstairs to the dining room, which was of course large enough to host a dinner party of at least thirty people. Isobel surveyed the precise table settings and pristine china and wrinkled her nose. "We'll eat in the kitchen," she told the young man, causing him to flash a comically panicked look behind her back as she turned back towards the stairs to the basement.

"I don't mind where w—" I began to say, at the same time as poor James, trotting after her, was saying, "Absolutely, but please just let me—" We were both silenced with a wave of Isobel's hand as she disappeared back down the stairs ahead of us.

The harried young man turned towards me with an apologetic look. "I'm afraid there will be just a slight delay while, um, we adjust."

I just smiled tolerantly, disinclined to add to his stress even by talking to him—I got the impression he was the sort of person who would be stressed no matter who he was working for because I couldn't see anything in Isobel's demeanour that warranted such nerves.

Just a few minutes later, we were seated in the kitchen, which had only recently been vacated by whatever chef or staff had prepared our meals. There was a large, rather nicked dining table in a windowed alcove, and it was here that we took our seats, cloth napkins folded our laps as we were served. Isobel poured us both water with lemon from the pitcher in the centre of the table, smiling at me as if this was the most natural thing in the world to be doing.

"You really didn't have to do this," I found myself saying. "I really wasn't expecting to be fed—I don't want you to think that—"

"Oh, it's nothing. Besides, I think it's apt. If you're going to be writing my book, you really ought to be spending more time with me—right?" She gave me a strangely piercing look.

I managed to shrug slightly and smile—I know it doesn't seem like it lately, but I'm actually quite good at appearing relaxed in unusual situations.

"Anyway, it's no bother, really. And besides, you haven't seen the paintings yet—I couldn't let you leave before we did that."

"Oh yeah, I'd almost forgotten about that." I hadn't, of course.

She arched an eyebrow. "Well, if you're not interested..."

"I am, absolutely," I said, reaching for some bread from the middle of the table between us. "I just don't want to put you out—how far a walk is it?" I teased.

She laughed, a rich, melodious sound that I'm sure sounded as good on film as it did across the dinner table. "Hey, just because I'm not searching out action roles doesn't mean I can't climb a few stairs."

"This is really excellent," I found myself saying. I tend to try to avoid pointlessly over-thanking people for favours—food, lifts in cars, whatever—as I think it's disingenuous. But on this occasion, I really had just taken a bite of one of the most delicately flavoured risottos I had ever had the fortune to taste.

"Mm, it is," Isobel agreed. "I'm lucky to have a very talented chef—do you cook, Nicola?"

I didn't start—visibly, at least, but I did internally register surprise. It had been Ms. Booth up until now—not in an unfriendly fashion, of course, but certainly not Nicola. Fighting the urge to correct her, to tell her it was always Nic to everyone but my mother, I swallowed before shaking my head slightly.

"Not really. I mean, I can do all the basics, but I'm not very imaginative. I guess I've never really had the patience."

"Ah," she replied, nodding sagely. "I'm an absolute wreck in the kitchen. Which is frustrating, because I'm used to being able to do anything I set my hand to. But there are only so many saucepans one can ruin before you have to admit that there are certain skills you'll never acquire."

"Oh, I'm sure you just need the right teacher," I said. I smiled at the mental picture of the woman in front of me frustrated or defeated by anything at all.

"Many have tried," she sighed. "All have failed. Hence the hiring of a very pricey but well-worth-it chef."

"Have you tried baking? Maybe you're a baker and not a cooker…"

"Or maybe I just shouldn't get nearer to a hob and stove than I am right now." She smiled, looking less than upset at this pronouncement. Apparently, she was over any frustration or embarrassment her lack of culinary skills might have caused her.

"I dunno. You should try baking. I'm quite good at baking," I commented. "Less imagination, more weighing and measuring and following recipes to the letter."

"Interesting. I would have thought you would be quite good with anything requiring imagination," Isobel mused.

"Hah, I don't even write fiction, remember?"

"Surely writing biographies requires imagination, though? I've read your work—it's very creative."

I shrugged. "A bit, yeah. But ultimately it's more like mixing cake batter than making soup—weighing and measuring every ingredient carefully, following the recipe to the letter to create a saleable work."

"How enticing."

I smirked. "Hey, you haven't tasted my cakes…"

"Are you offering?" she countered with a grin.

"Why not?" I said, ready for such a riposte. "It's been a while since I baked anything."

"Fantastic! Tonight?"

That did surprise me, however. "Pardon me?"

"The kitchen is very well-stocked, and I have a good many unused recipe books. You could show me how to construct a cake, and then while it's baking, we could take a look at the artwork."

This was turning into a very strange evening. "Okay."

"SO, YOU *CAN* use a food mixer for this bit, but I quite like to use my hands."

"What's the benefit of doing that?" Isobel asked, peering over my shoulder.

"No benefit. It's just… Here. You try."

To my delight, she delved right in, sinking her slim hands into the powdery mixture. "Oh, it feels…very interesting."

"Use your fingers to mix it through, keep it moving," I murmured, watching her work.

"I thought baking was supposed to be precise—this is just *fun*," she said with a grin.

"I didn't know the two were mutually exclusive."

"Well, apparently, they aren't always."

I could hardly believe Isobel was taking to this so easily – her enthusiasm was infectious. She let me talk her through the addition of the wet ingredients, mixing them in gleefully, though she kept glancing at me for reassurance. I got the feeling she was used to things going wrong very quickly in the kitchen, and I tried to reassure her, my voice slowing, my tone warming. It was strange because I never really thought of myself as a teacher. Perhaps Isobel was just a good student.

Eventually, we poured the mixture into several like-new baking pans and stuck them into the state-of-the-art oven, setting the timer for half an hour's time. "Now it's my turn to show *you* something," Isobel declared, washing her hands in the sink. She turned to me with a grin.

I spread my own freshly washed palms. "Lead the way."

The paintings were kept upstairs, lining a long corridor off which presumably were various studies and bedrooms. Isobel flipped on the lights as we reached the top of the stairs. "Here we are."

I blinked in the white light. The hallway was wide—surprisingly so for a house of this age—and so there was plenty of room to appreciate the two large paintings that hung along one side.

"They're...stunning. I don't think I've even *seen* this one before."

"I'm glad you like it." Isobel stood in front of the second painting, tilting her head as she looked at it. "I'm not really a collector, but when I saw it, I knew I needed to own it."

"She's...remarkable."

The painting wasn't anything special, at first—just a photo-accurate representation of a young woman glancing over her bare shoulder at the viewer. The longer one looked at it, though, the easier it was to spot the small details—the expression in her eyes that was half invitation, half question; the subtle freckling of her skin; the small, downy hairs on her arm illuminated by a golden light from behind her.

"Honestly, I can stand here and just stare at her for...well," Isobel said with a chuckle. "I don't know how long. I stop because I have things to do, not because I've had enough."

I glanced sidelong at her, raising an eyebrow at this.

For once, she looked slightly caught out. "Don't you have art that does that to you?"

I nodded. "Sure, of course. So where did you find her?"

"At a party, actually. I spotted her in the host's study and was so struck by her—well, my date for the evening wasn't pleased, let's just say that. I called the next day to make an offer, and after an annoyingly protracted negotiation, I finally got to take her home."

I smirked slightly, imagining some handsome young man—or woman, I suppose—thinking they'd lucked out in securing a date with Isobel Dewitt, only to find him or herself ignored in favour of a particularly lifelike canvas.

"I even tried tracking down the artist to find out more about the painting, but it turns out he died a few years ago. Nobody seems to know much about it other than it's not a model they recognize from any of his other work."

"Huh. Probably just as well," I murmured.

Now it was Isobel's turn to look at me, one eyebrow raised. "Pardon?"

"Well..." I shrugged. "She'd never live up to the picture, would she?"

"Ah. I suppose not," she said, shaking her head. "Still, I like knowing all I can about the people that fascinate me. What makes them tick. Don't you agree?"

I felt myself smiling again. "You do *remember* what I do for a living, yes?"

"Of course. Though, be truthful—does every assignment actually fascinate you? Every person you write about?"

"Absolutely. The only way I can do this is by becoming completely absorbed—obsessed, really." I felt a slight nervous twinge in my stomach as I said this—for a moment, I'd forgotten that, of course, Isobel herself was one of the objects of said obsession.

"Interesting." She turned back to the painting. "That sounds a lot like acting—the way certain people approach it, at least. Except instead of losing oneself in a fictional character, it's a real person you're becoming."

"You've portrayed real people."

"Usually long-dead, though. And never someone I've met face-to-face."

I found myself staring at her profile—far more fascinating to me than the painting, now. Even as I realized what a dangerous conversational line this was, and that I should probably draw back, I drove on.

"Perhaps that makes it easier," I said. "At least, as long as the person in question is penetrable."

"And if they're not?" She pursed her lips as she regarded the girl in front of her.

"Well. That's yet to happen. Everyone has a way in."

"Interesting." We stood in silence for some time—I couldn't judge quite how long—before the stillness was broken by the faint sound of a timer beeping. "Oh, that will be the cake, then," Isobel said, moving smoothly towards the stairs. I blinked in surprise—had it really been that long? Glancing at my watch to confirm that half an hour had indeed passed, I realized that Isobel was already gone from sight. I turned for one last look at the girl in the painting, my gaze trapped for another long moment, before I followed her.

Chapter Fifteen

THE REST OF the evening was uneventful—the cake turned out well, much to Isobel's delight (and my relief). It was a simple chocolate sponge with orange in the butter icing, and she insisted that we try it as soon as it was cooled, herding us back through to the basement lounge with our servings. I realized that this must be where she spent almost all her time when she was at home, leaving the rest of the house empty and untouched. It seemed a shame—it was a beautiful house—and I couldn't help but comment on it as we sat.

"So what do you use all this space for?" I asked simply.

"Oh," she said with a shrug, neatly scooping up a piece of cake with her fork, "the usual. Entertaining people. Impressing them."

"I wouldn't have thought you needed a beautiful house to impress people."

"I could hardly claim to have any sway in society if I didn't have an appropriate dwelling, Nicola," she chided gently.

I raised my eyebrows, involuntarily rankled by her use of my full name, just as I was when Laura did it. "And do you?" I said. "Claim to have sway in society, that is."

Another graceful shrug. "As much as any celebrity could, I suppose."

"And that matters to you?"

This time she took her time in responding, chewing slowly on a bite of cake as she pondered this. "Yes and no. On the one hand, I would like to think I'd be able to give this all up on a whim if I felt like it and still be happy. On the other...I like the things that fame grants me."

"The resources, or...?"

"Those, yes. But also being adored by so many people—or hated. It's a heady mix."

"So you *do* like fame."

Isobel smiled beatifically over her cake at me. "Did I ever claim otherwise?"

My stomach twisted with something that was part irritation and part something else altogether—I've always been a sucker for women who keep me guessing.

Eventually, I settled for a simple, "Why?"

"Why? Why does anybody like to be liked? It's like school, or a popularity contest, except on a much larger scale."

"So you're the, I don't know, the Prom Queen of the World?" I smirked.

"Hopefully nothing so crass as that!"

"But doesn't it...?" I pursed my lips in thought, sighing as I considered my words. "Isn't life in the public eye hard? Keeping your...private life private?" I was hesitant to go too far down this route, not least because I didn't want Isobel to think I was chasing that particular route of enquiry since it was one she so clearly didn't want in her book.

"But of course. It only seems a fair price, though, wouldn't you say?"

"Jesus, no." The words were out, along with their incredulous tone, before I'd even thought about it. Which in case you're wondering is absolutely not like me.

"So you think adoration should come for free?" Isobel's tone was amused but subtly edged. "It doesn't work that way, in my experience."

"Well, I suppose that depends on what you mean by adoration—and what you mean by 'free,'" I said slowly. This was turning into a conversation that, on the one hand, I was quite keen to have but, on the other hand, one where I would have to tread rather carefully, it seemed. "I certainly know, though, that conditional love isn't worth having."

"Oh, I didn't say anything about love," she replied, leaning forwards slightly. "That was you."

"Adoration is different?"

"It's not as nuanced. Adoration is..." Isobel Dewitt pursed her lips, casting her gaze towards the ceiling as she thought. "Adoration is something dogs do. It's fawning and scraping. Love is complicated."

"Ah," I said knowingly. "Fair enough. Although what's so good about being fawned over?"

She shrugged. "It can do as a stopgap?"

My brow seemed to furrow of its own accord at that. "That's..." *A little sad?* "Whatever works for you."

"I suppose I shouldn't expect you to commiserate—she of the budding love life," Isobel said slyly.

"What? Oh..." I shook my head, smirking. "I can commiserate, believe me. This...is very recent. And exceptional. And let's be honest, probably a blip."

"That doesn't seem like a particularly optimistic attitude. I thought it was going well?"

"Oh, it's fine. We get on well enough. But it's only a matter of time with me, generally."

"Before...?"

I just shrugged. What could I say, really? Isobel responded to my silence with one of her own, though by now she had set aside her half-eaten cake. I guess it was no surprise, with her figure. She seemed to be testing me somehow, letting the stillness stretch out between us as she steadily held my gaze. Eventually, I chuckled.

"Hey, who's the subject here?" I chided. "Me or you?"

"The recorder's off," she pointed out. "I thought we were just having a friendly chat."

So that was how she wanted to play it? Fine. "All right. I like her, but I worry that she's too young, too ambitious, and too much of a socialite to really be my type. She's altogether too polished for an indie director, and although she's obviously incredibly smart, her conversation is unchallenging. She's a good kisser, but there's no...*tension*. And I question her motives."

I sat back as I finished, fixing her with an expression that I knew was unreadable because I've practised it in the mirror.

It was obvious Isobel hadn't expected quite so much candour from me. She raised one eyebrow slowly. "Her motives? What do you mean by that, exactly?"

"I'm not sure it's really me she's interested in." There was no way Isobel wouldn't realize what I meant by this. The question was whether she would choose to pretend she didn't.

"Well, if it's not, she's being awfully foolish," Isobel said, shaking her head. "You're quite a catch all on your own."

I gave a derisive snort. "Not compared t—" I broke off, narrowing my eyes at her. "Now you're just making fun of me."

"Not at all. You're creative, attractive, intelligent, not to mention well-off, I assume? You have a sharp sense of humour but use it mainly to mock yourself; you're hardworking and dedicated. What isn't enticing about that?"

I almost laughed at this. Intelligent, yes. Well-off...moderately. Humorous, hardworking, and dedicated, sure. Creative...perhaps. But attractive? "I...don't exactly stand out next to a stunning film star."

"Is that what this is about, Nicola?" Isobel looked almost disappointed. "Does it seem to you that my looks have helped me at all in finding someone who truly loves me? You, who knows more than most about my life, should know better."

"Nor does the fact that *you're* intelligent, dedicated, creative, funny, rich..." I frowned, shaking my head. "We're getting off-topic." Not that I particularly liked the topic, either. "Foolish or not, the fact is that Laura spends as much of our time together trying to find out more about you as she does me."

"Well, I'm sorry to hear that. I'm afraid it will end up being her loss." I was pleased to notice she didn't rush to caution me against sharing information: at least she trusted me that much.

Now it was my turn to raise an eyebrow. "Really? You two seemed quite close. You wouldn't..."

Her expression was innocent. "I wouldn't what?"

Assuming you haven't already, of course. The thought hit me as it had, in passing, back at that screening. My mind's eye recalled the sight of the two of them, heads close together, Isobel's hand resting lightly against Laura's elbow. Now it noticed things that I hadn't at the time— details that in fairness I could now be filling in with my imagination rather than memory. A slight tilt to Laura's hip, a dilation in Isobel's pupils, a flush to their cheeks. Was I recalling or inventing?

"Well." I placed down my long-since-emptied plate and forced myself to sit back, to loosen my muscles, crossing one leg over the other and swinging my foot just slightly, toe lifting and falling to some imaginary beat. "Regardless of what her interest or otherwise is in me, it's as I said—I'm not sure *I'm* interested, I'm afraid. It's not unusual. I'm rarely really interested in anyone I'm not..." I remembered who I was talking to, then covered my lapse with a gesture towards the woman in front of me, realizing I might as well plough ahead regardless. "You know," I said. "Writing. Inhabiting. Whatever."

"And when you're done writing them?"

I'll admit, her response wasn't what I had expected. How could she continue to surprise me when I had spent so long trying to get inside her head? The answer to this one was simple, though I wasn't sure she'd like it.

"I shake them off again."

Whether or not she liked the answer, Isobel gave no outward show of emotion, merely nodding thoughtfully. "I see."

"I suppose I'm just not very well suited to relationships that have anything to do with *me*," I said eventually. A thought occurred to me and I smirked. "I suppose that sort of makes me the anti-celebrity."

"Or just alone," Isobel said darkly. Maybe I had struck a nerve after all.

"Then I suppose we have something in common, despite our opposite approaches," I parried dryly. No point in equivocating now.

"How comforting." She sighed and rose. She walked over to a small dark-wood cabinet, and opened it to reveal a few expensive-looking bottles and several neatly arranged glasses. It was all too easy for me to identify them by name just with a glance. "I suppose there's no point in asking you to join me for one," she said, glancing at me before selecting a single tumbler and a single malt that was older than I had been when I started voting. God, of all the things she could have chosen, why did it have to be whisky?

I smiled mirthlessly. "Thank you. No." So that answered that question, then. I had a feeling that I could count on Isobel Dewitt to be perceptive even when I'd rather she wasn't.

"Well, you'll have to stay until I'm done, at least," she said, pouring herself a generous measure. "I never drink alone."

"Happy to oblige," I murmured, my concentration on preventing my gaze from following the glass in Isobel's hand rather than the woman herself.

She raised the glass to her lips, and for a moment, I couldn't help but stare. Then she turned away to look out the window, her skin pale in the dim light of the room.

"So how is the book coming?" she murmured.

"It's..." I frowned. I heard a sigh and realized it was mine. "Impenetrable."

"Should I be worried?"

I smiled tightly. "I'll get there. I'm finding you...a slippery customer, I suppose."

"I'm not trying to be," she said, still speaking to her reflection in the window. "I'm...just not sure what you want."

I thought darkly that it would help if I had any idea myself. Oddly enough, although I had written for plenty of people with secrets that they'd rather didn't make it onto the pages of their book, both disclosed to me and discerned through other means, I'd never found myself writing something that seemed, while in-character enough, with Isobel's voice speaking the words in my head, somehow wasn't...*her*. It just didn't ring true.

When I came back to the present, I realized that Isobel had turned and was looking down at me with an intent expression that had me squirming slightly in my seat. "Maybe we ought to take a break from the interviews," she said quietly. "Give you time to sort things out."

I shrugged. "I don't really know whether that would help," I admitted in a tone that betrayed the fact I'd already considered it. "More time alone with my recordings and notes isn't doing to do any more good. I just need to...find my own way in, I suppose. Sorry—I don't mean to make you sound like...an exclusive club or something."

"Perhaps...something less structured, then." She sounded hesitant, as if she wasn't quite sure this was an offer she wanted to be making. "Would it help to shadow me? Spend some time in my shoes, as it were."

"I, er..." Well, I'd done it before. I'd followed Richard Fellows all over sub-Saharan Africa while he shot his last big nature documentary series, talking to him in the backs of jeeps, over meals, during long waits in tall grass for something interesting to come by. It had left me with no desire whatsoever to travel for years afterwards, but I sure as hell knew who he was by the end of it. This wasn't quite the same, though. Me, following Isobel Dewitt from party to opening to benefit, schmoozing, drinking— or in my case, not drinking—pretending to be sincerely interested in boring rich people? Could I really do that? Did I really need to see that?

"To be honest," I said eventually. "I know your shoes. It's the person you are with your shoes *off* that I can't get a grip on."

"I had thought tonight might help with that." She took a sip of whisky, closing her eyes momentarily. "But no?"

My eyebrows raised of their own accord this time. She'd planned this to let me get better under her skin? I'd been working up until now on the assumption that our tension was born of her reluctance to let me get any closer to her, but could it be that the reluctance wasn't hers at all? Was I sabotaging myself by assuming that she didn't want me prying when she was actually perfectly happy for me to do so?

"I...suppose I'll find out when I sit back down at my desk," I said.

"Well." She opened her eyes and looked down on me once again. "Let me know. Because I understand that sometimes creative partnerships just don't work—and that it's better to be honest about it earlier rather than later. You were my first choice, Nicola, but if this isn't working...then I'm not going to waste your time. Or mine."

Chapter Sixteen

I LEFT ISOBEL Dewitt's house that night determined of two things. The first was that I was going to stop seeing Laura Maguire. My conversation with Isobel had reminded me why I *didn't* date—the reasons it didn't work for me—and it had reminded me that I was actually okay with that.

The second was that by whatever means necessary, Melody Graham was going to be the factor that turned this project around. Because I was damned if I was letting go of Isobel before I'd cracked her, and this woman was the only avenue I had left.

IT WAS AFTER the breakup with Laura—which I thought had gone well, even if I did conduct it over the phone—that things got a bit weird. Isobel and I had scheduled another interview, as I figured there was still information to be gathered even if I wasn't sure what to do with it. We were once again seated in the hotel restaurant, chatting over cups of tea, when an angry redhead bypassed the protests of the hostess and stormed over to our table.

I confess that the first person I looked to for a reaction was Isobel and not Laura—I hadn't even mentioned to her that Laura and I had ended things, although I wouldn't be surprised if, somehow, she'd already figured that part out.

"Hello, Laura." Isobel greeted her calmly, as if she hadn't just caused the beginnings of a scene with her dramatic entrance. "What are you d—?"

"You know very well what I'm doing here!" Laura snapped. "How could you say those things to me, Is? I'm not a child!"

I started in surprise. She was here to rage at *Isobel*? My dinner companion seemed to be taking it in her stride, however, smiling carefully despite her apparent confusion. "I'm not sure what you mean,

Laura. Are you referring to the email I sent? I thought it was quite measured."

"Clinical is more like it! You can't just pretend like you're concerned for my well-being. That's a load of bullshit. Say what you really mean to say. Right now."

"I don't think that would be appropriate, but if you'd like to make an appointment with—"

"I'm not going to make a goddamned appointment!" Laura interrupted, her freckled face looking redder by the second. "Just tell me you don't care for me, and I'll leave."

I watched Isobel do a very passable impression of surprise. "*Care* for you? Laura, if you want to discuss my decision to take a step back on the film, you can make an appointment. If you want to discuss anything else, then we can do that, but we're *certainly* not doing it here. Can't you see I'm in a meeting?"

Hazel eyes flashed my way and then back to Isobel as Laura ground her teeth. "Fuck your meeting, and fuck you!" she shouted, loud enough that everyone in the restaurant was now openly staring at us.

"Laura, I'd like you to go now, if you don't mind," Isobel said quietly as I glanced around as surreptitiously as I could. It was only the particular clientele of this place that was stopping people from pulling out camera phones, and it couldn't possibly be long before even this crowd would.

Thankfully, it seemed Laura had had her say, and without any further invective, she turned on her heel and stalked out, leaving a trail of murmurs in her wake.

Isobel made no move to say anything, simply lifting her wineglass to her lips and picking her fork back up. On this occasion, I couldn't let it lie.

"That was...interesting," I offered, giving her the opportunity to expand upon what had just happened without having to be cajoled.

"Mm?" Isobel replied, lifting one eyebrow slightly in a mockery of curiosity. "I'm sorry you had to see that."

I stifled a sigh but took the bait. "What happened? Did you two fall out?"

"That certainly wasn't my intention, though it seems the choice may be out of my hands," she said, considering the matter. "I merely realized I had overcommitted myself somewhat and decided to take a step back from my involvement on Laura's next project."

My brow furrowed of its own accord, my voice dropping as I spoke again. "That's...not quite what it sounded like. Or not the end of the story, anyway."

"Well," she said, a little shortly, "you're the author. I'm sure you'll be able to make one up."

I blinked in surprise. Usually, even when Isobel was delivering some cutting remark, her tone was such that you couldn't be too hurt by it. I personally found it one of her most attractive traits, albeit one that could be infuriating at times. But that...stung.

"My apologies," I murmured, my gaze sliding to my meal and putting roots there. "Clearly none of my business." Except that it was. Except that it wasn't.

Chapter Seventeen

THINGS COOLED AFTER that meeting, and my writing output slowed to a halt. I felt I was getting further from where I needed to be, not closer. I kept thinking of that night in Isobel's home, watching Isobel as she looked out the window, a glass of amber whisky in her hand, dark hair curled at the nape of her neck. And then, Isobel sitting across from me at the hotel, tight-lipped, fingers wound around the stem of her wineglass as Laura berated her for some unspoken rebuke.

The weekend passed at a snail's pace, and to say that I was nervous by the time I reached Melody Graham's meeting place of choice (a rather nice café in the West End) on a rainy Tuesday afternoon was something of an understatement.

I didn't spot her at first, and it was only on my second sweep around the café that I noticed the slight woman with mouse-brown hair sitting... Well, sitting exactly where I would have chosen if I hadn't wanted anyone to notice me.

Thinking that at least I now knew where to sit if I ever came back here and wanted to be left alone, I made my way over, hovering for a moment rather than just taking a seat.

"Ms. Graham?" I hazarded, though I knew perfectly well that it was her.

She glanced up from her notebook, which she had been scribbling in quite busily. "Ms. Booth. Hello. Take a seat."

I remembered her voice as quite thin and tight on the phone, but today she sounded a lot more at ease—not entirely free of tension, but certainly less unfriendly. I felt myself relax.

"Just let me grab some tea, and I'll be right with you."

A few minutes and some foot-tapping later, I had my giant mug of tea and was slipping gingerly into a seat opposite the critically acclaimed Melody Graham. The moment seemed anticlimactic. She was older than me—which of course I knew since she was a couple of years older than Isobel—average height, slight build, brown hair, brown eyes, pale skin.

Attractive but not out of the ordinary. It was strange to me, having built her into this semi-fictional "one great love" in Isobel Dewitt's life, to see how... *normal* she looked.

She glanced up again as I sat down, not quite smiling but not giving me the evil eye, either. "So," she said, without prevarication, "Isobel is writing her life down."

I held back a smirk. "Some of it, yes."

"I used to say that anybody who chose to do that before they were old and infirm was just a money-grubbing fame whore."

"And what do you say now?"

She sighed and shrugged, sliding her fingers through the handle of her mug. "Izzy always did like her recognition."

"Mm, I'm getting that." I pursed my lips briefly before going on, using the line I always did when people questioned why anyone would write an autobiography before their life was *over*. "I don't think that autobiographies written in the middle of a person's life perform the same purpose that one at the end does—they tend to lack the full benefit of hindsight, for a start. But if they make for interesting reads, they're fair game, these days."

"And does hers?"

"Her life? Sure. She's done a lot. She's had an active creative life."

"So you're finding it a stimulating project?" I realized Melody Graham had fixed me with a steely gaze, one that I couldn't quite pull away from.

I narrowed my eyes—almost as though the act might protect me somewhat from that penetrating stare. "She's a very complicated person. And I can't get past the surface."

"And that's why you called me." The statement was flat, less of a challenge and more of a concession. "Because you thought I might be able to help."

I just shrugged and nodded. "More or less."

"Despite me reminding you that I haven't had any contact with Isobel Dewitt in nearly a decade. And yet you still did. So why?"

"Because it seemed as though at one point you probably knew her better than anyone. And I could use some insight." Yep, I'd decided to level completely with her.

"Ah." Melody sat back, her mug still clutched between both hands. I could see her nails had been bitten down to the quick. "And you think she's going to let you put any of that...insight into the book?"

"Oh, Christ, no. I mean…" I smiled, shaking my head. "I don't know. I can't see how…some things…could possibly go in. She's clearly not ready for that. But I'm having trouble finding her voice. I think…" I tried to find the right phrasing. "I think that although she trusts that I know what goes on the record and off it—although she trusts *me*—there's a part of her that I'm not touching that I need to, not so I can spill her secrets but so that what I *do* write actually feels like her to people." My eyes were drawn back to Melody's. "D'you get what I mean?"

Instead of answering my question, Melody Graham took a sip of tea, casting her gaze to the now-closed notebook before looking back up at me. "I've never written a biography before. I can imagine it would be difficult."

"An *auto*biography." The distinction seemed particularly important under the circumstances.

"I'm sorry," she said solemnly. "If you had spoken with me earlier in the project, I would have told you to quit while you were ahead."

I raised my eyebrows. "I got into *Karl Golden's* head in the end. You really think I can't get into Isobel Dewitt's?"

Again, she bypassed my question with one of her own. "How much have you written so far?"

I pursed my lips. It looked like getting information out of Melody Graham wasn't going to be much easier than getting some genuine human feeling out of Isobel was.

"A fair amount. None of it quite right."

"Mm. Can I see it?"

"What? No!"

"How am I supposed to know what you need if I don't know what you have?" she queried, cocking her head to one side.

"I…" I frowned. This was all very irregular. "I'm not really in the habit of sharing works in progress with anyone but my editor."

"And *I'm* not in the habit of granting interviews with, well, anyone." It was true. In all my background research on Isobel and to some extent Melody, interviews with the playwright were few and far between. "I'm sorry," she said, gathering up her things. "I can't give you something for nothing."

"I wasn't… Hey, waitaminute…" I was standing myself, now. "I'm sorry, please, hang on, please, sit down."

Melody paused, her hand on her bag. She frowned. "I'm not trying to blackmail you, Ms. Booth. But I can't see a way for this to work without input from *both* of us."

I hesitated. Could I? Graham was probably the last person on the planet Isobel would want to see her words—even filtered through me. Still, it wasn't as though I didn't have information that *Graham* wouldn't want getting out, either. Not that I ever would, but it did mean I could probably trust her...

"All right. But listen, this can't—"

"I haven't spoken to Isobel since the cast party for *Home and Hearth*, Ms. Booth. She's not going to hear it from me, never fear."

"All right." I sighed. And frowned. "Okay."

THAT MEETING DIDN'T last long—without a draft of the autobiography, there wasn't much we could do—but it lasted long enough for me to at least get a better read on Melody Graham. The problem was, what I read slightly worried me.

Don't get me wrong—I was expecting smart, incisive, and I'd even discerned enough from Isobel to expect difficult. But Melody was all those and more so—and I didn't know if I'd be able to wrangle her long enough to get anything useful out of her. Still, for all that, I was also kind of looking forward to it. And *that* worried me as well.

After all, this was supposed to be research for Isobel, not a separate and equally confusing diversion of its own. I thought I'd just *rid* myself of other distractions.

Chapter Eighteen

"SO...LET ME get this straight. You broke up with a perfectly good woman, had some late-night heart-to-heart with Isobel Dewitt, and *now* you're sharing your most intimate of intimates with her ex-girlfriend...so you can get inside her head?"

I laughed, and reached to grab the bowl of popcorn from Julie's grasp. "I guess so."

"You're insane. You know that, right? Completely insane."

"Thanks, I'd already established that," I said through a mouthful of popcorn. "Besides, it actually makes a lot of sense. Laura was pushing me further from Isobel. Melody will hopefully get me closer." Why had she been *Melody* in my head since the moment we'd met? I didn't have more than a split second to consider this before Julie was talking again, more at me than to me.

"Except if Isobel finds out. And then you'll be out on your arse before you can say 'advance refund.' Are you really sure this is a good idea, Nicky?" I hated when she called me that, and she knew it. "Besides, isn't Graham some sort of weirdo recluse? How helpful can she be?"

"I think... I think possibly very. Possibly not at all. At the very least, I think she can be trusted. After all, I know stuff no one else—well, no one else who isn't Isobel or you—knows. She may be a recluse, but she still has a partner, remember?"

"Yeah, and if what you've posited is true, she's cheated on him once, if not several times with the esteemed Ms. Dewitt. Classy lady." Julie tossed a bit of popcorn up in the air, tipping her head back and opening her mouth, only to miss it completely. "Gross, it went down my top."

I smirked. "Well *I'm* not fetching it out."

"Hey—this is probably the best chance at getting close to a pair of breasts you're going to get now that you've dumped Laura. You couldn't have shagged her first?"

"I..." I frowned. "I didn't want to. You know that's not how I work."

"I know, I know." She sighed. "Besides, I don't blame you—she was cute, but she's no Isobel Dewitt."

I snorted. "Not that that's any basis on which I should be making romantic comparisons. I mean, assuming I was making them at all."

"Riiight. So the fact that she offered you 'unlimited access'—bow-chicka-wow-wow—had nothing to do with the breakup."

I made another face—this time an incredulous one. "When I talk, you actually just make up a story in your head and listen to that instead, don't you? I don't have 'unlimited access' to Isobel Dewitt. I had dinner at her house, and we talked, and I don't know if you noticed, but I also observed that since things have been worse, not better. I don't think that I'm going to be at her house again."

"So invite her round here," Julie said with a grin and a shrug.

"It's finally happened. You've actually gone insane."

"What?" Julie looked hurt. "You said she's not opening up, letting you in. Maybe she still regards you as a reporter when what you need to be is a friend."

"I'm neither a reporter *nor* her friend." I frowned. Was there any reason I *shouldn't* be her friend? Julie had a fair point in some respects—it was no help at all for Isobel to approach me as a reporter, out for dirt. She had final approval on whatever went to press. I had signed numerous confidentiality agreements and had several glowing client references to back them up. My interests were *her* interests, not a newspaper's. Maybe, for all her apparent trust, that was still how she felt?

"Well, it was just a suggestion. You're the expert at this stuff. Anyway..." Julie began telling me about her day, which was less celebrity-filled but a lot more satisfying—perhaps the two were related.

I WAS TRYING to avoid shifting nervously. I don't think I'd been further out of my comfort zone in some time. After all my mocking of Julie for suggesting I invite Isobel over, Melody Graham was in my home, and she was reading my work.

You see, although I take my laptop nearly everywhere, it never has anything on it—I plan my days out, decide what I'm going to be revising, take encrypted memory sticks with those segments with me, safely zipped up in my bag, used one at a time, never saved onto my hard drive, all backed up at home every night on my external. I do keep hard copies, printed and reprinted in segments, but again, they never leave the house—in their case not even in bits—not until the day they go to my editor. Sure, if my flat burns down or is burgled, I'm screwed, but that aside, no one gets to see the whole of my books before they should. So if Melody wanted to read Isobel Dewitt's autobiography, she had no other choice but to sit and read it on my couch.

Which she was doing quite happily. She was a fast reader, unsurprisingly, and in the completely silent forty-five minutes since she had started reading, had gotten through a significant part of the first few chapters.

Eventually she stopped and set the laptop aside, looking a bit like a skin diver coming up for air. "I can see what you mean," she said. "You're very good, but this isn't."

I nodded and sighed, slumping down further into my armchair. "I know."

"It's fine. But it's not good." I could tell Melody had high standards, both for herself and now, apparently, me. "She's holding back. These are all sound bites. You need stories."

"She tells stories," I said with a sigh. "But they're...just what happened. You know?"

"Mm. Yes. I wonder..."

I raised my eyebrows expectantly, waiting for Melody to finish her thought. In the conversation we'd had over tea before she started reading this afternoon, I'd learned that she had a tendency to begin a sentence while still thinking of the end and occasionally had to stop to let herself catch up.

"Well. Perhaps I would be able to help," she said. "I don't know everything you're going to need—only Isobel does. But I could point you in the right direction, give you somewhere to start from."

"If you think you can give me an idea of where to go with this stuff, I'd be eternally grateful," I said, gesturing towards the laptop.

And so began one of the strangest collaborations I had experienced in my entire writing career, Melody Graham and I working together to piece together a line of questioning that would hopefully get Isobel to open up about her life to me. She seemed keen to begin right away, clicking immediately to a page in the first chapter and beginning to talk about what Isobel might not have been saying. A little surprised, but pleasantly so, I became completely absorbed in discussion with her, a couple of hours passing before I even thought to get up to make us another pot of tea.

Over two steaming mugs, we sat quietly, both of us musing over the words we had exchanged so far that afternoon. It was obvious that Melody was right—she knew enough to suggest certain lines of enquiry that I was sure would lead to something fruitful. The only challenge would be convincing Isobel I had come up with it all on my own.

"Thanks for this," I said eventually. "You...weren't obliged to do any of this. I really appreciate it."

"You're welcome. I hope it helps," she told me solemnly.

"As long as I can manage to sound this insightful by myself, I think it will."

She nodded her agreement. "Isobel is not the most trusting person. You'll have to tread carefully."

"Yes, I..." I hesitated. Then, "Knowing what I do now, actually, I'm surprised that she worked with you again. Even all those years later. Not that you...but just *because* she finds it so hard to trust people."

"I think there were several factors at work there," Melody replied. Unlike Isobel, she had clearly decided that whatever secrets she might divulge were safe in my care. "Firstly, her career. It was a very good script, and she knew it would only boost her career to be involved with it."

I smirked. Clearly, for all her reclusiveness, Melody bore no false modesty regarding her work. "And secondly?"

A shrug. "There's always a temptation to revisit the past, no matter how painful."

I tipped my head to one side and took a risk. "And did you?"

Melody hesitated, looking for a fleeting moment as if she might clam up into total silence. "Yes," she said, after several long seconds. "We did."

"I see." I nodded, realizing that now, of course, I was not only going to need to watch that film again, I was going to be viewing it with a completely different eye. "That must have been... Well, I don't know. Painful, ultimately, I imagine."

See, here's the thing. I knew by now, having checked what Isobel had told me, that Melody Graham had been in a relationship with the same man since university. His name was Harry Whittaker, and he came from a notable line of aristocracy who made up most of the old, pre-industrial money in the North West of England. He had studied English with

Melody at Cambridge and was now a Green political activist and columnist, writing mainly for the *Guardian*. I knew of him. I wasn't a huge fan of his writing or manner of expression in general, but I knew that was partly down to my general prejudice against the "idle" rich. Sitting with Melody now, It was very hard to imagine that Whittaker, with his foppish hair and pithy but largely empty opinions, could possibly be the love of her life. Why she had stayed with him this long I didn't know, but I *did* know that, were I in her position, even a short revisiting of an affair with Isobel Dewitt would have left life feeling just that little bit more unbearable.

Of course, as we've established, I was a lesbian and Melody, presumably, was not. So I probably had it totally wrong.

"Yes. But what is pain to us if not fuel for the creative fire?" She gave an empty chuckle. "Part of the reason the film was so successful, I'm sure."

"I don't believe that you need pain to be truly creative," I said, frowning slightly. I had once. It was one of the hardest convictions I'd ever had to break, but in the end, I'd been able to admit that my work was no worse when I wasn't hurting, that pain was not the source of creativity but rather that those dark moods had prompted the clarity and single-mindedness that caused me to create. Separating the two and finding one without the other had been hard, but I'd got by—well, until now, at least.

"And I don't believe it's me you should be talking to in order to write this book," she said, with no hint of anger in her voice. "And yet—here we are."

"You've helped a lot," I said, entirely seriously. "I do think I needed to talk to you. The last time I spoke to Isobel, I had no idea whether I'd meet her again—if this hadn't given me anything, I think we'd be done." Of course, that wasn't strictly true—I had had no intention of ending my project with Isobel, but only because I had been completely determined that, one way or another, speaking to Melody *would* work.

She gave a small, private smile, reaching for the teapot between us. "I'm glad to have helped, then. I think we've done enough for today, however."

"Oh, absolutely, I don't want to..." I stopped before reaching "keep you" as she refilled her tea. Not that I was annoyed that she was apparently going to stay a little longer—indeed, I'd actually enjoyed her company. I was just surprised. "So you'll meet with me again sometime?" I hazarded to cover my previous hesitation.

"If you need me to, yes."

"I...suppose I don't know yet if I *need* you to," I admitted, leaning over to top up my own tea, surprising myself by leaving open the implication that perhaps I just *wanted* to.

"Well, I suppose you know how to get a hold of me." What was reassuring about Melody was that while she was perceptive and intelligent, she didn't make me feel like I was constantly under scrutiny. I had a feeling she turned most of that on herself. "Don't hesitate to call if you want to."

"I will. Thanks." And I was fairly sure that, whatever came of my next meeting with Isobel, I would.

Chapter Nineteen

IT SEEMED I spent most of my days in a constant state of anticipation now, waiting for my next meeting to arrive. I was supposed to meet Isobel at nine—she had a dinner engagement but had promised to squeeze me in afterwards "for as long as I needed"—and spent most of the time from eight p.m. onwards nervously looking over the notes Melody had helped me make.

We were meeting back at our usual hotel again, this time in the lounge bar, where Isobel had apparently gathered with a couple of friends—or at least cordial acquaintances—for the evening as they were talking animatedly as I entered.

She didn't shoo them off but instead waved me over, which surprised me, since I didn't think my presence was something she particularly wanted to advertise. She seemed to get around it by introducing me as "a writer friend," and it was on that round of (very effusive) introductions that I realized that she was quite drunk.

What I should have done at that point, of course, was politely excuse myself and got the hell out of there right away. What I *did* was head to the bar and return with a glass of clear, sparkling liquid with ice and lime, which to anyone who wasn't me could have been just about anything.

"So," Isobel said, patting the cushion next to her with a smile, "how are things coming? Have you had a productive few days?"

"Actually, I have," I said, returning her smile with a tight one of my own as I sat. "I may have had a bit of a breakthrough. Hard to say yet, though—a few questions have come up."

"Oh?" she asked, leaning close enough that I could smell the slight scent of the perfume she was wearing—something dark and spicy. "I'm all ears."

I swallowed, hard, but managed a reasonably congenial smirk. "Maybe later," I murmured.

"Why not now?" She glanced around at the other people gathered around the table, most of whom seemed caught up in their own conversations, though I had no doubt they would be ready to entertain Isobel at a moment's notice. "Go on—no one's listening."

I shook my head. "Not here."

Which is how we ended up in a private room—one I didn't even know they had—all alone, just me and Isobel Dewitt. She had brought her drink through—an obnoxiously bright coloured cocktail—and was lounging in a comfortable-looking chair, her little black dress hugging every curve just perfectly.

"We really don't have to talk about this tonight," I started, all my concentration on not looking nervous or uncomfortable (and I was reasonably sure I was still failing). "I can go home, leave you to your friends."

"No, no—I said we'd talk tonight, and we shall. Besides, I'm interested to know what *questions* you have for me now," she said with a smirk. "So, go on. Ask away."

I held back from sighing but pulled out my recorder and clicked it on, leaning to rest it on the table between us. "All right," I said, my voice feeling unnaturally loud in the quiet room after the bustle and chatter in the main bar. "I've been going back over my notes—what I've written and recorded so far—and I'd like to go back and begin filling in some gaps now that we've been working together a little longer." I left a pause, then, but Isobel only did that single arched eyebrow thing and nodded for me to continue, so I went on. "I thought we'd start with *Single Figures*—how did the experience of playing a single mother affect you?"

This seemed to surprise her a bit; obviously, she had just been expecting to clear up confusion on dates and names and that sort of thing. "That, ah... I'm not sure I understand what you mean," she said, shaking her head. "It was a challenging role, but..."

"Well, I just...got the feeling that something about that role had a profound effect on you, that's all," I hazarded.

"Yes, well. Of course. My, ah, experience was very intense—I'm sure you saw that I donated most of my payment to Mother's Aid. They offer financial aid to single mothers attempting to gain higher education."

"Can we talk more about why it was so intense for you?"

Isobel frowned, taking a large gulp of her drink and shifting in her chair. I had never seen her look so ill at ease; clearly Melody had known what she was talking about.

"It reminded me of a girl I knew," she said eventually, her gaze firmly directed off to one side. "Someone I had modelled with when I was younger. She and her boyfriend—she got pregnant and he left her. Everything in her life began to fall apart, and I watched it all happen. So doing that role...it brought back those memories, I suppose."

I nodded, fighting against a satisfied smile. "Tell me more about her."

It was probably the alcohol, lubricating the conversation, but I got more out of Isobel Dewitt in the next half hour than I had in our entire collaboration. Including tears, which I definitely wasn't expecting. This girl had been more than just someone she knew—they'd been close friends, and Isobel had been there with her throughout the whole ordeal to the point where it impacted on her own happiness and stability, drained her completely.

Eventually, her cocktail now drained, Isobel sat forwards, resting her elbows on her knees as she wiped her fingers over her tear-streaked cheeks. "She's...doing all right now. But things were so hard for so long, and all because she was trying to do the responsible thing. It didn't seem fair."

"It's not," I agreed, leaning in to better meet her eyes.

"I haven't talked about that in years." She let out a deep breath and gave me a look. "It can't go in the book, Nicola. I can't do that to a friend."

I nodded. "I know. That's not what this is about."

"What *is* this about?"

"Scraping the surface."

"Oh." She straightened up, hands going to her hair, her jewellery, her empty glass. "If this is what scraping the surface feels like, I'm not looking forward to seeing what happens when you get underneath."

I didn't say anything, just kept my gaze steadily on her. I'll confess, it was nice to shift the balance of power in this direction for once. Isobel continued to squirm under my scrutiny, until she couldn't take it any longer and stood up, glass in hand.

"I'm going to the bar."

I watched her go, clicking the Pause button on my Dictaphone and sitting back in my seat. That had been...interesting. Was it useful? In itself, perhaps not—there was really nothing about Isobel directly there and certainly nothing we could share regarding other people. But it *had* scratched the surface—that was for sure.

Isobel returned a few minutes later, drink in hand, though she didn't sit down immediately. She paced around the room, taking frequent sips and glancing at me nervously, like I might spring more tear-jerking questions on her at any moment.

"I've told the others to leave. They were just hangers-on anyway."

I hesitated, almost expressed my surprise that she hadn't used her "friends" as an excuse to cut our meeting short. I recovered in time, though, nodding.

"So go ahead. Ask me something else." It was as though she was daring me—or herself.

"All...right. Do you want to sit down?"

"No, thank you."

"Are... all right." I glanced back to my notes, leaning forwards to turn the Dictaphone back on. "Tell me more about working with Grace Martinez." This one was risky, as I'd already prodded at this topic before, but I figured that if there was ever a time, this would be it.

She made a face, turning to pace to the end of the room and then back again. Even though I was eagerly awaiting whatever story she might tell me now, I'll admit to being temporarily distracted watching her move. I hate high heels, but they do amazing things to women's legs.

"I made a complete fool of myself with Grace. I was incredibly attracted to her, and I threw myself at her—multiple times. She never reciprocated and...that was embarrassing, to say the least."

Wow. "You didn't worry that she'd out you?"

"Grace is a very private person. She might not be gay, but I never thought she would do something like that." Isobel shrugged. "I suppose it was only to be expected. I always go for the women I can't have."

I nodded. "Did you...?" I cleared my throat. It was really important that I gave my best performance here because I was about to delve into territory where I most certainly knew more than I was saying, courtesy of Melody. "Did you ever find yourself in situations where you *did* fear exposure?"

"Well, yes—I mean, it's impossible to go forever without *some* risk," she replied, resting one hand on the back of the chair she was now standing beside. "And there have been one or two times when things were...slightly tricky."

"Yeah?" I prompted, unwilling to sound *too* keen lest she thought I'd suddenly developed a one-track mind.

"Mostly when I was younger... Less discreet. Before I had learned it was better just not to bother at all."

"So you're just, what, celibate now?"

She looked at me, lips pursed, eyebrow raised, and something deep inside me squirmed. If she *was* celibate, it was a damn shame. "Anyway, there was this one girl—back when I had just started doing films. She was a terrible actress, but *God*, what a body. She was dating the director of my newest project. The things we would get up to behind his back..."

I chuckled, though in light of what must have been years of loneliness, secrets, and pain, I really shouldn't have, I suppose. "So..." I hesitated again. I was straying off script now, but there was something I'd been wondering, and it looked like this was the time to ask. "Are you actually gay, or...? I mean, over the years, you have had a couple of relationships."

"And look at how lasting those have been." Isobel snorted. She sobered almost immediately, though, dropping down into the chair with her drink in her hand. "I...don't know. The only person I've ever loved was a woman. Does that make me gay?"

"Well, when you put it like that... It becomes sort of a daft question, doesn't it?" I muttered, feeling sheepish now.

"*All* of these questions are a little...pointless. None of this can go in the book," she told me, frowning.

"That's not really the point, though," I said. "We've talked about plenty of things that can't go in your book before. It's just about finding your voice."

"And is this helping?"

"I think it really might be," I said—and I didn't have to fake my sincerity.

"Mm. Well, good." With that, she knocked back the rest of her drink, slinging an arm over the back of her chair. "Because I don't know why else I'd still be here."

I raised my eyebrows again. "You don't like talking to me?"

"This isn't talking, Ms. Booth. This is baring my soul while you sit there and record it. It's not reciprocal, and it's certainly not something I'd categorize as *fun*."

I guess she had me there. "I'm...sorry. I'm not saying this is fun. I just..." I frowned. Now I felt guilty. "Is there something I can do to make it easier?"

"You could offer as good as you're getting," she said pointedly, uncrossing and crossing her legs.

"I..." I wasn't at all sure how to respond to this. "I really wouldn't know how. I don't have any secrets. Just...other people's."

"I'm sure there are things you could tell me of interest."

"I won't betray other clients' confidences…"

"I wasn't talking about other people."

I fought the urge to squirm—and not pleasantly this time. "As I say, I doubt there's much of interest to you about me."

"Are you refusing?" she asked, arching an eyebrow.

"Just saying that you'll be disappointed."

"Why don't you let me be the judge of that?"

I frowned. This was not the way this was supposed to go. Why did she even care? Was this just about making me suffer because she felt uncomfortable? "Whatever makes this easier for you."

With a satisfied smile, she sat back, looking placated at least for the time being. "Lovely. Well then, I think it's your turn."

I opened my mouth, then let it shut again, just shrugging and gesturing for her to start. I might be about to be hanged, but I wasn't about to make my own rope.

"All right then. Tell me about your family."

I raised my eyebrows. That was an interesting choice. Not, fortunately, one that particularly bothered me. I let myself relax just slightly, and began to talk—about my teacher father and stay-at-home mum now happily retired together back home in Exeter, my academic brother sitting safe and sound in his lecture seat in Durham. I even threw in some extra bits about my early years, the summer trips, and big family Christmases. My childhood, up to a point at least, was comparatively idyllic. When I'd finished, I reached for my water glass and sipped carefully, watching Isobel for signs of disappointment.

Surprisingly, I saw none. Isobel had been nodding along with the concentration of the quite drunk, though I suspect, even so, she was catching everything I was saying and storing it away for…some purpose.

"Thank you," she said, giving me a slight smile. "That was perfect."

Perfect for what? But I just nodded, shrugging again.

"I suppose it's my turn, now."

I frowned, unsure where to go from here. If her intention had been to derail my train of thought, she'd managed to do just that. "I…was going to ask you about your time in Quebec—I understand you have family there?"

This time, she launched quite happily into speaking about the time she had spent in Canada, including details about her father's side of the family, which up until then she had barely said three words about. They sounded, quite frankly, a bit insane, and I wasn't surprised she hadn't mentioned them before, but even so, the tales of their exploits (illegal and otherwise) had us both gasping with laughter before too long.

Part of me knew I was allowing myself to be swept up by "charming chatty drunk Isobel". This was not the soul-searching that had been going on earlier, and that I'd intended on instigating. That being said, I reasoned internally, was it any less useful for the fact it was less intense?

At the very least, she seemed more comfortable around me, no longer perched on the edge of her chair as though she might flee at any moment. The sounds from the bar outside had grown noisier, and on checking my watch, I realized that it was nearly midnight.

Isobel caught me looking and arched an eyebrow imperiously. "I'm sorry, was I boring you?"

"Mm?" I feigned mild surprise. "Not at all. Do you want to tell me about David London?"

"What about him?"

"Well, I assume your relationship wasn't a *complete* sham..."

Isobel looked offended. "No, of course not."

"And yet we haven't talked about him," I said, my tone entirely innocent. "So, tell me about it."

"We had a relationship. It ended. Honestly, you can read all about it in the tabloids, I don't see why y—"

"I swear to *God* if you are about to tell me I should pick up your life's story from *OK!* magazine to put into your own *book* you *do not* want to finish that sentence," I snapped. Okay, so maybe discussing my family *had* left me brittle, for all their unremarkability.

Isobel jumped as if I had bitten her; maybe she wasn't used to the press or media being quite that aggressive with her. When she spoke again, it was quiet; I almost had to move my chair closer to hear her.

"David and I met on the set of *Three Fingers* and began dating after it wrapped. He has a strict rule about not dating co-stars, so he waited until I had begun my next project to ask me out."

"Sounds sweet," I offered, almost by way of apology. Almost.

"It was. He was a true gentleman, in every sense of the word. Opening doors, red roses sent to my trailer... I felt like I was being courted, and part of me wanted to be offended. This was 1997, for God's sake. But I couldn't quite feel outraged about it—just flattered."

"You two were very much the golden couple that year. It was a mercy the media hadn't starting doing portmanteaus yet—you could have been Isovid. Or Dasobel."

She laughed, though it didn't really reach her eyes. "I think that would have ended the relationship even sooner than it did."

"So what did end it? I mean, really?"

"He asked me to marry him. I said no."

"Why?"

"Because...because it wasn't right." She sighed.

I nodded. Of course it wasn't—I had just started to put the timeline together. "You were still in love with Melody." I watched Isobel's face, the way it didn't so much freeze as very carefully remain unmoving. "You were...*sleeping* with Melody."

"Yes. We...when we came back together for our second film. Things happened and we briefly resumed our affair. And I knew I couldn't marry David."

I nodded, all my concentration on not looking as though I knew this already. "So you broke things off altogether."

"Yes. David was upset, understandably, but he handled it with grace. He didn't know about Melody," she hastened to add. "Just that I couldn't commit to him the way he wanted me to."

"Do you think you would have married him if Melody hadn't...been around again?"

"I don't know. Would you marry someone you weren't in love with?" She fixed me with a determined gaze.

"We're not on me right now, are we? Would *you* marry someone you weren't in love with?" I swear I didn't mean for the question to sound so accusatory.

"I think *you* skipped a few questions," she shot back, frowning deeply now.

I frowned again. "No. I wouldn't."

"Well. I nearly did."

In the strained silence that followed, I eventually nodded, sitting forwards again. "All right." I sighed. "Your turn."

"No," Isobel said, shaking her head and shifting before she suddenly got to her feet. "It's late, and I'm going to my room."

"You're staying here? You live, like, a half hour's drive from here. Well, taxi," I added as she swayed slightly.

"It's late," she repeated flatly. "And I'm drunk. I just want to go to sleep. You can save your judgement of my profligate lifestyle for later." Isobel made to head for the door but took a misstep in her high heels and stumbled, yelping with pain.

I was up and off the seat and by her side with a speed that surprised even me. "I've got you…"

She grasped at me even as she kicked off her shoe, leaning heavily on my shoulder. "Goddamn it," she hissed, smelling of perfume and sweat and alcohol. "My ankle."

"Here, sit down, let me take a look…" I muttered, helping her into the nearest chair and kneeling in front of her, my pulse racing in my ears. I tried to tell myself that it was the adrenaline of surprise and not her sudden unexpected proximity. I'd seen her walk over on her foot, and it didn't seem serious, but her slim, shapely ankle was already beginning to swell. I could imagine how painful it must be. "I'll help you up to your room," I said. "We'll get you some ice. I'm sure you'll be fine in the morning."

"I had better be, I have a—ow—lesson in the morning."

"Well, hopefully a good night's sleep and some Alka-Seltzer and ibuprofen and your *ow* lesson will go without a hitch," I said with a smirk, helping to her feet only for her to stumble again with renewed yelping. I sized her up for a long moment. A couple of inches taller than me but maybe a few pounds lighter—unless she was all muscle. "Here, put your arms round my neck?" And in a gesture that my back hated me for almost instantly, I hooked my arm under her knees and was carrying her, Prince Charming style, in my arms.

"People are going to talk," she murmured as we pushed through the door and into the main part of the bar. Despite the fact that they almost certainly would, she didn't struggle or ask to be put down at all, though I told myself it was only because her ankle must have been extremely painful.

"You'll get over it. Besides, never underestimate my ability to not be noticed." Although whether I could avoid notice while carrying one of the most famous women on the planet was significantly less likely, but perhaps I could at least minimize the issue. At least, by now, the bar had closed to non-residents. Head down, expression closed, I made no eye contact and brooked no attempts to talk to me until we were safely out of the bar and into the corridor—at which point my only questions were, "Which is Ms. Dewitt's room?" and "Could we have an ice pack, please?"

The second question seemed to clear up any confusion regarding the first, and we made it to her room without any further delays—thankfully in the lift, as her room was of course on the top floor of the hotel. She waved the way to the bedroom and sighed with relief as I set her down on the acre-wide bed.

"You certainly are a full-service ghostwriter. I'll make sure you're compensated accordingly," she joked, leaning down to rub her foot gently.

"Don't worry about it," I muttered. The rushing in my ears and the plunging in my stomach were abating slightly now that my senses were no longer filled with that heady mixture of alcohol and Isobel, and irritation at the situation she'd put me in was replacing it. I *knew* I should've turned around as soon as I'd walked in that night—this sort of thing was *exactly* why I avoided drunk people as well as drink.

Whether or not she sensed my annoyance, she seemed to realize where we were now and straightened up, her cheeks still somewhat flushed. "I'm sure I can manage from here," she told me. "Thank you for your help."

"There'll be an ice pack up in a minute," I said. "I can hang on for a few." Then I realized that of course she probably wanted rid of me. "Actually, no, I can go. I'm sure whoever it is can let themself in." I took a couple of steps back, wondering idly whether the staff would realize that I'd left my bag and jacket—and Isobel's shoe—downstairs in our private room.

Looking back at the bed, it struck me how small and vulnerable she appeared, and it wasn't just because of her swollen ankle. She had told me more revealing information about herself tonight than in the entire rest of the time we had been working together, and I was reasonably sure I was only beginning to understand how lonely she was, all alone in this palatial hotel room, hurting, with only someone who was essentially a member of staff to help her.

I heard a long sigh and realized it was me. Fine. We'd make sure she wanted me gone before leaving. "I'll make you some tea," I murmured, turning and heading out of the bedroom to hunt down the kettle and teabags that would surely still exist *somewhere* even in a suite like this one.

I heard the sound of a sheet rustling, along with a few muttered oaths as Isobel presumably readied herself for bed, and a few moments later, a quiet knock came at the door to the suite—a maid with the requested ice pack. Abandoning my tea-making for the moment, I made my way back through to the bedroom and knocked on the door myself in case Isobel was midchange.

"Come in," came the response, and upon entering, I found that Isobel had indeed already finished changing and was already in bed, the duvet pulled up in such a way that I was left with next to no debate about what she was wearing underneath—which was very little at all.

Christssake... "I've got your ice pack," I said, making my way over to the bed, where I hovered, unsure where to go from here.

"Thank you," she said. One long, shapely leg emerged from beneath the duvet, and she leaned over to take the ice pack from me.

I could've just dropped it and ran, to be honest, but somehow, I succeeded in passing it to her carefully before I turned tail and disappeared back into the other room to finish making the tea. I hoped that, by the time I did, the burning sensation that was slowly creeping across my ears would have abated somewhat.

See, I'm good at the whole resisting temptation thing—you may remember how this story starts. I know how to want something, *really* desire something and not take it. But that doesn't make it easy and, honestly, this stuff wears you down.

My palms had been prickling since the moment I smelled Isobel's spirit-soaked breath on my face right after I arrived that night, and after hours of sitting around watching her drain cocktails, I was now expected to withstand an assault of a very different kind. It was safe to say I looked displeased as I re-entered the bedroom with a steaming mug of strong, milky tea.

My foul mood *almost* dissipated at the look on her face, however, as she spotted me (and the tea). "You're a godsend," she murmured, cradling the ice pack against her ankle.

"Wouldn't go that far," I muttered, bending to poise myself ready to take the ice pack from her as I proffered her tea.

Isobel accepted the mug gratefully; our fingers made contact, though it didn't seem intentional. She sighed and sank back against the mountain of pillows, her dark hair spreading over them artfully as if arranged by an underpaid PA.

I busied myself with the ice pack, my concentration apparently on keeping it pressed lightly to her swollen ankle. I cleared my throat, figuring I should probably make some sort of conversation, but under the circumstances, words escaped me.

I heard her sip at the tea and sigh again, that small sound of pleasure resonating through me as I focused on anything but her proximity and state of undress. Julie would never believe me when I told her where I'd ended up this evening, and I pondered with amusement showing her the tabloid headline—DRUNK DEWITT TWISTS ANKLE, RESCUED BY ANONYMOUS NOBODY. The clink of ceramic on the nightstand got my attention then, however, and I glanced up to see Isobel's eyes fluttering closed as she set the half-empty mug aside.

I straightened, lifting the compress from her ankle and gingerly tugging the blankets back over most of her leg. "I'll...get going, then," I murmured quietly, not really expecting a response.

"Mhm, g'night," she murmured, gathering the duvet up against her chest with one slim arm. She mumbled something else then, and though I couldn't quite make it out, I *swear* she had said "I miss you, Mel," with a final, sleepy frown. My mind still racing over the various revelations of the evening, my pulse a little faster from its end, I made my quiet escape.

Chapter Twenty

"AND WHAT DID you do then?"

I shrugged, tapping my short nails against the sides of my mug.

"I went downstairs, picked up my bag and jacket, gave her shoe to a steward, and left," I said simply. In the silence that followed, I dragged my gaze back to Mary's. "I know what you're thinking. And I agree. It was stupid, and I shouldn't have risked it. I guess I had enough other distractions that..."

"You *did* put yourself in a dangerous situation. And you *did* come through it without making any mistakes. You should be rightly proud of that," Mary told me. "But you should also be careful about repeating it—don't let it make you cocky. Just because you were okay this time doesn't mean the next time will be the same."

"I know. Believe me, I have no intention of doing that again." *Even if it did probably give me the kick I needed...* Of course, it was hard to know whether that was as much a product of the alcohol as it was Melody's careful coaching.

"Intentions are all well and good, but... Just be careful, Nic. The tighter you wind yourself, the easier it is to snap."

I smiled weakly. "I got it."

"Have you heard from her since then?"

I shook my head. "Although our next meeting was already scheduled since we have a regular Thursday thing, so I wouldn't necessarily expect to."

"And do you think it will be difficult?" Mary asked, reaching for her ever-present pack of tissues to stifle a sneeze.

"I have no idea. I'm seeing Melody again this evening—I guess we'll see if she has any further insight."

"I suppose so. Is there anything else you'd like to talk about? Any stresses, challenges, problems?"

"Well, I'm currently wrestling with the temptation to email Laura Maguire and ask her about that thing in the restaurant. She looked just about angry enough to tell me if she thought it'd drop Isobel in it…"

"And would you? Betray Isobel, I mean."

"What? No!" I frowned. "You know me better than that."

"Then why ask at all?" Mary queried, ignoring my outrage. "What would it gain you?"

"More insight, I guess. And it would satisfy my curiosity about a couple of things." Like whether she was ever interested in me at all.

"Hm. You couldn't just ask Isobel? It seems she's growing to trust you, at least more than she did."

"Only because I have Melody feeding me prompts," I contested.

"And you're sharing more of yourself as well. You don't think that has anything to do with it?"

"Christ, I don't know. I don't think she's even that interested—I think she just wanted to pay me back for pushing her buttons."

"Maybe you ought to see how your meeting on Thursday goes before you start making any assumptions." Mary more often than not ended up acting like the good angel on my shoulder—a fact for which I both loved and hated her. "And I would stay away from Laura Maguire if I were you. She's obviously trouble."

I raised my eyebrows. It wasn't like Mary to make such a black-and-white pronouncement—at least not without meeting someone. "What makes you say that?"

"Because people who are into public confrontations and shouting matches generally are."

"Ah, but she's an artiste…"

"And those are usually trouble too, I've found," she replied with a smirk.

"Hey…"

"Teasing, teasing. But still, I don't think she's a good influence on you, Nic. Although I'm not sure Isobel is, either. Maybe you should write a book about Melody Graham instead. She seems nice."

I smirked. "I don't think Melody Graham would ever want to put out an autobiography. And if she did, she'd write it herself."

"Fair enough. You could always try writing your *own* book…"

"Because we all know how well that goes." The last time I'd started writing original fiction, I'd also started drinking again.

"Yes, well, things have changed. *You've* changed."

This time, my raised eyebrow expression was sceptical. "I haven't changed that much."

"You were out until past midnight, in a social situation, with a woman who you're attracted to *and* who was increasingly inebriated, culminating in an encounter in her hotel room. And you still didn't drink. I'd say you have," Mary said, sniffing.

I smiled grimly. "You have no idea how much I wanted to."

"And yet you didn't."

"Y'know, maintaining a healthy sense of self-loathing is much harder when you're around."

Mary smiled. "It's in the job description."

Chapter Twenty-One

"SO WHAT DO you think? Better?"

Melody nodded slowly, looking up from the draft she had just finished reading. "Yes, much. Things are really starting to come together."

"Just as well, I suppose, it was hard won." Melody and I had spent the first half hour of our meeting picking over the other night's events before I'd given her my redrafted chapters to read.

"Mm. You really seem to have gotten a better feel for her voice," she said, narrowing her eyes at me.

"I...did," I said carefully, unsure what was lying beneath Melody's tone but disinclined to say or do anything to put her out.

She looked at me closely for another few seconds, then nodded, turning back to the computer. "And you have another meeting with her on Thursday?"

"Mhm. Day after tomorrow," I added redundantly.

"And do you think you'll need to...'prepare' again? With me?"

"Do you?"

"I don't know," Melody said, shaking her head. "It sounds like you've got her voice, basically, but it'd take more than one night of drunken rambling to really get inside her head. Beautiful she may be, but she *is* deeper than that."

I rolled my eyes, although in frustrated agreement rather than argument. "You're not wrong."

"So. Do you want my help?"

"Teach me, sensei."

WE SPENT ANOTHER couple of hours going over the rest of the manuscript—Melody pointing out things I should ask Isobel about and prompting me to use my newfound knowledge to deduce things she might not have elaborated on particularly the first time we talked about them.

It was an interesting discussion—I'd never let anyone see my work at this stage before, but somehow Melody inspired complete trust in me, and I began to realize how, out of everyone she'd ever been involved with, this was the only person with whom Isobel had let herself fall in love. The dichotomy in the fact that what Melody was doing now, for me, was essentially a betrayal of that trust was not lost on me, and later that evening, eyes tired from hours poring over manuscripts and computer screens, now sitting next to her on the couch with mugs of hot chocolate (just for a change), I plucked up the courage to ask.

"So why are you doing this? I mean, you've kept these secrets so close for so long, if you'll pardon the melodrama. So why are you talking to me now?"

She didn't look altogether surprised that I had asked; however neither did she look eager to answer. "I...suppose I was curious," she said slowly, thoughtfully. "And I want Isobel's book to be as good as it can be. So I justify it to myself as helping."

I didn't quite disguise my wry smirk. Yet another woman spending time with me to find out more about Isobel. Not surprising, of course, and exactly as I'd thought. Still, it was a shame.

"Plus," Melody went on, finishing the thought she had begun a bit too early, "I had heard of you and was intrigued. I'm good friends with Professor Banks, and he said you were very talented back when he taught you; I guess I wanted to see for myself."

Okay, *now* I was surprised. "You know Martin Banks?"

"Of course. We met years ago, at some literary event or other. He's a great man."

"He is..." I narrowed my eyes. "He talked about me? We didn't get on at *all* in uni."

"He's not the easiest person to get along with—and I can imagine he would be a difficult teacher to have. Regardless, that didn't sully his view of your writing ability. He said you were one of the most promising talents to pass through his class in years."

"Hah, and yet here I am," I said with a dark chuckle. "Oh well."

"What do you mean?" Melody asked, tipping her head to one side inquisitively. "You don't value the writing you do?"

"I do," I said. "I just don't know that it's the sort of end point he might have expected from a promising writer. And I imagine he'd agree with you about young people writing memoirs."

"Yes, well. He is an old grump," she said, giving me one of the first genuine grins I had seen from her yet. I thought how different she was when she was at ease—all that mousiness disappeared and her intelligence, wit, and general good nature shone through. That unfriendliness and reclusiveness was, it seemed, just a front. Although what was it for?

I hesitated—dare I ask? Figuring that she would at least know I wasn't asking out of a desire to spread the information by now, I charged ahead. "Melody, just tell me if I'm stepping over a line here, but I'm curious... I know you're reserved, but you're not unfriendly and you clearly don't actually hate people. So why the famous need for solitude? I mean, if the stories are to be believed, you don't even see your own partner for some months of the year."

Clasping her mug, she pulled her lower lip between her teeth, worrying it for a moment before blinking and shrugging. "It...isn't a personal thing. I mean, it's not because I don't like people. It's just...what happens when I write. I go into my own head and I don't really come out until the book is completely finished. I can't just turn it off, and over the years, I've found it's easier to shut myself away rather than try to explain to people where I am or why I haven't said a word in three days."

"And when you began to get a reputation for it?"

Another shrug. "I don't really care about my reputation. It only made it easier to get work done when this mythos rose up around me, so I guess I didn't do anything to disabuse people of the notion."

I smiled. "And here you are, not terrifying at all," I teased gently. "Or at least different-terrifying."

Melody looked intrigued, though I could also tell she wasn't about to fish for anything, compliments or otherwise. "And here you are, just as talented as you were made out to be. I suppose not all rumours are false."

I smiled in spite of myself, unable to remain entirely unfazed in the face of a compliment delivered in such a sincere fashion. "I can see what she sees in you," I blurted out in my mild bemusement. "Saw in you. Whatever. You're really quite disarming."

"That's certainly something I've never been called before," Melody said with a surprisingly throaty chuckle. I wondered all of a sudden if she was a smoker—or used to be. "But it's better than eccentric recluse, so thank you."

"That surprises me. You certainly have a habit of cutting straight to the heart of things and making your mark on them. You're... It's remarkable, really." I glanced sideways at her but didn't turn my head, instead looking back to my mug of hot chocolate. Somehow it can be easier to say things sitting side by side with someone that you could never say if you were face to face.

"Well. Some people might agree. Other people don't like having the truth waved in their faces," she murmured in reply. She shifted then, and our knees touched, and I zoned out briefly, only to realize she was speaking again. "The heart of things and you get inside people's heads—it's just the same talent, applied differently."

I did turn to look at her now, raising my eyebrows sceptically. "Whatever you say," I murmured. I was surprised by how quiet it sounded.

She glanced up, her eyebrow arched exactly the same way Isobel arched hers when she wanted to needle me. I got the feeling that Melody wasn't trying to get at me—at least, not like that.

"What is it that you don't believe? That it's a similar talent, or that you and I are alike in any way?"

"Oh, I dunno," I said, shaking my head, dipping my gaze away from hers. "I suppose I just can't see why anyone would want to compare themselves to me."

"I thought my opinion counted for something, Nic. Otherwise, why am I here?" she asked.

"I..." I frowned slightly. That wasn't what I'd meant. I just... "Sorry. I don't...compliment well. Take them well, that is. Sorry."

"That's all right." Melody paused but, instead of leaving me to stew in silence, cleared her throat a moment later and continued speaking. "I'd like to take another look at that most recent chapter; a few things just occurred to me that might be useful..."

Relieved, I let her take us back to the computer screen, shifting closer on the couch to read over her shoulder as she annotated my text, made suggestions not just regarding things I might ask Isobel, places I might probe for more information, but also giving advice on turns of phrase, words, manners of expression that she would use. I lapped it all up, grateful not just for the help but for a distraction from the new layer of complication that was my growing interest in Melody Graham herself.

WE FINISHED THE edits, and she departed around ten o'clock, leaving a loud silence that made the flat feel emptier than it had in years. I liked living alone—preferred it, especially when I was trying to write—but somehow, having Melody around was relaxing in a way that being on my own wasn't. Maybe it was just her gentle reassurance and guidance that I was lacking; maybe it was something more. Either way, I didn't want to dwell on it and instead dove back into my writing, tackling a chapter on Isobel's first years at university, which up until now had stymied me. It went surprisingly well, and I stayed up until nearly four in the morning, busily typing and rereading my notes until I finally fell asleep on the couch, the laptop balanced precariously on my knees.

Chapter Twenty-Two

I WOKE WITH a start at around midday to a ringing sound in my ears—it took me a few moments' prodding and poking at my phone to realize that the intermittent, insistent sound was actually not my phone at all but my front door.

A look through the peephole showed only an unfamiliar young man; upon opening the door, I was suddenly assaulted by a riot of colour and scent as he brandished a large bouquet at me.

"Delivery for Miss Booth," he said sullenly.

I was stunned—who on earth would be sending me flowers? But I signed for them and sent him away and was already on my way to the kitchen, puzzling over the mysterious bouquet, before it occurred to me to just check for a card.

There was one, of course, and a written message, though not in a hand I recognized.

Nicola,
A small token of my gratitude for your chivalrous acts the other night. I almost expected you to show up in the morning and fit me with the missing shoe.
Thank you again.
Isobel x

I stared at that card for a long time, a slow smile growing on my face in spite of myself. This didn't redeem her entirely for knowingly putting me in that position, of course. But it helped.

BETWEEN THE COLOURFUL bouquet and the residual warmth of Melody's visit, my flat was practically glowing by the time I settled down to do some work. Not writing this time—instead I cued up the DVD I had rented for a second time from the online shop and settled down on the couch to watch *Hearth and Home* with a critical, more knowing eye.

Mostly, it was just the same—Isobel's immersion in her role was, as always, near-complete as she inhabited the lead character, Melody's script sparkled and stimulated in turn, and the direction was as slick-yet-unaffected as before.

The difference—and indeed the bit I had been looking forward to (although I'd forced myself to watch the film first anyway) were the behind-the-scenes extras. As with most DVDs nowadays, there were the usual barrage of useless features—an informational video about the town where the majority of the filming had taken place, a few different cuts of the theatrical trailer, some mildly interesting chat from the costume designer and set dresser. What I really wanted to see, however, were the various interviews between different members of the cast and the production team, including several with Isobel herself and another dual interview with Melody and the director.

I was immediately struck by how much younger she looked—I'd come to know her features quite well since I last saw these interviews and although at first it seemed she'd barely aged, I could now see where her face had changed, the absence of the fine lines she wore now rendering her somehow less interesting, less finished. Her manner was unchanged, I thought at first, but the more I watched, the more I became convinced that there was *something* there, just under the surface—a lack of her usual control, a slight giddiness that didn't seem to match up with the Isobel I had come to know.

Melody, by contrast, really *was* just the same, surprisingly so. Not knowing then what I did now, I hadn't even bothered to watch her interviews before, but looking at her, she seemed hardly a day older and her demeanour was just as it had been the previous night—calm, reserved but quietly confident, congenial but not overly affectionate.

"So, Mrs. Graham," the interviewer was saying, obviously gleeful at the opportunity to speak to the famously reclusive author, "how does writing for the screen compare to writing for stage or a novel? It must be a big change for you to make."

"It's Ms.," Melody corrected her gently before continuing. "It is a change, yes, but not as difficult as you might expect. I was already used to writing dialogue, and I really left most of the staging up to the director."

"It was a very collaborative process," the young director hastened to add, leaning forward in his canvas-backed chair. "We all worked together to create the best screenplay we could—the actors as well. I know Isobel and Melody spent quite a lot of time getting Marie's voice just right."

I smirked to myself. *I bet they did.* I rewound slightly and listened to this snippet again, this time watching Melody's face. It didn't betray the slightest flicker of nerves or private thought at this. I wondered whether that had been quite upsetting for Isobel. It couldn't have been easy for her, fighting to keep her own simmering excitement under control, watching Melody appear just as she always did—intermittently serene and eloquent or nervous and distracted, neither demeanour dependent on the presumably torrid affair they were currently having. *Mind you I'm only* assuming *torrid...*

I'll hand it to them, though—they were very discreet. If I hadn't known there was something going on between them, I never would have noticed...and that must've been hard as well. I'll admit it did inspire some slightly unkind feelings towards Melody; to have broken it off so soon after, with Isobel so obviously happy, was bordering on cruel. Just because she had a long-term partner to rely on didn't mean she couldn't have exhibited a bit of self-control.

That being said, when I thought about it, I had no idea how reliable her relationship with Whittaker was. She'd never mentioned him in the times we'd spoken and the pair were almost never seen in public. If I hadn't been so absorbed in Isobel, it was a question that I would probably find quite diverting.

For now, though, I had plenty of material to work with, as well as a couple of questions that would probably get me into plenty of trouble (and possibly lose me the job) if I were to ask them.

Chapter Twenty-Three

THURSDAY ROLLED AROUND all too slowly, with me spending the best part of a day over-prepared and with nothing at all to do. We were meeting at a restaurant I hadn't been to before; I wondered if perhaps Isobel wasn't reluctant to be seen with me at the hotel so soon after the night of her sprained ankle.

I was immediately glad, when I arrived, that some underlying paranoia had made me dress up for the occasion in a smart pair of trousers and a button-down shirt, because the restaurant in question was far more upmarket than I was in the habit of frequenting—and I'm used to some fairly upscale places.

To my surprise, Isobel was already there, wearing an incredibly flattering maroon-coloured dress and checking her makeup in a compact mirror at the table. She looked up as I pulled my chair out, face lighting up as she saw me.

"Nicola! Right on time, as always."

I almost stumbled—Isobel was by no means a reserved person, but she'd never greeted me quite so effusively before. My returning smile wasn't even dimmed by her calling me by my full name again, although I made a mental note to correct her the next good chance I got if she was going to keep using it.

"I think that's my epitaph, right there," I said as I sat.

She laughed, reaching for the glass of mineral water next to her plate. "I've heard worse."

I chuckled, with relief as much as amusement. This was altogether not quite how I'd expected Isobel to behave after the other night's events, but the surprise was most certainly a pleasant one.

"What would yours be?" I challenged her.

"Oh, God, I don't know," she said, grinning and shaking her head. "'Died old but still left a good-looking corpse'?"

"An aspiring Helen Moran, eh?"

"Always strive for the best, I say." She smiled again, reaching up to play with the gemstone pendant around her neck.

"So you were early," I commented. Not that she had ever been very late, but she was usually a bit behind me.

"Mm, I had a meeting nearby earlier. One of the reasons I chose this restaurant, actually. Anyway, it finished early, and I didn't see the point in going elsewhere only to come back here, so here I am."

"I take it you'd rather eat before we start."

"If that's all right," she said, raising her eyebrows slightly.

"Of course."

This seemed to be the cue for the waiter, who had been invisible up until now, to suddenly appear, menus in hand. Isobel spent some time looking over hers and asking for his recommendations before finally making her choice—a seafood salad with fresh oysters and fennel.

I went for a rather less exotic risotto, and soon we were left to ourselves again, me with my water and her a small glass of white wine. Eventually, I brought up the topic that I knew she was waiting to see if I would comment upon.

"I got the bouquet," I started, after a rather longer than usual clearing of my throat, which I'm sure she noticed. "It's lovely. Thank you."

"I should be thanking you," she replied with a shake of her head. "You went above and beyond the call of duty that evening."

"Well, I did feel a little responsible." Inwardly, I cursed myself because of course if there's one thing I know it's that the responsibility for overindulgence, and any resulting chaos, lies with the drinker alone.

"Let's just say I am grateful and leave it at that, shall we?" Isobel said lightly, though there was a certain amount of "the less said the better" in her expression.

I nodded, realizing that I hadn't asked about her ankle and now unsure that I should. I did know, at least, that there'd been no media attention drawn by the incident—either we'd been more discreet than we thought or Isobel's people had dealt with it.

"And anyway, I've been on my best behaviour since then. What have you been doing with yourself?"

I shrugged. "You know. Writing. Meetings. The usual."

"And how is the writing?"

"Better," I said with a nod and a smile. "Much better, I think."

"Really?" She looked pleased, and that in turn pleased me. "I'm so glad. Would I be able to see what you've done, or...?"

"I..." I hesitated. I could hardly show my work to her ex and then not let her see it. "Yes, if you like. Oh, although..." What I couldn't do, of course, was compromise my security principles and let the full manuscript out of my flat. "I don't really carry it around with me. Ever, I mean. Not in its entirety..."

"Really? Not even on a memory stick or something like that?"

"Have you noticed what happens to memory sticks in this country?"

Smirking, Isobel took a delicate sip of her wine. "Fair enough. I don't need to read *all* of it... I just admit to being very curious about what you're putting together."

"Well, I can certainly show you some excerpts, or..." I thought better of the suggestion that Isobel could come to my flat just a shade too late, and she looked at me expectantly. "I was going to say you'd be welcome to read whatever you want on location, but I really wouldn't want to put you out like that, and if you're just looking for a feel for what I'm doing..."

"Oh, well. I suppose we could do that," she said. "I mean, I go to business meetings at people's homes all the time. And you *have* been to mine..." It sounded for all the world like she was trying to convince herself that this was an acceptable idea, not just me.

"Believe me, by comparison my place is a hovel," I warned her. It wasn't that I was remotely ashamed of my place, it was more... Well, I almost didn't want to give her the opportunity to embarrass *herself* with her attitude, somehow.

"I'm sure it's not," came the response, along with a dismissive wave of her hand. "I would love it see it—the manuscript, I mean."

"I'll...do a printout of the latest draft for you," I said eventually, slightly confused as to how we'd reached this point.

"Oh, I wouldn't want to trouble you like that... I'm sure I could stop by and take a look at a chapter or two."

"A chapter or two I *can* just bring to a meeting," I offered.

Was it my imagination, or did Isobel look slightly disappointed? She soon banished the expression, however, and smiled brightly. "That would be lovely. I can't wait to see what you've done so far."

"Well, I hope you won't be disappointed."

"I'm sure I won't."

WE SPENT THE rest of the meal avoiding any talk of business, which meant that I had nothing to talk about. Isobel didn't seem to mind supporting most of the conversation on her own, sharing with me news of the projects she was considering taking on next and how her dealings in that sphere had been going. I listened eagerly, having in spite of myself become quite a fan over the course of my investigations and as such enjoying the inside scoop on her future almost as much as I did that of her past.

The food was, of course, exquisite, and after we'd eaten, we retired to a quiet corner of the bar area that I hadn't even known the restaurant had before we were led through there.

"I think I want to talk about some of your more moving experiences tonight, if you think that would be okay," I said as I placed the recorder between us and sat back again, my post-dinner espresso resting on the table untouched as yet.

"You mean like when I moved from Milan to London?" Isobel asked with a smirk. She had another glass of wine in hand, though she had only had the one during dinner.

I chuckled. "That's not quite what I meant, as well you know. Be serious."

"All right," she said, putting on a comical serious expression, her lips slightly pouted. "What do you want to start with?"

I pursed my own lips in thought. "Do you think we could start with the aftermath of your father's death?"

Well, *that* sobered her right up. "I...suppose so."

I nodded, sitting back a bit. "All right then. I don't want to...overstep any boundaries here. So just...start wherever you're comfortable."

She sipped her wine and reached up to run a hand through her artfully-tousled hair. "All right." She sighed. "But if I start crying again, our meeting is over."

I tipped my head to the side, slightly. "Why? There's no shame in crying about something emotional, is there? I've had plenty of clients burst into tears in front of me."

"Not here. And besides, I've made enough of a fool of myself in front of you already."

I frowned. "You didn't... Well, you crying isn't making a fool of yourself."

"Still. I don't want to do...that, here."

I nodded. "All right. I want you to be comfortable, no matter how emotional you feel. There's hardly any point in me trying to probe deeper into those places in your life where you feel uncomfortable. Is there somewhere else we could go?"

She gave a humourless laugh. "How far away do you live?"

The surprise flashed over my face too quickly for me to hide it. "Maybe twenty minutes at this time of night?"

"Fine. If you want to pursue this line of questioning, we can go there. I'll pay for the taxi."

"I have my car."

"Okay, well...it's up to you."

Chapter Twenty-Four

I COULD HARDLY demand that Isobel share her deepest emotions, then back off to prevent her from seeing my home, so drove us both in my modest but fortunately recently cleaned Golf back to my flat. Isobel seemed perfectly composed, if slightly more closed off than she had been at the start of the evening. At least she wasn't drunk—when I had suggested we go elsewhere, she had put down her wine and gathered up her bag and coat, ready to go.

My flat was fortunately as clean as my car, although nothing could hide the age of my furniture or the slight distress to the floors and paintwork.

Whether it was because I had warned her or because she just didn't care, Isobel betrayed no surprise as we entered, setting her purse down on my kitchen counter and shrugging off her jacket.

"Oh look," she remarked suddenly, turning to me with a smile. "You still have them."

"Well, they only arrived yesterday," I said, surprised that she thought I might've gotten rid of them already. "Um...tea? Coffee? Hot chocolate? Water?"

"Coffee would be lovely, thank you."

"Just sit down wherever, then, I'll be through in a minute."

When I returned to the sitting room, Isobel was settled on the couch, thumbing through one of the books I had left out on my coffee table.

She glanced up as I entered, smiling. "This is very interesting."

"Really? I mean, it was interesting to *me*... I guessed milk and one brown—hope that was right..."

"Absolutely perfect."

"All right then." I passed her mug and took a seat in the armchair in front of her, silently noting the fact that she had chosen the same spot on the couch that Melody had before.

"Thank you. I'm sorry if this seems like an overreaction to you—after the fiasco the other night, I really didn't feel like attracting any more attention to myself in public."

I shook my head. *What happened to less said the better?* "Not at all—it's fine." Right now, I was wondering firstly whether that coffee was going to be okay, and secondly, having done some mental calculations, why we were here and not at Isobel's own house, given she hadn't actually been much further away than my place from that restaurant. Had I been played, just slightly?

"Well then," she said with a deep breath and a pitifully brave smile at me, "shall we?" At home, I didn't need my little Dictaphone—I had a decent miniature multi-directional mic that plugged into my laptop, which I could use to record directly through to my external hard drive. This all took a couple of minutes to set up, through which Isobel waited patiently, sipping at her coffee and nibbling slightly at the biscuit I'd provided with it.

Once we were all set up, I sank back into my chair, shooting her an apologetic smile. "Wherever you'd like to start," I said.

It took a bit more prompting for her to begin; though she maintained her composure, it was (understandably) not an easy thing to discuss. Her father had died when she was still a budding actress, before she had really made it big, and she didn't work for almost six months as she supported her mother and siblings, hiring lawyers to deal with the financials and sifting through his things and apportioning them out to various relatives.

"Honestly, I look back on it and I'm not sure how I coped. I suppose it was only the support of my friends that got me through it—and my family, of course."

"What sort of role do you feel you played in that? I mean..." I qualified. "What I'm asking is where you felt you stood with those around you. Were you mostly supportive, mostly in need of support..."

"I...don't know. Even though I was the youngest, my family always viewed me as an adult—mostly because I travelled so much, with my touring and modelling. So when Father died, I had to be an adult then as well, even though I felt like a lost little girl."

I nodded, filing this new information away. Isobel's family had been a happy, stable, supportive group all through her life, which was great, but it didn't really help me to figure out how they had shaped her character. The idea that she had been left exposed like this, expected to be strong and supportive of others while her world was falling apart, that was a little more useful.

"And, being young, most of my friends were as well. They didn't really know how to help me, even though they tried," she said, looking down at the coffee mug in her hands. "There were only a few people who were actually aware of what I was going through, in the end."

"Who were they?"

"My agent, James Stockwell—he was very supportive and never pressured me to return to acting before I was ready, even though I had to pass up some very good opportunities."

"Of course." I'd met James, when we'd been in early discussions. He'd struck me as a decent guy—still an agent, of course, with all that that entailed but much less self-interested than some I'd seen. Certainly, he was very keen to get the measure of me before he let me near Isobel.

She nodded, and I realized she wasn't going to elaborate any more unless I pushed her. Well, why not? We had gotten this far already. "You said there were a few more people?" I prompted.

"Oh. Yes. Well, mostly friends, people who were slightly older and more mature."

"Uh-huh?" I raised my eyebrows, nodding for her to go on, making sure that I looked for all the world like I was waiting for the inevitable rather than pressuring her into saying something she'd rather avoid.

With a sigh, she continued. "It was mostly Melody Graham, actually. She heard about Father's death—I'm still not sure how—and contacted me. We hadn't seen each other in about two years at that point. Anyway, she was very helpful, since she had lost her mother when she was younger and could understand what I was going through."

This was, of course, more or less the exact response I'd expected. The question was whether to call her out now or later on the fact that she'd claimed she hadn't seen Melody from leaving university right through to when they next worked together—and this was almost in the middle of that period. Rather than get too clever with her now, I simply moved on to something less emotional—I'd carefully picked out a few logistic questions to throw in the mix to keep things from getting too bogged down.

"Your first film after that was *Seamstress*—d'you want to tell me a bit more about that? I don't have much on the filming yet."

She gratefully grabbed onto the topic and began to share her stories with me; they were interesting as always, though I'll admit I was only half listening, knowing that my recording equipment would pick it up for me to transcribe later. I was mostly preoccupied with the idea that she and Melody had yet more contact that she hadn't admitted to before—why not? Had she been that afraid that I might pick up on Melody drifting in and out of her life and draw conclusions that she didn't want drawn? Or was it some kind of coping mechanism, ignoring their past because of the lack of a future?

Of course, now I felt that by prying further into this I was going to cast suspicion on myself, and that I didn't need at all. Suddenly, I was regretting contacting Melody in the way that I had—I had assumed there was no way the pair's paths would ever cross, but it seemed that they were considerably less estranged than Isobel had led me to believe. Was there a chance that she still had some small level of contact? Would Melody's loyalty to her supersede any to me? It seemed plausible, perhaps even likely.

Eventually, I realized Isobel had stopped talking and was looking at me with a strange, curious expression. "Is everything all right, Nicola?"

"Nic," I said without even thinking about it. Then, shaking my head to clear it and looking back at her properly, I cleared my throat and clarified. "I go by Nic. I'm fine, sorry."

"I just realized I was babbling away to myself after a while. Would you prefer I talk about something else?" she asked, arching one eyebrow at me.

"We can talk about whatever you like," I said. "Although I was interested to know more about your trip to Paris in 2000—you sort of glossed over it when we last spoke about it." This was another one of Melody's tip-offs, so I wasn't surprised to see Isobel hesitate and then shake her head.

"Actually, I'd like to hear more about your life—this all feels a bit unbalanced to me, don't you think? I enjoyed hearing about your family the other night."

I had doubts that my smile reached my eyes. "You know, you're not actually writing a book about me," I contested.

"Maybe not yet. But I have a feeling one day your life might make an interesting film. So tell me more about it."

I made a face, resisting the urge to argue with this sweeping remark that made so little sense and raised so many questions. "First, tell me about Paris," I said eventually. "Then you can ask me anything you want." After all, she already knew the worst of my secrets—what could she really ask?

Perhaps getting into a bargaining war with Isobel wasn't the best idea, because she seemed to relent awfully quickly, shrugging and sitting back on the sofa. "I went to Paris to help launch a new campaign for one of the designers I used to work with when I was younger—Thierry St. Michel. There were several events over a three-day period, including a fashion show in which I was an honorary model."

I nodded. "Sounds interesting." Then, surmising that I was, after all, going to answer her questions, I added, "So why did you skate over it before? I presume something happened in Paris that you'd rather didn't go in the book."

She gave a short laugh; I had never been quite so upfront about her evasions before. "There was a slight incident at the party on the last night; it was rather unpleasant and I don't like talking about it."

"I see." I waited. If she was going to refuse to discuss said incident, then I wouldn't make her, but I sure as hell wasn't going to help her skirt past it either.

After several seconds of silence, she went on, looking like a sulky child. "David was there. He was incredibly drunk, which is very unlike him, and he confronted me about the end of our relationship. He knew there was someone else—though not who, thank God. He was very upset."

"How did you leave things with him?"

"I...attempted to assuage him," Isobel said, her gaze sliding away from mine, coming to rest somewhere along the arm of my chair. "I couldn't have him going to the press about it."

"Presumably, though, things had ended with Melody again by then?"

"Yes."

I nodded thoughtfully. It couldn't have been easy, having turned this poor guy down, left him for someone she knew she couldn't be with, to then have him coming up to her and reminding her at once not only how much she hurt him but also that it had left her alone. Again, I felt a stab of anger towards Melody—I felt sure that she had been in love with

Isobel in return, possibly still was. And yet she'd refused to leave her comfortable, settled, heterosexual life to be with her.

"All right," I said. "Thanks." *So what do you want to know about me? I guarantee you'll be disappointed...*

Isobel was ready with her question. "How long have you been an alcoholic?"

I blinked, stunned into silence for a moment. There was no way, of course, that she *didn't* know how little I would want to talk about this. And that meant that she was asking as much to throw me off-guard, to lay me vulnerable, as out of curiosity. This new combative element to our relationship was at once unpleasant, worrying, and (I couldn't help but admit it at least to myself now) exciting.

The answer, however, was perhaps less exciting. "I really don't know," I said. "Since shortly after uni. Maybe before. Maybe always." After all, who knew if the only reason I wasn't drinking too much before then was because I didn't feel the need? That didn't mean that I wasn't addicted. "I always saw it as a way to manage my moods."

"I see. And now that you don't drink, how do you manage them?"

I smiled dryly. "Mostly I avoid having them," I quipped. Then I sighed and shrugged. "I do what normal people do. Try to work through things when I can and try to keep my mind off them when I can't."

"What do you do to keep your mind off things?" Isobel asked eagerly, leaning forwards now, looking rapt. The questions were getting rapidly less discomforting, but I could tell she liked this—being in control again, being the interviewer instead of the interviewee.

"Write. Tidy. Bake. Go for walks. You know, mundane things," I said. "Well, mundane things that don't involve places that sell alcohol," I added, figuring I should probably give her *something* beyond the minimum information possible. "Which does cut down the options a little."

"And how long has it been?" she replied, raising an eyebrow.

"A couple of years. Well, since I last relapsed. Three since I decided to stop drinking."

"I see."

I raised my eyebrows expectantly. "Anything else?"

She smiled enigmatically and shook her head. "I think it's your turn."

"All right." I reached for my notepad, suddenly unable to remember what else Melody had given me. I had some more bits and pieces from a few years before, during the high point of her acting career. Instead, I found myself asking a different question altogether.

"Did you sleep with Laura?"

"*Excuse* me?"

My expression didn't flicker. *Hey, we are long past pretending that this is just about the book. You don't need to know about* me *for this book. If we're playing Lecter and Starling, I'll ask whatever I like.*

"Did you have sex with Laura Maguire?"

"No, I did not. And even if I had, I hardly see how that's relevant to anything," she responded icily.

"I think it's probably *as* relevant as my alcoholism."

"Well. You have your answer. Ms. Maguire and I are business colleagues, that's all."

"Interesting."

"Why? Did you?"

I sighed. "No. My best friend thinks I should have before I ended it. But I didn't."

"Oh." Isobel shifted, reaching for her now-empty mug and setting it down again. "I see."

"What on earth did you email to her to get her so angry?"

She frowned for a moment, obviously thinking back, then shook her head. "I told her that I valued our professional relationship and hoped our collaborations would continue, but that I could not commit to being so closely involved with her current project and would have to step back to a lesser role. And...oh, the rest isn't important."

"Tell me anyway?" I suggested, nothing in my tone now but genuine curiosity.

"I may have included an opinion about her treatment of you and what a fool she was being," she replied measuredly, her expression unreadable.

My brow furrowed. "She didn't treat me *badly*, you know. I really think we just weren't that interested in each other, in the end."

"Perhaps that explains her reaction, then."

My frown gave way to a darkly amused smile. "No. She was reacting to your rejection. Not mine. That's why it seemed to me as though you two..."

"No. I've adopted David's rule—never sleep with anyone you're working with," she said, shaking her head. "It just complicates things."

"I suppose that's true." Why did I feel a slight pang of something like disappointment? I had *never* entertained the notion that Isobel might sleep with me, nor did I particularly want to—that is, any more than anyone would want to sleep with such a beautiful, talented woman.

"Besides," she added, biting back a smirk, "she's too young. I prefer my lovers with a bit more experience."

This I wasn't sure how to respond to, so I returned the almost-smirk with a half smile and moved on. "So, you drew back from her because she was becoming romantically interested in you?"

"I suppose so. She's a talented young woman and I do have an interest in her career, but I didn't want that interest to be muddled by or confused with any misunderstandings. And, as you saw, she's not very good at concealing her emotions. It only would have ended badly—or at least, worse than it did."

"Have you spoken since?" To Isobel's nod, I added, "Has she calmed down a bit then?"

"She seems much more reasonable now, yes. Funding is going very well for her next film; I believe they expect to start casting shortly."

"Good for her. She's very talented."

Isobel nodded, winding the long golden chain of her pendant around her finger. "Yes, she is. I hope you wouldn't expect me to invest my time and money in anything less," she said, giving me a pointed look.

"Certainly not."

"Speaking of which... I would love to see the book now."

"Oh... Well, that would be...fine, although I don't have the latest version in hard copy right now. Would you be okay with reading from a laptop screen?" I began running through the manuscript in my head for the slightest of signs that I'd spoken to Melody, realizing with some relief that I'd never made notes with her anywhere other than the notepad I held in my hands.

"Of course."

Chapter Twenty-Five

WE SWITCHED FROM coffee to a pot of tea (half-caf, although I didn't tell her that), and soon Isobel was seated on the couch, reading my latest draft straight from my external drive, with me alternating between sitting in my chair, trying to read a book (a *Very Short Introduction to the Cold War*) myself, or finding ways to occupy myself tidying or simply organizing in other parts of the flat.

It was hard, however, with the subject of my book hunched over the screen, busily scanning away. She didn't read quite as quickly as Melody, and occasionally I heard her tap-tap-tapping the up arrow to reread a section, but she still finished the chapter thankfully fast, sitting back with a thoughtful expression on her face.

I sat forwards as she tipped the lid of the laptop to look over it at me, meeting her eyes, my expression expectant and, I'm sure, more than trepidatious.

"It's very good," she said, sounding almost surprised. "How did you do that?"

"You know, it's a funny thing. I hit the keys that correspond to the right..." I stopped at her warning expression. "Do what?" I said.

"Make it sound so much like *me*."

"Well, that's the bit that I've been wrestling with," I said, relief flowing through me that I'd got it right even as something like nerves twisted in my stomach at how I'd managed it. "That's what these last couple of meetings have been about. I...know you."

"You're not putting those things into the book, though, are you?" She looked worried for a moment, colour actually draining out of her cheeks at the thought.

I shook my head. "That's not what it's about. It's about...leaving the right spaces. If I'm..." I frowned, looking for the right words. "If I'm *you*, and I'm leaving something out, I need to know what I'm leaving out to continue with the right voice..." I narrowed my eyes slightly at this because it wasn't quite right, but it was as close as I could get. "Do you understand?"

She breathed a sigh of relief. "It sounds a bit like when scenes are cut from a film—they're still incorporated into the others even if no one else will ever see them."

"Sure, maybe a bit like that? I just... Without wanting to sound creepy, I need to be in your skin."

"I understand." Isobel looked at me a bit longer, lashes lowered over her dark eyes, her chin tipped up just slightly. "And how much longer do you think this will take? Being in my skin, I mean."

Right now, my own skin was beginning to feel increasingly tight, but I swallowed and managed a nonchalant shrug. "As long as it takes, I guess. Who knows?"

"Well, I thought you might, which is why I asked," she teased gently.

I allowed for another smile and managed not to physically squirm in my seat. "Drink your tea," I said, nodding to the cup. "If you want the next chapter, it's in the same folder."

"Don't mind if I do."

BY THE TIME Isobel had sated her curiosity, reading several more chapters and drinking several more cups of tea, it was nearly midnight. I hadn't intended on having her over so late, but she seemed content to sit on the sofa and scroll through the manuscript, occasionally chuckling with delight or furrowing her brow as she read a particularly evocative passage.

Not that I was tired, obviously—I hadn't got out of bed until about half one that day, albeit after falling asleep around seven in the morning, but the longer she sat there, the more awake I felt. It was almost as though just by sitting there on my couch she was slowly filling the flat with her presence until even when I went through to the bedroom a bit, ostensibly to fold some laundry, I could feel her.

Eventually, I heard her stand and stretch, her stocking feet tousling the sitting room rug as she stepped away from the couch. "Nic? I think I'm finished, for now—if I stay up much later, I'll regret it in the morning."

She was bent over, placing my laptop back onto the coffee table, as I re-entered the lounge, and I can't say that I'm proud but I enjoyed the view in silence, not speaking until she straightened again.

"All right. I hope it all met with your approval."

"It did. And I'm looking forward to seeing the finished product." I couldn't tell if this meant she wasn't going to ask to read anything else—and if that was the case, shouldn't I feel glad? No one liked an impatient client breathing down their neck.

"Well, if you need to see any more..." I said, not quite understanding why I was offering.

She smiled. "It would be a bit narcissistic of me to insist on reading everything, don't you think?"

I shrugged. "Whatever you need."

"I'll keep that in mind," she murmured, and I *know* it wasn't my imagination that her gaze dropped to run over my body for a long second. At least, I think it did.

I reminded myself what she'd said before about people she was working with. I also reminded myself that it was completely implausible that she would be remotely interested in me. Neither of those facts stopped my heart from leaping into my throat, and all I could do was nod in reply.

With that, she began to gather up her things, slipping back into her shoes and pulling her mobile out of her purse. From the way she was scrolling through it, I was aware that she had quite a few messages, and it made me feel inordinately proud to think she had ignored them all in favour of reading my book. "Is Monday still the best time to meet?" she asked then, glancing up at me.

"Um, sure," I murmured, still standing by the lounge door watching her prepare to leave, the weekend suddenly stretching out in front of me, impossibly long.

"All right. Why don't you pick the place this time? I trust your tastes."

"All...right. I'm sure I'll think of something."

"Good." Having replaced her mobile into her purse, Isobel began to put on her jacket, looking every bit as poised and elegant as she had at the restaurant.

"I'll...see you on Monday then," I said. Why, oh why did I sound so hesitant and shy all of a sudden? Then to make matters worse, I remembered that I'd driven us here. "Oh, shit, I forgot, can I call you a cab?"

"Mm? Oh, no, it's fine, I'll call one now and wait downstairs." With one last smile and a glance at the flowers on the table, Isobel put her hand on the doorknob and let herself out, heels clicking on the concrete landing.

I was left staring after her for some time, heart still beating in my throat, though it had slowed by the time I reached my armchair and sat back down, my now-cold tea sitting on the table in front of me. I did absolutely nothing for a very long time, just processing the evening's events. I seemed to have gotten away with this new, scary approach so far. But I wasn't sure how much more tension—of any kind—I could take.

Chapter Twenty-Six

W*ITH* I*SOBEL'S* P*RAISE* still ringing faintly in my ears, I was eager to get stuck into writing again. The next couple of days passed in a blur— I'm sure there was eating and sleeping and showering in them, but I don't really recall it. The thing that *did* stand out was the phone call I got on Saturday afternoon from Melody Graham.

"Nicola Booth."

"Nic, hello, it's Melody…Graham."

"Er, hi. How goes it?"

"Just fine, thank you. I was calling to see how your last meeting with Isobel went."

"Oh! Right. Yeah, it was…interesting. Good, though, I think. Pretty good," I said. "Thanks for all your help."

"Of course. I'm glad that it went well." There was a long silence. "Are you meeting with her again?"

"Always," I said with a chuckle. "I'm apparently choosing somewhere for dinner on Monday—any suggestions?"

"Try the Ethiopian restaurant in West Kensington."

"Copy that," I said, noting it down. "So, how's the first half of your weekend been?"

"Very quiet. Just the way I like it. Yours?"

"The same. Climbing the walls a little," I admitted.

"Oh?"

"Mm, yeah, usually when I'm on a roll like this, I'd be delighted to get a few days to blitz through my writing, but for some reason, I'm just aching for the weekend to be over, you know?"

That throaty chuckle surprised me again. "Looking forward to seeing her again?"

"That's…not quite what I meant," I said, in a tone that I knew screamed "busted."

"Well," she said, ignoring my obvious guilt, "I understand if you're busy writing, but if you want some company I'm free tomorrow afternoon. I'd like to see what you're working on now."

"That would be great," I said immediately, surprising myself with how quickly I responded.

"All right. Shall I come by yours?"

"If you want to read the latest couple of chapters, certainly."

"I'd like that. What time is good for you?"

"Oh, whenever, really. Well. Not before midday."

"Three p.m.?"

I was glad that Melody wasn't in front of me to see the way I was grinning down the phone. "See you then."

SUDDENLY, THE WEEKEND seemed to drag past even more slowly, stretching out until I thought I would go mad with a mixture of boredom and anticipation. Saturday night found me in the oh-so-swinging venue of the church hall once again at my AA meeting, listening to familiar voices drone on about their problems and challenges.

Don't get me wrong—I understand the value of the process, and more than once, it's saved me from heading down a slippery slope, at the bottom of which is a vat of Long Island Iced Tea. It was just that today my thoughts were not taken up with cocktails and hidden bottles of vodka but with a temptation of an entirely different sort.

Not that there was any real danger of me giving into this temptation— or at least, if I did, of anything coming of it. My preoccupation with getting into Isobel's skin had somehow blossomed into wanting to just be *near* her skin, and not only that but had spilled over until there were thoughts of Melody there as well. I mean, on one hand, it's not surprising I felt that way about Isobel, since the whole point of celebrity was that the majority of people want to either be them or do them. But I hadn't felt this way when I was still getting to know her; a bit in awe, yes, and even slightly jealous, but not this. It was only once I started to really break her down, see the more human side of her that she became desirable, and I don't know what it said about me that I was having the same sort of feelings about her ex, a wholly different but still fascinating person.

The thing about Melody that confused me was that she was, well, to put it frankly, the "me." Sure, the non-fucked-up, practically married to a guy me, but where Isobel was the beauty, she was the brains, and that's the role I was used to fulfilling back when I actually had relationships. Without wanting to brag, I tended to date very attractive women (admittedly all the time wondering what the hell they were doing with me), one or two just as pretty as Isobel was, in ordinary lighting anyway, and so I'd always sort of assumed that I was hopelessly shallow and I was basically okay with that.

But then, Isobel was more than just a beautiful face, and Melody looked prettier every time I saw her, so all my usual labels were going out the window a bit now. Nonetheless, the fact that Melody made something inside me jump every time our hands brushed was either a testament to how long it had been or a sign that something strange was happening. Was it because some part of me was busy transforming into Isobel as it always did when I was writing someone? And if so, was it actually a good sign for the book, even if it was a bad sign for my continuing, tentative friendship with Melody? And which of the two did I care about getting right? And if I cared more about Melody, then what did *that* say?

You'll be able to tell by now that the reason I don't date or even befriend most women is because I have a slight tendency to overthink things, which meant that I didn't get much worthwhile sleep on Saturday, only dropping off as the sky was lightening into dawn. I woke up in a panic at one in the afternoon, sure that I'd hear the buzzer go at any moment and I'd have to greet her in my robe and bedhead.

Fortunately, although Melody was a timely sort, she wasn't the type to arrive early, and my flat was pristine in any case, so I had only myself to prepare, meaning that I was washed, dressed, and lunched successfully and reviewing some of Thursday's recordings when my buzzer went.

Opening the door after she had climbed the stairs to my flat, I was greeted by the sight of Melody smiling warmly at me, cocooned in a rose-coloured sweater, and carrying a small canvas bag in addition to her ever-present leather satchel.

"Hello, Nic."

I broke into a wide smile in return in spite of myself (not that I'm not friendly, but I had a feeling I looked like I'd just won the lottery), which was quickly wiped off my face by the way Melody's suddenly disappeared, her gaze shifting past me towards the interior of my flat.

"What's... *Oh...*" Too late I realized that I'd left the recording playing in my lounge, Isobel's rich, resonant voice drifting clearly along the hall to where we stood.

"...vid was there. He was incredibly drunk, which is very unlike him, and he confronted me about the end of our relationship. He knew there was someone else—though not who, thank God. He was very upset."

"How did you leave things with him?"

"I...attempted to assuage him... I couldn't—"

"Jesus, I'm sorry, I'll just—" I practically ran through to the lounge in my eagerness to turn off the recording, unheeding of the woman hot on my heels until I felt her hand on my arm, stopping me just as I reached my laptop.

"...had ended with Melody again by then?"

"Yes."

I whipped around to find her standing right by me, almost uncomfortably close, and she was gazing right into my eyes as Isobel went on.

"How long have you been an alcoholic?"

I had forgotten about this, but I was frozen now, Melody's fingers feeling like hot wires on my bare forearm, and although she really wasn't gripping me that tightly, it could have been a vice for all the difference it made to my ability to move.

"I really don't know. Since shortly after uni. Maybe before. Maybe always."

"Oh Isobel," Melody breathed, her voice hitching in her throat as her fingers contracted on my wrist. She seemed to come back to herself then, blinking and wetting her lower lip with the tip of her tongue. "I'm sorry. You should...turn that off."

I nodded mutely, disengaging myself from Melody's grip with a combination of relief and reluctance and turning to click the Stop button on my media player. She stepped back, looking around herself as if she wasn't quite sure how she had gotten there.

"I, um, brought some tea," she murmured, sliding the canvas bag off her shoulder. "And biscuits. If you like."

"You really didn't have to," I said, trying to keep my voice light. "But thanks. I'll...go get the kettle on."

Somehow, we managed not to speak until we had both settled back into our usual spots around the coffee table—me in my armchair, Melody on the sofa. If anything, she seemed *more* distracted when she sat down, brow furrowed and manner distant.

I'd been ready to move on and pretend that nothing had happened, but then I realized that if Isobel was the whole reason we were here, skating around her probably wasn't going to help with anything.

"I'm...sorry about that," I said, leaning over to lift the teapot. I moved it in little air circles to help it brew. "I should've thought."

"It's all right," she replied with a shake of her head. "It's not your fault. I should be used to it. I was just surprised, hearing her talk about David in that way...and then what she said to you. I had no idea what she was putting you through."

I shrugged. "It's just quid pro quo—she isn't the first client to try it." *Although she's the first to get under my skin like that.* "About David in what way? I mean, she seemed matter-of-fact enough..."

"Oh, I'm sure it was," Melody said, giving a short, humourless laugh. "Her 'appeasements' usually are."

I frowned, thinking back to what Isobel had said. *I...attempted to assuage him... Ah.* "I see."

"Mm." Thought she was obviously still lost in thought, Melody leaned forwards, arranged the mugs on coasters, and opened the package of ginger biscuits she had brought. The pink sweater set off the rosiness of her cheeks, and again I wondered how I ever could have considered her at all plain-looking.

"I suppose that's why you're here," I said with a wry chuckle. "Reinterpretation and all that." I poured our tea, but rather than reach for the milk, I just set the pot down and sat back, my mind wandering back to the other night, sitting opposite Isobel, listening to her talk... And it occurred to me that of course, Melody was sitting in the same place. I wondered briefly whether she knew, and then remembered the look that had flashed over her face as she'd sat down and knew that Isobel's perfume still rested lightly on the fabric.

"I guess so. Though I'm not sure if it's such a good idea any more..."

The unpleasant tug I felt at these words was one that I could only try to pretend was related just to our working relationship. "Er...all right. Can I ask why?"

She turned a conflicted gaze in my direction. "I don't know if it's a good idea for me to be reinterpreting these things for you. You seem to have gotten her voice down, and anything else I give you is just gossip, really. Gossip that she doesn't want you knowing."

It looked like hearing Isobel's voice had caused an attack of conscience, then. Well, I could hardly blame her—after all, it had been eating at me too. Only now, though, did I find myself thinking about how much I would miss her.

I managed a nod. "I understand. All right. Thanks for all your help."

Apparently, my poker face was better than I thought, since she frowned slightly and then shifted, beginning to rise from the sofa, obviously taking this as a dismissal of her services.

"You're not even going to drink your tea?" I completely belied the nonchalance of my tone by practically leaping out of my seat as she stood.

Melody looked shocked, then flattered, then amused as we stood staring at each other over the low table. "Do you mind I stay?"

"I'd...like you to." Okay, now I felt about fifteen.

"Then I'd like to as well." Slowly we both returned to our seats, and Melody added milk to our cups, managing to do so without a splash on the table (which was better than I achieved most days).

"So...what are you working on right now?" I asked before biting into one of Melody's ginger biscuits, unsure how to proceed now that our main topic of conversation was *verboten*.

"I'm researching for a play at the moment—it's historical, based on the Massacre of Glencoe," she replied.

"Sounds gory."

She laughed. "What's theatre without a little blood and guts, eh? Honestly, though, there probably won't be much gore involved. I'm more interested in the personal side of things."

"Ah, I see, the fictionalized drama that goes on behind it all—the human element."

"Something like that. It doesn't sound too wanky to you, does it?" she asked, giving me an uncertain look.

I grinned at this. Perhaps it was the pink but she was kind of adorable right about now. "Wanky is in the execution," I said. "I'm sure it won't be with you writing it."

"Oh God, don't say that—I've written some real stinkers in my time."

"And they've quietly disappeared thanks to your sheer volume of really excellent work," I finished, my grin still in place.

"Are you sure you don't want to go into publicity? Forget ghostwriting, I could use someone like you on my team." It was clear Melody was joking, though I'll admit it still made my stomach flip to consider being recruited to her *team*. "Or maybe a personal motivator."

"Hah. I don't think so." I shook my head, sipping my tea. "I'm too honest."

"And yet you write what people tell you about their lives."

"Mm, well, tiny lies of omission are one thing." *And huge lies of omission are another*, I mused, considering Isobel. Perhaps Melody sensed my thoughts, or they matched hers, because she cleared her throat, leaning forwards to reach for another biscuit.

"I would suggest we just avoid talking about work altogether, but I think that might leave us with nothing to discuss," she said, sounding half amused, half regretful.

I smirked. "I suppose we'll have to discuss other people's," I offered. "Have you read the latest Carmen Gould?"

This proved to be a good question, as Melody had, and we quickly fell into discussion. She was articulate, observant, far more up to date on her literary criticism than I, and she *loved* talking about books. It became clear that most of the time she wasn't writing she spent reading, as she had a vast knowledge of literature and an impressive knack for recalling certain quotes and excerpts to prove her points.

In my case, of course, said novel was the first fiction I'd read in over a year and even then, I'd struggled to get through it out of basic loyalty, but I think I managed to hold up my end of the conversation—more or less. Afterwards, I steered us towards older books by the same author, passing the time pleasantly hopping from book to book.

"...did a film adaptation of that one that I loved. Did you see it?"

"No," Melody said with a shake of her head. "I honestly don't watch many films. I know that must seem strange, but I guess I'm just not a very visual person."

"Oh, but it's about so much more than *just* the visual—it was written and directed by Fred Kane, and he basically pulled it to pieces as a book and put it back together again as a film," I enthused. "I swear, it's one of the best novel adaptations I have *ever* seen—I mean, you know how different writing a screenplay is from writing a novel and he's really *thought* about that, you know?"

"Well, I guess I'll have to look out for that, then," she said, tilting her head to one side and giving me what looked like a fond smile. "It sounds good enough that I might break habit and watch it."

"I actually own it, if the mood ever takes you." I offered, fighting the blush that threatened to spread from my ears at that smile.

"Really? I don't suppose you have it on VHS..."

I laughed. "Oh, dear me. Er, no, sorry..."

"Well, I guess I could watch it on my laptop," Melody said, pursing her lips thoughtfully. "Unless...well, would you mind watching it with me?"

Somewhat relieved that she was taking my reasonably transparent implication, I shrugged and nodded. "Always happy to watch *In Light of That* again... I could actually throw it on now if you don't have anywhere to be for a couple of hours?"

Another one of those smiles that inspired hot cheeks and a silly grin of my own. "My evening is free."

Chapter Twenty-Seven

A FRESH POT of tea was made, some lightly salted popcorn was popped, and soon we were seated side by side on my couch, viewing the aforementioned film on my respectable-sized, recently purchased flat-screen TV.

As the light outside dimmed and the room warmed, the rose-coloured jumper was gone. Underneath it she was wearing a little red T-shirt that testified that however much time she spent hunched in front of a computer screen, she hadn't let it affect her figure.

I hadn't watched *In Light of That* in a while, actually, but it was as good as I remembered, and better yet, Melody seemed to think so too. I could tell she was a bit dubious at first, but soon she was sitting rapt, leaning nearer to the screen just slightly and chuckling at every deftly executed turn of phrase.

As the film wore on and Melody relaxed back against the couch cushions again, I *think* it was my imagination that she seemed to be leaning over a bit, closer to me now, but this conviction didn't prevent the little tingle that ran through me at the proximity. Fortunately, my attention to the film—and hers—was such that I wasn't in a position to do too much obsessing over this point. I thought wryly that, for all her distracting good looks and wiles. Laura had never quite managed to excite these long-buried feelings. Not, of course, that Melody was an eligible fixation, something I tried to remind myself of even as I got up to visit the loo with the express purpose of sitting back down just the *tiniest* shade closer when I returned.

Of course, it turned out not to be necessary, since this time I was certain she was sitting closer to my side of the couch when I came back from the bathroom. Not only that, she glanced up and gave me a warm smile, reaching for the remote.

"I know you've seen this before, but I thought I'd wait until you got back."

Shooting her a smile in return that I hoped wasn't as shy as I suddenly felt, I sat back down and found there was no way that I could prevent our thighs from touching without making a huge show of it.

Not that I particularly wanted to. Though she wasn't as poised and perfumed as Isobel, Melody *did* smell nice—a mixture of shampoo, tea, and something familiar that I finally realized must be the scent of paper and ink.

"Do you write by hand?" I asked, albeit keeping it to a murmur beneath the dialogue for the film. I wasn't even sure at first whether Melody had heard me.

"First draft, yes," came the eventual response. "Why?"

"Mm, no reason," I hummed, eyes still on the screen. I forced myself to settle back on the couch, my shoulder perilously close to hers. I could actually feel the slight warmth emanating from her as we sat, and I realized this was probably the closest I'd been to anyone who wasn't Julie—or Laura, I suppose, but that didn't seem to count somehow—in a very long time.

The rest of the movie played on—it must have done, since I at least remember the credits rolling at the end. The rest was a blur, however, as I was caught between paying attention to what was happening on screen and trying not to give into the temptation to shift ever slightly closer to Melody so that we were properly close. She certainly didn't seem to mind our current situation—I suppose I expected her to be much more standoffish, but she seemed quite content (almost) cosied up to me on the couch.

I cleared my throat, and reached for the remote to turn off the television. "So," I said, my voice a little hoarse, although that was presumably partly from not speaking for a while. "What did you think?"

"You're right. It was very good," Melody said, turning towards me. "Certainly the best film adaptation I've seen in quite some time."

"I'm not usually a fan of writer-director efforts," I said, my concentration now on preventing my gaze from straying to her lips as I spoke. "Too few cooks. But in this instance..."

"It definitely worked. Thank you for the recommendation."

"It was my absolute pleasure. The only person I ever get to sit down and watch a film with usually is Julie and she talks through them..."

Was it my imagination, or did Melody look too interested all of a sudden? "Julie?"

"My best friend. My *only* friend, just about. We've known each other since my first job in London temping in some horrible little publishing house."

"Ah," she said, nodding sagely. "When was that?"

"God, fifteen years ago? Longer?" I shook my head. "Feels like forever ago. She's a fully fledged editor there now."

"Presumably able to stick out less-than-stellar working environments better than some?"

"Better than me, certainly, although that was never going to be my sort of job, I don't think." Maybe I was wrong and Melody's interest in my social circle was purely friendly curiosity—after all, we'd established that Julie and I weren't involved and she was still asking questions. I silently chastised myself for entertaining the idea that it could have been anything else.

"Well, you know what they say: Those that can, write. Those that can't, edit," Melody said with a chuckle. She reached up to run a hand through her hair, and when she let it fall again, it landed not back on the sofa but partially on my knee, lightly resting there as if it was the most natural thing in the world.

"I don't know," I murmured, my gaze straying to Melody's hand in spite of myself. "I'm not sure what I do isn't closer to particularly imaginative editing than it is writing..." Alarm bells should have been ringing in my head right about then—this woman was basically married, had a history of doing, well, this, apparently, and I already knew she'd ended one such affair to the ruination of another woman's life. Said bells, however, if they rang at all, were ringing far, far away. I thought wryly that this, at least, gave me more insight into quite what had happened between her and Isobel. Another part of me wondered how much more *insight* I might have the chance to gather. I must have smirked at this, because she leaned slightly closer, tipping her head to get a better look at my expression.

"I think you do yourself a disservice. And I was only joking about editors, anyway. I certainly wouldn't publish without one."

"So you're not like whatserface with the vampire novels, then," I said with a smirk. "Good to know." I dragged my gaze back up to hers and it felt like she was closer still, and it was all I could do not to lean in and kiss her. Back in the day, I was accustomed to being the one who made the first move in situations like there. Now, it seemed, I was destined to always be the passive one. With Laura... Well, that had been a strange and not entirely satisfactory situation from the start. In this instance, I *couldn't*—if Melody was going to jeopardize her relationship, I had come past the point where I would stop her, but I wasn't going to be the one to make the first move. The little voice in my head that had been telling me up until now that this was all in my imagination had fallen silent, it seemed, at least for the moment.

There was a long pause, at least enough for a couple of very loud heartbeats to thud their way through me, before Melody closed the gap between us and touched her lips to mine. It was a hesitant kiss, but I could tell by the shuddering breath she gave and the way she clenched her fingers on my knee that it was not lacking in its own kind of passion, and I reciprocated immediately, lifting my hand to cup her jaw as I opened my mouth against hers.

She gave a slight whimper, but a second later, she pulled back, catching my hand in hers. "Nic, I need to... We should talk."

Not yet, God, not yet... My brow furrowed as I reopened eyes I didn't even know I'd closed. "All right," I managed, trying not to sound too disappointed. "Let's talk."

"I know what you probably think of me... Mostly because I've done nothing to disavow you of that fact," she murmured, squeezing my hand tightly. "But this isn't as...sordid as it seems."

I swallowed. All the things I'd managed to push out of my head—the fact she had someone, a *male* someone, the way she'd treated Isobel—came flooding back, and I pulled away further. "All right..." I said, nodding for her to go on.

"Harry and I... It's not what it seems. We're friends."

My frown deepened. It wasn't that it didn't make sense. It just...didn't track with what I knew about her and Isobel, the way things had gone. "I don't... I'm not sure that I follow."

Melody sighed, but a moment later was looking at me entreatingly again. "I mean that we're not together. We are in the public eye, but in private...we're just good friends. Do you understand what I mean?"

This was, of course, what I thought she meant, but again I kept coming back to that inconsistency, that, "But...what about Isobel? If you and Harold aren't...then why did you end things with her? That second time... She broke things off with David, but you—"

"Had already been dumped by that point," she finished for me with a sad smile.

I'm a little embarrassed to admit that my mouth fell open slightly at this as my whole image of lonely, done-wrong Isobel came crashing down around my head. She had let me think—had downright *encouraged* me to believe—that Melody had left her. She had not only subverted my perception of the part that she'd played, but that perception had meant I had spent all this time thinking twice about everything that seemed to be the case about Melody. Melody's depth of feeling, her integrity, her respect—all these things I'd called into question, all these things had made me resist what I'd felt growing between us... I dread to think what expressions passed across my face as these thoughts ran through my mind because when I finally drew my gaze back to Melody's, she looked almost scared.

"I'm...sorry." I turned my hand in Melody's grip to wrap my own fingers around hers. "I didn't know. I thought..."

"It's all right," she said, shaking her head. "I let you think it. I had thought that maybe once you started pressing her, she would tell you what really happened, but I guess there are just some things she still won't admit to anyone."

"I can't believe she..." I shook my head. It wasn't as though Isobel *knew* about Melody, that we'd been meeting. She *certainly* didn't know about this. "I'm sorry," I said again. So what now? After all, if she and Harry *weren't* an item, and if she *hadn't* betrayed Isobel and left her... Well, that meant there was nothing stopping us from...following through to some kind of logical conclusion what we had just started, was there? My pulse was still racing, my face still hot from that short kiss. There was definitely time to find our way back to where we'd been...

Except, of course, that Melody seemed to have drawn back now, turned in on herself even as she still grasped my hand. The spectre of Isobel came between us as clearly as if the woman herself had swanned into the room and plopped down on the couch. Melody's reaction to hearing Isobel's voice earlier was understandable now—it hadn't been guilt but hurt that had caused her to want to stop all talk about her, and I suddenly wished more than ever that we hadn't discussed it at all, only continued the kiss.

Then again, this was certainly more typical territory for me. Near-misses, almosts, and might-have-beens were very much my forté these days, and it was with a resigned rather than disappointed sigh that I turned to sit facing forwards on the couch, my hand shifting once again in Melody's to lace our fingers together between us.

"I really like you, Nic," she murmured. "And I think...once you finish this project, I'd like to see you again—properly, I mean. Just the two of us."

I almost laughed. I managed to keep it to a wry chuckle. "Sure," I said, nodding. I didn't shrug, although I think it must have come through in my tone, because she looked hurt as she drew her hand away and reached for her jumper. I turned, then, to look at her again, reaching to catch her arm to still it, although I stopped myself at the last moment and only laid my hand lightly on it.

"I'm sorry. I just... I can understand that the situation will have changed for me after this is done with, but I don't really see what will have changed for you. After all, it's been five years, and you're still..." I was wary of making any assumptions any more. In love with her? Hurting? Certainly, I knew that while I could face a passionate, fleeting encounter (or series thereof, as I'd dared to hope for that exhilarating few seconds) with someone who would ultimately always belong to someone else, I certainly wouldn't enter into a relationship on that basis—the modicum of self-respect that I had clawed back in the past two years just wouldn't allow it.

"Hung up on her. I know." Melody's shoulders slumped, and she rubbed her fingers idly over the knit of her jumper. "But I've never had a reason to get over her, really. Even though she made it perfectly clear there was no cause to hold out any hope. But then—and I know how clichéd this sounds—we met, and I just thought... Here was a person worth moving on for. But I know that can't really happen while you're still writing, not while you're still in her head. It would just be strange and fucked-up for everyone involved."

Now I was completely taken aback. It wasn't that I wasn't attracted to Melody—I was well down the road to crushing quite heavily on her before I'd even noticed. But the idea that *I* was "the one" who could allow her to move on from *Isobel Dewitt* was more serious and more of a bombshell than I was in a position to process right now.

"Melody, I..."

"It's okay. Please don't say anything," she told me, shaking her head. "I think we both need some time to think." This time she did pull away, gently. She tugged her jumper on and then smoothed it with nervous hands. "I'll go now."

Shit. Shit, shit, shit... I pushed to my feet as Melody did, fighting the urge to do something stupid, to grab her hand, pull her back into a kiss. Sure, it would all collapse and it would never last, but it would clear the air and maybe, just maybe, at the end of it, we'd have that growing friendship that I'd come to appreciate so much without even realizing it was there. As it was, I couldn't help but feel I was letting us consign ourselves to a sort of permanent limbo of tension and ultimately disappointment for both of us, one that might leave Melody at least disinclined to even be friends.

But I didn't do anything. I didn't even say anything, looking at her with what I'm sure was a pathetically helpless expression, one that said, "I have so many problems with the way this is going, but I don't actually care enough to change it." And I suppose that was exactly how I stood. Gutless and apathetic. Better than self-destructive and angst-ridden, right?

God, I hated myself sometimes.

She departed then, leaving behind the tea and cookies and a twisting, roiling feeling in the pit of my stomach that I knew no amount of ginger would settle.

I SPENT THE rest of my Sunday distracting myself, to varying degrees of success, with further annotation and planning. It was with a pang of both satisfaction and regret that I realized, around two in the morning as I headed to bed, that the whole book was now planned out. After tomorrow, there was no reason to meet with Isobel again.

Chapter Twenty-Eight

ISOBEL WAS EARLY again. I'd gone with the Ethiopian restaurant that Melody had suggested, and when I arrived, Isobel was already there, sitting near the back in a little booth, scanning the menu and sipping at a glass of wine. She glanced up and smiled widely when she saw me, apparently choosing to remember the friendly nature of our parting on Thursday rather than the less comfortable moments that preceded it.

"Nico—Nic," she said by way of greeting. "I hope you had a nice weekend?"

"It was...fine," I said with a tight smile, sliding into the booth across from her. "Yours?"

"Oh, you know, the usual—nothing terribly exciting. I certainly found myself looking forward to tonight for a nice change of pace," she told me.

My smile widened in spite of myself. "I'll take that as a compliment. Or did you just mean the restaurant?"

"Well, the restaurant was an excellent choice—but it wouldn't be the same without the company."

I hesitated—best to broach the status of our meetings now, or later? Surmising that there was no good reason to wait, I decided to charge ahead now. "Yeah, about that... I've been reviewing what I have, finalising my plans, and I think we're actually done."

"Done?" Isobel's eyebrow arched upwards. "I see."

"Well, that is to say, I think I have all the recorded material I need, and all the extra insight too," I explained. "Now I just need to get properly writing, mapping out the rest of the book, and so on. I may need to fill out some names and dates and so on, but ultimately, we can do that by email. It'll be a while longer before it's ready," I added quickly. "I mean, I don't want you to get the impression we're ahead of schedule—if anything I'd usually be done with client meets by now under normal circumstances. I think we'll finish about when I expected." Okay, I was babbling now, and I finally noticed and shut up.

"Well. I'm glad to hear all that," Isobel said smoothly. "Not that I was getting impatient, but it will be nice to put this project to bed, so to speak." *Okay, that was just a funny choice of words on her part...* "And it will also be nice not having to dredge up old memories as an excuse to see you."

My first reaction was to frown at this. Was she openly expressing relief that we didn't have to meet any more? That seemed a little... Something made me track back across her words—*as an excuse to see you...* She wanted an *excuse*? "Well, now you don't have to see me at all if you don't want to," I said anyway, although I accompanied it with a slightly teasing smile.

"Well, I wouldn't want to take away from your writing," she countered. "But again, I wouldn't want you to be too overworked, so I think it might be in my best interests to make sure you get regular breaks."

"I...suppose that's true..." I said hesitantly. After Melody's revelation, I felt as though I should be angry with Isobel—I certainly was yesterday. This evening, though, sitting across from her, with her smiling at me with an almost hopeful expression, I somehow couldn't find any of yesterday's anger inside me. It had all turned into some sort of soft, gooey sensation that I couldn't quite get hold of but that had me almost melting under her gaze, just like always.

"Well then. That's settled." And I had the feeling that it was, whether I was entirely on board with it or not. "Do you know what you want? It's my treat—a celebration of our successful collaboration."

I blanked for a minute—I had *no idea* what I wanted right now. Then I realized she meant food. "Oh! Yes, I think so," I said, turning to the waiter who had been waiting patiently next to us for a few moments. "I'll have the chicken and rice."

Isobel chuckled, and then proceeded to order several other dishes—far more than two people could eat alone. The waiter looked slightly surprised but scurried off, obviously betting on a large gratuity at the end of the meal.

"Are we expecting company?" I asked with a smirk.

"I think you ought to try something different tonight," she replied knowingly.

"Several things different, apparently..."

"Well, until you know what you like I thought it best to provide options."

Feeling as though, unless my imagination was running away with me again, I was shaping up to have altogether too many options, I just grinned stupidly, and nodded

PERHAPS UNSURPRISINGLY GIVEN that Melody had recommended it, Isobel seemed far savvier with Ethiopian food than I was, and had managed to choose a variety of inviting dishes for us to try. I played along willingly, sampling as instructed. Isobel kept up that same level of charming, "could be harmless" flirtation. Though when she leaned across the table, a food-topped scrap of flatbread proffered towards me, and I found myself being fed by her, her fingers brushing lightly against my lips as she did so, I was left with more than just my mouth tingling slightly from the contact.

When we had finished the main meal (with plenty leftover, despite the fact that we both tried some of everything), Isobel ordered us both a cup of strong coffee, settling back on her side of the booth with a satisfied expression on her face. She seemed to be waiting for something, though I had absolutely no idea what it might be.

Me, I was still melting—if anything more so. She'd filled the gaps between mouthfuls with her usual brand of meaty but unchallenging conversation—intelligent without being too dry or academic, like, I don't know, an *Independent* columnist or one of those "good" chick lit novels that invariably get made into films. I resented her easy likeability— particularly given that I had, the previous day, felt so betrayed by her. And yet here I was, grinning away and giving as good as I got, relaxing into my role as Judas on two counts.

Maybe she was firmly decided to control the situation after our last few encounters; maybe she truly wanted nothing more than to celebrate the end of the interviews. Whatever the case, I couldn't claim to dislike the amount of attention she was paying me, nor did I want it to stop. Which is why I almost agreed point-blank to her next suggestion without even a hesitation.

"So, you should come with me to the premiere on Wednesday. I think you'll like the film."

Chapter Twenty-Nine

AND SO HERE I was once again, on tenterhooks. I had plenty of writing to do, of course, but every time I took a break my thoughts would stray back to one or the other of the two women who right now seemed to fill every waking moment of my day, one way or another. On Tuesday, I broke concentration long enough to come to a decision, and found myself picking up the phone and dialling Melody's number.

It rang for quite a while before someone picked up—Melody, to my surprise, not one of her secretaries or assistants. "Hello?" She sounded tired.

"Hi, it's, um, Nic."

"Hello, Nic. How are you?"

"I'm... yeah, I'm all right, listen, I've been thinking, about Sunday..."

"Oh?" At this her tone brightened.

"I'm not done with the book, yet, obviously, but I've been reviewing what I have from Isobel and I realized that our interviews are, to all intents and purposes, finished."

"Well. That's very good. Congratulations."

"And, look." I took a long breath. "I know that I must've seemed a little hesitant, and I wanted to make sure you knew that it isn't... Well, that it's me stuff that made me seem that way. I mean, you probably already know I'm not the least damaged person you'll ever run into. At least, if you don't know that already, well, this is me telling you now."

"That's all right, Nic," Melody said soothingly. I could almost see the faint smile she must've been wearing. "I understand, and...it doesn't change anything that I said."

"Okay." Now I exhaled, slowly. Then, "Okay, so here's the thing. *I* understand where *you're* coming from, and I agree. But I don't think it should mean that we can't get to know each other better in the meantime anyway. If...you think you'd be okay with that." I found it hard to believe that Melody would be so overcome by lust in my presence that she couldn't just be friends. Frankly, I was still confused on the lust point at all to start with, though, so I was still uncertain as I made my proposition.

"Of course. I never meant to interrupt our friendship over...this." I could tell she had wanted to say something else, but she didn't elaborate. Whatever she'd left unspoken, however, my relief overwhelmed my curiosity—for now, at least.

"Well, in that case, there's a talk by Esme Whitethorpe at the Kingdom's End tomorrow afternoon. I don't suppose you're free?" I tried not to sound too hopeful.

"I was going to be at the library for most of the day, but I suppose I could cut my visit a bit short..."

"Oh, I mean, if that doesn't work we can always find something else..."

"No, no, it's fine. Kingdom's End you said? What time?"

"Four-thirty—it's the end of an all-day workshop but I figured we'd skip that bit."

"All right. Well, it sounds lovely—I'm looking forward to it already. Thank you for inviting me."

I grinned like an idiot down the phone in silence for slightly too long before finding my voice again. "Good. Great. I'll see you tomorrow?"

"Mm-hmm. Have a good evening, Nic."

"You too."

"SO LET'S BE clear, here. This woman, who you think is smart, sweet, and sexy—okay, pretty at least—she wants to date you once your book's done, and you tipped water over her, metaphorically speaking?"

I pursed my lips, my eyes on the film in front of us, although I don't think I'd heard a single word of dialogue the whole time. "Sounds about right."

"Right... Have you had your head examined lately? Because if they let you away without certifying you, you ought to file an incompetency suit."

"I just don't..." I sighed. "I'm not *ready* for this, Jules, I need more time. She said...she said that *I* could be the person worth getting over Isobel for. You know. That sounds huge to me. Doesn't that sound huge to you?"

"It sounds big, sure," Julie said with a shrug. "But Nic...sometimes the best things come along when you're not ready for them."

"*But I'm not ready.*"

"Hey, hey... Calm down, honey." Turning to me, Julie gave me a worried look. "So don't do anything. She's still hanging out with you, you're not actually missing out on anything, so don't freak. Okay?"

My frown stayed in place, and I still had my arms wrapped defensively around myself, but I let myself nod. "Yeah. I'm not. I'm okay."

I WAS STILL telling myself that I was okay at half-past four the next day as I waited in the foyer of the Kingdom's End—what was once a theatre, now converted into a "bar and conference centre."

Except that every *other* thought was trying to convince me that this was a mistake, or that Melody was going to stand me up, or that she would be able to read my guilt just by looking at me. Not exactly conducive mental meanderings for a "just friends" afternoon out, but somehow I managed not to completely lose it by the time she showed up, leather satchel under one arm, a little after the minute hand on the clock in the lobby ticked past the six. She was simply dressed, her hair pulled back in a stubby ponytail that made her look much younger than I knew she actually was.

"Sorry I'm late—we haven't missed anything, have we?"

My face broke into a grin far too bright for the occasion, but I reassured myself that, after all, we had every reason to be a bit nervous, and Melody seemed largely unfazed. "No, no, no, we're good. We're good—Esme's always late anyway. Shall we go in?"

"Yes, let's. I'd like a seat near the front if we can."

Of course, we could, if only because of one of us was Melody Graham, and recluse or not the literary set could recognize the genius in their midst. She nodded at a few people and accepted the proffered seat in the front row, but unlike Isobel, who would've delayed the talk a few minutes longer to schmooze and greet people, Melody settled in and turned her attention towards the podium at the front, expectantly waiting for the speaker to begin.

I guess I'd cheated, choosing the event that I had. I knew Esme Whitethorpe—I'd been tutored by her for a while in one of my Masters, and she and I had hit it off quite well, so I'd seen most of her talks several times by now. Today she was talking about characterisation, and I knew for a fact, particularly in light of the discussions we'd had a few nights previously, that Melody would enjoy it.

Despite having heard it before I enjoyed the talk; Esme was an engaging speaker and she stimulated some lively discussion in the Q&A portion at the end. Afterwards she spotted me and immediately made her way over, her many bracelets and necklaces chiming together as she moved through the crowd. "Nic! You made it! God, it's been ages, hasn't it?"

"Little while, yeah," I said with a grin, dutifully returning her effusive hug. "Esme, I'd like you to meet my friend Melody..." I began when we'd pulled apart, gesturing to my companion for the afternoon.

"Oh, no introduction needed here," Esme gushed, greeting Melody with the same huge grin she gave all friends, old and new. "Talk about moving up in the world—did you suddenly become a serious novelist when I wasn't looking, Nic? It's about damn time..."

"Not likely, I'm still hiding behind famous people," I admitted freely. "Melody's just doing some charity work."

"I'd hardly call it that," Melody said with a chuckle and a shake of her head. "I enjoyed the talk very much. I particularly enjoyed the section on motive—I thought it was very compelling."

Esme looked pleased at this, although she echoed Melody's chuckle in force. "Oh, I doubt there's much I could teach you about writing," she said, "but I'm flattered all the same."

Melody smiled, glancing at me and reaching up to rub the back of her neck bashfully. Esme beamed at us both. "Are you two running away just now, or can I drag you to the café for a cup of tea?"

"I, um...don't know," I confessed, on the one hand happy to see Esme again but on the other keen to maximize my time with Melody before I had to head home to prepare for the evening's festivities. "What do you think, Melody?"

"I don't mind—I mean, if you'd like to have some time to yourselves I can head back to the library..."

"No, no, that's not what I..." I shook my head and grinned. "Let's all just go for a cuppa, shall we?"

Chapter Thirty

Tea with Esme and Melody was an interesting affair—as I had expected, Esme dominated the conversation, though she peppered it with plenty of questions for both me and Melody. My companion seemed slightly more reserved than I had seen her, though I couldn't tell if she was overwhelmed by Esme or just quieter overall because of remaining tensions between us.

Whether by chance (she was a rather busy woman) or design, Esme wasn't able to stay long, and was soon making her good-byes, promising, as usual, to "be in touch for a proper catch-up"—something we rarely if ever actually achieved. We said (or hugged) our farewells and soon Melody and I were alone again.

"So," I said with a smile that I'm sure didn't quite cover my nerves. "What did you think?"

"She's very nice," Melody said, leaning forwards to top up her tea with what remained in the pot. "And I can see how she would be a very good tutor." She glanced up, hefting the teapot in my direction. "More?"

"Sure, thanks. Well, I meant her talk actually, but I'm glad you liked her."

"The talk was nice as well. Thank you for inviting me." Melody smiled, carefully filling my cup and setting the teapot back on the table. "I don't really go to many nowadays."

"Well, as Esme said, there isn't much anyone could teach you," I said with a slight smile.

"I hope that's not the case. If I'm not capable of improving my writing any further, then I don't know why I'd bother continuing."

"I said there wasn't much anyone could teach you, not that there was nothing left for you to learn," I corrected her, my smile warming as my nerves slowly thawed. "There comes a point where you've got all you can from books and lectures and everything else has to come from inside. Don't you think?"

Melody tipped her head to one side thoughtfully. "I suppose, to a certain extent. Though there's always a danger of being *too* introspective."

"God, if I believed one could be *too* introspective..." I mused with a smirk.

"Well, it must be different for you. Introspection is good in a biography—as long as it's not yours."

I raised my eyebrow. "Was that a subtle dig?" I asked, amused rather than annoyed.

"Not at all," Melody said, looking surprised. "Just a speculation. Maybe I'm wrong... I just assumed that the whole point of getting into someone's head was to minimise the chance of letting your own voice seep in."

"Ah. Well, I mean, yes, that's the trick. It helps not to be too judgemental. Getting to know someone really, really well without deciding you either love them or hate them is nigh-on impossible."

"I can imagine." I suddenly admired Melody's ability to keep a perfectly unreadable expression. "Still, you seem to manage better than most."

I sincerely hoped that my smile didn't betray my thoughts. "I do my best."

WE CHATTED FOR a while longer, mostly about writing, though we never strayed too far into our own works. Eventually, Melody glanced at her watch and apologetically began to gather her things, which was just as well since there wasn't too long before I had to start getting ready for the film premiere with Isobel. I had worried initially that Melody might see pictures—in the news or magazines—and realize what I was doing, but she didn't seem very inclined to seek that sort of thing out. Still, I made a resolution to hide from the cameras as much as possible that evening.

I received an irritating text from Julie en route home.

So, how was date 1 of 2?

I opted to ignore it rather than attempt to refute the suggestion that it had been a date in favour of panicking over clothing. It wasn't that I didn't have smart clothes—I actually had quite a few very nice suits that I tended to wear to events. But they all looked...let's be honest, really *gay*. For my own part, this didn't bother me in the slightest but I couldn't help dwelling on the fact that Isobel was going to be seen with me, and I knew better than most how she might feel about any questions that might arise. Not that she wasn't friends with plenty of reasonably high-profile gay actors, and she seemed to take her lesbian following in her stride, but this would be different—I wasn't a "known" face *or* name, and that made me more suspicious.

In the end, I went for one of said suits, but paired it with some subtle jewellery and makeup and left my hair to fall in its natural, rather unruly waves to my shoulders rather than scraping it back as I usually did. The effect seemed to offset something of the masculinity of my outfit, although it also left me feeling on the vulnerable side as I arrived at the hotel—where Isobel had said to meet her, presumably with her entourage. The opening would be small, but a premiere was a premiere.

AFTER PACING THE lobby for about twenty minutes, I was graced with what had, a few years ago, been deemed by *People* magazine as "One of the Seven New Wonders of the World"—Isobel Dewitt in an evening gown. It was a dark blue, nearly black sparkling affair with criss-crossed straps over her shoulders and back and a plunging neckline that seemed far too precarious to exist without double-sided tape. She paused momentarily at the foot of the stairs, obviously enjoying my gobsmacked expression, before crossing the carpet towards me.

"Nic, dear, don't you look gorgeous," she said, leaning in for a cheek kiss.

I opted to smile and say nothing until I could trust myself not to stammer, receiving her kiss without returning one of my own, my senses immediately filling with a combination of her subtle perfume and whatever else it was about her that made her smell so damn good. After what seemed like forever we pulled apart and I was able to find my voice.

"You look stunning," I said simply.

"Thank you," she said graciously, her own smile growing at the compliment. "There's still time before we go—do you want a drink? Coffee? Something to eat?"

"I'm almost positive I shouldn't have any more caffeine today," I said with a wry smile.

"All right, well, the car should be here to collect us shortly."

"Then I suppose we should find somewhere to sit, for now," I said, at least attempting to be more decisive. "Assuming you *can* sit in that," I added with a slight smirk.

"I've had years of practice," Isobel replied with a laugh, heading for one of the nearby couches. "I think I'll manage."

I echoed her laugh with what I'm sure was a hopelessly goofy grin, but I at least managed not to make a fool of myself walking in my slightly heeled shoes.

We settled down on the sofa facing the window so that Isobel could see when the car arrived, though she promptly turned away from it to look at me. "So. How was your day?" she enquired, lifting an eyebrow.

"Nice, actually," I said. "I went to a talk by an old tutor of mine, Esme Whitethorpe. Yours?"

"Business," she said with a graceful shrug.

"Sounds fascinating."

"It's certainly a bit more complicated than learning your lines and showing up on time ever was."

"Do you miss that, then? Acting?"

"Oh, always," Isobel said with a surprised look at me. "Not just because it was easier—it was challenging in its own right."

I nodded. I knew this, of course—there was a whole segment in my archives of Isobel talking about the differences between acting and directing or producing. But it was hard to make conversation with someone about whom you knew almost everything. My companion didn't seem to mind; indeed, I imagined she was probably relieved *not* to be obliged to talk about everything that ever happened to her.

"So tell me more about this film," I said eventually, breaking our companionable silence.

THIS FILLED THE time well enough until the car arrived a few minutes later, sliding up in front of the hotel inconspicuously. Luckily Isobel noticed, gathering up her small purse and wrap and beckoning for me to follow. I've been in hired cars before, obviously, but this was the nicest of the bunch—tinted windows, sleek styling and, I discovered as I slid into the backseat, heated seats. As the car pulled away from the kerb my mobile beeped annoyingly, and I pulled it out to see a text from Julie.

I'm totally going to stand outside the cinema and paparazzi you x.

Isobel glanced over, looking curious.

I shook my head and grinned ruefully. "My friend Julie making fun of me," I explained, waving the phone before turning it on silent.

Isobel chuckled. "I find it hard to believe many people manage to get under your skin."

"Oh, she's fine. Although she does know how to push my buttons. She's threatening to turn up at the carpet with a camera."

"Ah. And you're embarrassed to be seen with me. I knew it."

"Mm, yes, that's it. I don't think I could bear to be caught by some camera-wielding thug arm in arm with the most beautiful woman on the planet," I deadpanned. Not that I actually expected us to be that close, mind you...

"Don't worry, I'm sure there will be lots of stubble-sporting hunks for you to cosy up to instead," Isobel replied with a smirk.

"God, spare me... I don't even like *women* with stubble..."

"Oh, a princess, are we?" Was Isobel really teasing me in the backseat of a private hire while we were on the way to a film premiere? Life was surreal sometimes.

I managed to smirk and reply, "Definitely a prince. If we're getting all heteronormative, anyway..."

"Who said we were? I just didn't know if maybe you were an equal-opportunities amoureuse."

"Ah," I said. "Not me, I'm afraid."

"Ah, well" She looked strangely pleased. "Poor Prince Charming, then."

"Prince Charming would set his sights a little higher, I feel."

She reached over to pat my knee, her nails short and painted with a dark shade of varnish. "Not if he saw you all cleaned up like I have."

Now Old Nic (if you'll pardon the reference) would have taken this opportunity to rest a hand over hers. Would have made some suave remark—would, let's be honest, probably already have manoeuvred a hand somehow up underneath that gorgeous dress by now. Old Nic would also have been drunk but wouldn't have cared. I was always at my best when slightly pissed (except that I could never just stay *slightly* pissed). New Nic just about managed a slight smirk. I did glance up and meet her eyes, though, and was mildly shocked at quite how dark hers looked as they bored into mine in return.

"Prince Charming would, I hope, know better than to think my cleaning up had anything to do with him."

Her long, slow smile had me just about toppling over where I sat. "I would hope so too."

The screening was at a well-known film house and in honesty as we approached I did find my nerves growing a little. How big would it be? Would there actually be press there? Was I about to make a fool of myself? Isobel still hadn't indicated what I was going to *do* exactly, except, presumably, walk, which I was *fairly* sure I could still do. Although the likelihood of that was reducing with every minute that Isobel's hand remained resting lightly just above my knee.

Eventually, the car pulled up at the kerb; it was difficult to see through the dark windows but I was relieved it didn't seem *that* crowded. Isobel turned, flashed a smile at me, and, moments before the door was opened (presumably by the driver, although what did I know about such things?) gave my knee a quick squeeze before removing her hand altogether. She then slid out the open door to a dazzling array of camera flashes, leaving me in the suddenly cavernous car interior alone.

Guess that answers that question, then. I waited a suitable amount of time for Isobel to get further along the carpet—short enough that all the cameras were still on her, but long enough that they wouldn't catch me as well—before getting out of the car. My usual good coordination had returned in her absence, so I made a controlled, unostentatious exit.

Nobody even bothered to look my way, and it suddenly dawned on me why Isobel had worn quite so ostentatious a gown for such a small premiere—it kept the attention firmly on her. I wandered up the short length of red carpet, avoiding getting caught in the crossfire of the journalists, and made my way towards the lobby inside. Presumably, Isobel would detach herself soon enough and join me.

Other arrivals were milling around the foyer as I entered, the only person paying any attention to me being the doorman who checked my name off the guest list.

Now, I don't read the tabloids and I hardly ever watch any gossipy news, but even still as I looked around I was struck by how many people I recognized, at least by sight if not name. Producers, actors, directors... If I had been somebody who was impressed by fame and money I would've been bowled over right about then. As it was, I was mainly struck by how much I *didn't* have in common with any of these people, a fact which I found more reassuring than upsetting.

Eventually, I heard shouts of "Isobel! Isobel! Just one more!" from outside. A moment later, she swept inside, causing a ripple of commotion through the other guests. She smiled and greeted a few of them, but didn't seem too invested, glancing around until she spotted me and giving me another of those dazzling smiles.

Okay, *now* I was star-struck. By some miracle, I wasn't a puddle on the floor by the time she reached my side. "You know, when I go to the cinema I have trouble just getting attention from the popcorn vendor," I jested quietly.

"I'm sure if you were wearing a dress like this you'd have no trouble getting any attention," she told me, her hand coming to rest briefly on my elbow.

"No, I suspect not," I said with a chuckle, "given that on me I doubt that dress would actually stay up—and that's assuming I could even fit it over my hips."

As I said the word, I felt Isobel's gaze slide down to them, sending a shiver running through me that I was sure everyone in the lobby must've been able to see. How did she get away with doing this in a public place and not get caught? Regularly turning women to jelly surely must attract *some* attention.

"Mm. Sadly, there will be no popcorn here tonight."

"Wasabi peas then?"

"If you like."

"Not really," I confessed. "That was me trying to be witty."

She smiled fondly down at me. "Of course. How could I miss it?"

I wasn't even sure *what* to say now. I had a vague idea that our accompanying one another this evening was probably something of a quasi-date, but she was behaving for all the world as though we were already secret lovers—those intimate, private looks, the lowered voice, the light touches. I lost count of how long we stood there, gazes locked, me rendered dumb by what seemed for all the world like the unstoppable steamroller of Isobel Dewitt...seducing *me*.

Luckily, I was saved from having to come up with anything else to fill the space between us when the doors to the cinema opened and people began to filter through. I'm sure there was still plenty of time before the film actually began, but Isobel murmured something about wanting to get good seats and guided me towards the door with another subtle touch of my arm. It was all I could do to follow without tripping over my own feet.

The theatre was quite small and steeply staged, so in this instance it seemed "good seats" meant right at the back—or that was apparently Isobel's opinion, since it was the centre of the back row where we found ourselves sitting. The rest of the theatre filled slowly, though of course the seats next to Isobel were among the first to go, and we found ourselves surrounded by eager chatter from well-meaning well-wishers. Isobel was all smiles with them, of course, making cheerful conversation, although I noted that the hand that rested on the armrest between us was gripping it tightly enough to make her knuckles white.

I felt a twinge of sadness for her, and annoyance that I couldn't do anything to relieve her obvious discomfort. What was I going to do, distract them all with my witty and urbane conversation skills? No, I mainly sat there smiling at people who were already ignoring me and wished the film would start.

When it finally did, the hangers-on quieted down; by the time the lights were fully dimmed it was just like any other theatre, albeit without the pervasive smell of stale popcorn clouding the air.

Chapter Thirty-One

THE FILM—A tense, claustrophobic thriller that reminded me of nothing so much as Hitchcock's more low-key efforts like *Rope* and *Marnie*—was actually much more my cup of tea than the Laura Maguire film we'd seen a few weeks ago. This time Isobel had only had an Executive Producer role, but once again she'd clearly recognized an up-and-coming young talent and given him a helping hand. It was clear that he had chops, and that this film was sure to be the beginning of his ascent to success.

I'm sure the ending was a fitting conclusion to the deftly woven story, but I really couldn't tell you. See, about three-quarters of the way through, I was nearly shocked out of my seat by the soft, slim hand that slid over the armrest and over my own hand, and the strong fingers that wove their way through mine. At the time, I fought the urge to glance wildly around, but told myself that Isobel clearly wasn't concerned that anyone would see us, otherwise she wouldn't have done what she had, and certainly wouldn't now be stroking her thumb lightly across the suddenly super-sensitive skin of the back of my hand.

The lights flickered on the screen ahead of us, and the actors spoke, and yet none of it seemed to make any impression on me whatsoever. My full attention was focused on those few square inches just above my wrist—well, that, and wondering what might happen when we got back into that private car after the screening.

I was in such a daze as Isobel left the cinema in front of me, making polite conversation with her hangers-on but miraculously not allowing herself to be drawn in, that I didn't even notice us exiting by the back of the building, her car already waiting, until she made reference to it herself.

"I always leave premieres this way—the press always know and wait at the road end anyway, but it does make for a marginally faster exit." She was holding the door open—for me, I realized a moment later, and

I practically tripped over in my attempt to move quickly to cover up my brief bemusement.

"So, what did you think?" she queried once she had gotten inside and shut the door firmly behind her. "Any good?"

"Very," I said with an emphatic nod. "I..." Jesus, what was it even about again? "I liked the way he built the tension—very classic thriller, but with the edgy cinematography it became something new."

"Mm, yes. I was quite pleased with how it turned out." Slowly, Isobel leaned back against the leather seats, managing to avoid the embarrassing squeaking that seemed to happen every time I moved. She tipped her head to look over at me, a lazy smile playing on her lips. "And I'm glad you enjoyed it as well."

"I did." I swallowed—I don't *think* it was audible. "Very much."

"Good. Then we'll have to do this again sometime, hm?"

Yes, because I haven't nearly had a heart attack five times this evening already. "Absolutely."

The car drove on in silence; Isobel continued to hold me with her gaze, and I could only hope that whatever was going on behind her eyes wasn't some silent mockery of my pathetic inability to look away or indeed come up with *anything* to say.

The thing is, right about now I was thinking that there was a strong possibility that she was trying to entice—nay, practically *intimidate*—me into making a move on her. And frankly, coward though I've become in my perpetual sobriety, by this point I was pretty much convinced enough of her intentions that, had we been alone, I would have. Unfortunately, the tiniest possibility that this was not the place, that her driver, while clearly discreet, wasn't *that* discreet, hovered at the back of my mind, rendering me completely impotent. I was only able to raise my eyebrows expectantly, hanging onto the small mercy that I, at least, had been the last one to speak.

Eventually Isobel stirred, smiling to herself as she turned to look out the window. "There's a fundraising dinner next week. Would you be my guest?"

I cleared my throat. It was now or never. Vocalize that I felt there was something going on, level with her about Melody, apologise, clear the air... Get kicked out of her car and have her never speak to me again. Oh well...

"I'm...not sure that I can," I said. Why did I sound so damn hoarse all of a sudden? "If I'm honest, and this is probably my imagination so I'm sorry about that, but it seems as though there's a...something...going on here, and I'm not sure I can handle much more of this tension."

"Tension?" She didn't turn around for a moment, though I could see her reflection in the window. She looked amused, though there was that slight quirk to her eyebrow that I knew meant she was intrigued. Then she turned to look at me, and her expression was all innocence. "Have I made you feel uncomfortable, Nicola?"

"Nic," I corrected her levelly. Whatever was going to happen here I was sure as hell going to at least take back a modicum of control over it. "You make me feel a lot of things. Uncomfortable is certainly one of them."

"Well, I'm sorry for that. I had hoped that after the interviews were over our relationship might become a bit more pleasant."

But no more transparent, apparently. I began to seethe internally and I could tell that she knew it. What the hell was she playing at? Was this just her idea of *fun*? I lapsed back into a now somewhat less friendly silence, unwilling to give her the satisfaction of me joining in with whatever little game she was playing. This wasn't the Isobel I'd first met *or* the one I'd recorded the life of. Subtly, this was someone new.

Eventually, she sighed, looking a bit deflated as she leaned in again to put a hand on my knee. "Nic, I'm sorry. Will you forgive me?" The look she gave me was pure heart-wrenching enticement.

I felt my lip curl in the distaste that I hadn't even realized I felt until now. In an interesting juxtaposition, I also felt that slight hot stinging sensation behind my eyes that one gets right before tears form. I had so wanted to give in, earlier tonight. I wanted nothing more than to play along, to let her reel me in, bemused as to why she'd want to but a perfectly willing victim all the same. Let's be frank: if she wanted it, I was going to be an easy lay.

Now I felt...disappointment. I felt as though I was being held at arm's length and given how close I'd been it felt like a betrayal. I felt as though I'd left myself completely open to attack and she'd chosen to sneak up behind me anyway. I felt as though she was trying to take something that had seemed like it might be comparatively straightforward and twist it, make it feel complicated and perverse for...what? Her own amusement?

"I don't know," I said. Then, "I don't like mind games."

Her expression flickered for a moment; I could tell she wanted to protest but bit it back, dropping her gaze to the seat between us for a long moment before she looked up again at me.

"I'm sorry." This time it was genuine. "This isn't... I don't know how to do this. Normally. It's been a long time since I've had any opportunity."

"Normally you don't intentionally try to drive the other person insane to the point where they either explode or fuck off never to be seen again," I said dryly. I did manage a somewhat sympathetic smile, although my sympathy was limited. "I shouldn't have to tell you that I would be the latter. I'm prepared to play these stupid games to get my job done, but this is my *life*."

"I know, I know," she sighed, and she looked so downtrodden that if I hadn't been annoyed at her I probably would've been melting all over again. "I'm just used to flings—mind-fucks, you know? That's all I'm good at, really. And I shouldn't have tried that on you."

"You can't do one without the other?" I tried to keep the disappointment out of my voice as the last hopes I had that anything would happen with this woman began to fade. It felt very much as though the longer we talked about it the less likely the whole thing became.

This seemed to incense her slightly, and she leaned closer, frowning at me. "I never said I couldn't—just that I haven't had the chance to in a long time. Do you know how difficult it is to get a fuck in this town without *some* sort of drama?" Her breath was hot on my skin.

"Apparently not," I said, hardly moving my mouth, my composure thinner than ever, but holding for now.

It was threatened again a moment later as I felt her hand on my knee again, though this time she wasn't content to just leave it there but instead began dragging it slowly up my thigh, her eyes locked on mine all the while.

"Well then," she said in a low voice, "aren't you lucky? Some of us just *dream* of that."

Even as my heart leaped into my throat I remembered the other thing I was meant to say. "Listen," I murmured, unable to tear my gaze away from hers. "There's something you sh—"

All my good intentions were swept away then by the irresistible force of Isobel's lips against mine, her spicy perfume filling my nostrils as she pressed me back against the car seat. Her hand reached the top of my thigh and then slid between my legs, pressing against me with a sudden urgency that shocked me, but nonetheless seemed to trigger some instinctive response because I felt my hips shift slightly, my thighs parting. Suddenly my dress trousers, thin though they were, were not thin enough, my mouth was open against hers, tongue flickering out to taste her, and I was sliding my hand up her arm and across her shoulders and up her neck to cradle her face, the other hand flat against the seat of the car and, I'm quite sure, the only thing keeping me upright.

When she pulled back a minute later, it was as if the world had stopped spinning suddenly—but then I realized it was just that the car had stopped moving. "Come to my room," Isobel said hoarsely, taking my hand in hers and holding it so tightly it almost hurt. "Come upstairs with me—no drama, no mind games, I swear. I need you right now."

Thinking that she could've saved us both a lot of discomfort by saying this a lot earlier, I hesitated, but really, there was only ever one choice, and after a curt nod I followed her through the hotel foyer towards the lift to her suite, looking as nonchalant as I could with a flushed face and tousled hair. Isobel, on this occasion, didn't seem to care.

We had barely made it back into the room before she was on me again, her hands sliding over my sides and hips and pulling me flush against her as we stumbled past the creamy-white divans and armchairs in the direction of the bedroom. Insistently her lips sought mine, parting as she let out a low moan and touched her tongue to mine.

Suddenly, finally, everything was very, very simple—there was me, and her, and there was this crazy but unbelievable thing that was happening between us and she felt, tasted, smelled amazing, and this, this I could work with. As she pulled me down onto the bed on top of her I searched her back and sides for the elusive zipper that I finally found neatly hidden down one discreet seam. I eased it down, helping her remove carefully the dress that I got the distinct impression she would just as happily have torn off. And my own clothes were shed just as easily, her slim fingers finding each button and pulling it apart. She pressed her lips to each inch of exposed skin until I was tingling all over with anticipation. As I sank down against her, we both shuddered, our legs weaving together until there was nothing between us but need.

Although the room was warm, I could feel goose bumps rising on the skin of my back as she slid her hands down it, finding my hips, pulling me closer. I rocked into a gentle, and then less gentle rhythm against her, the perfectly firm yet soft mattress beneath us giving just a little beneath us with every thrust, the sensation delicious and yet only really an anticipation of what was to come.

Now that Isobel had me right where she wanted me, however, it didn't look like she was going to let me go anytime soon. With amazing self-control, she steadied my hips, slowing their movements, then smoothing one hand up my front until she reached my breast. Teasingly she began to trace her fingers around it, brushing the underside, coming ever closer to the small pink bud of my nipple without ever touching it.

"I thought you said no more games," I murmured, but it was with a slight smirk now.

"Oh, I'm sorry... Do you want me to stop?" Isobel said, arching an eyebrow as she stilled her hand.

I could only shake my head, the one arm supporting me above her beginning to ache, my free hand sliding slowly up the perfect curve of her side. Isobel had been no stranger to nudity as an actress and her figure had barely aged in the years since she'd stopped taking her clothes off for the camera, but for all I'd seen of her in high definition on the screen it just didn't remotely compare with being this close. At my touch, she smiled slowly, and then, before I knew it, she had pushed herself away from the bed, turning and flipping me onto my back and pinning me beneath her. Dipping her head, she began to lay kisses across my body, starting at the sensitive skin of my neck and drifting downwards, across my collarbone and chest.

Although not a strong believer in stereotypes about tops or bottoms, butches or femmes, it did take me by surprise that it seemed, on this occasion at least, I was to be passive. Nonetheless, I submitted happily to her ministrations, my back arching of its own accord, my hands now both seeking her skin again, coming to rest briefly on her hips before beginning a fresh ascent across those soft, supple curves.

With a drawn-out moan, Isobel's crested my breast with her lips, her tongue flicking out to tease my nipple as her other hand slid up my side. I bit back a gasp of my own, my hands stilling, and I squirmed beneath her, trying to insinuate a thigh back between hers.

"Mm-mm," she purred, her tongue tracing a circle around my nipple. "Not yet..."

I shut my eyes tightly for a few seconds, steeling myself against the sensations that were running through my body, and I settled for running my own hands up and across Isobel's unfeasibly perfect breasts, quickly establishing that no, any rumours of "work" were entirely false and, furthermore, her nipples were every bit as sensitive as mine.

Isobel raised her head, her dark eyes heavily lidded, her lips moist and slightly parted. "God, Nic... I've wanted to do this for so long..."

Rather than answer—what could I say to that?—I lifted my head to kiss her again, hard, catching one of those nipples between my thumb and forefinger, and rolling it gently between them. This time it was Isobel who arched against me, her breath catching in her throat. Try though she might, she couldn't quite seem to keep her cool and it was me—*me*—that was driving her mad.

My free hand found its way to the small of her back and I pressed her closer, shifting against her, my tongue touching to hers. Isobel shuddered and sighed, closing her eyes as she melted against me, and this time when I shifted my leg hers parted willingly, and I lifted my knee to increase our contact, my teeth catching her lower lip lightly. It seemed that some things I could remember drunk or sober.

From there things get hazy—I mean, I was a full and (very) willing participant in all of it, but I don't really think it bears getting into. We had sex, very *good* sex, and in the morning, I had a cup of coffee with her before heading back to my flat, grinning, I'm sure, like an oversexed loon.

Chapter Thirty-Two

WHEN I ANSWERED Julie's phone call later that morning, all it took was my, "I'm fine," response for her to know that something had happened.

"You did it, didn't you? You shagged the author."

I rolled my eyes. "No. No I didn't."

"Like hell you didn't. I texted last night—you didn't answer. Because you were busy. Getting frisky."

"No, Julie. I really didn't." I said levelly, frowning down the phone. Why did it annoy me so much that she thought I'd slept with Melody?

She seemed to take the hint, at least for now. "Okay, fine, whatever. Where were you? The film couldn't have been *that* long."

"I was...with Isobel."

"Oo-er, were you? Doing what? Schmoozing at some boring afterparty?"

"Something like that."

"Lucky you. So, how was it? Have you become a starfucker yet?"

I laughed at this, couldn't help myself. "Sure, maybe a little," I murmured. *Maybe a lot, depending on the famous person.*

"Well, just don't forget about me when you've become some big movie executive, okay? I expect a cut of all that."

"Yeah, I can't see that happening but I promise that if I ever do you will get free popcorn forever."

"That's what I'm talking about. Speaking of which, you got any more Dewitt films that need watching? I could help you with your important research..."

"I'm actually done with research," I said, and now I didn't have to fake anything—I really was glad that was all over with. "Just writing now."

"Ah, well. I guess I should let you get on with that..."

"Hey, I'm not saying we shouldn't hang out."

"Well, you know how to reach me. When you're not busy partying with the hoi polloi."

"Oh, I don't think that's going to be a regular thing."

"OH, MY *GOD* you're amazing." I rolled over, burying my head in the cool pillow beside me for a moment before lifting it away to catch Isobel's damp lips in a long kiss. "Thank you."

Her answer was a quiet chuckle and a long kiss back, after which she slung an arm over my waist. "You don't need to thank me, you know."

"After *that* I think I need to do more than just thank you," I said with a grin, moving my mouth to Isobel's collarbone.

"Mm, well, *that* you can do as much as you like..."

"SO TONIGHT, I'M going to show you the best film last year that got no attention at all from anyone," I said as I sat down beside Melody and passed her a mug of tea.

She smiled at me, settling back in *her* spot on the sofa. "I can't wait to extend my education further. Thank you for inviting me, Nic."

I smiled but shook my head. "You don't need to thank me, you know. I like spending time with you."

"So do I. I'm glad we're not... Well. I'm glad we're doing this."

"Me too." I hesitated, then reached to rest my hand lightly on Melody's knee for a moment. She hesitated, obviously unsure about my motives or how exactly to respond, but in the end settled for a shy smile and a friendly shoulder bump.

"So, shall we?"

Removing my hand, somewhat reluctantly, I settled back on the couch and pressed play. The movie rolled on, and we spent a companionable hour and a half, mostly in silence. After it finished, we discussed it at length; Melody had enjoyed it but found it flawed from a writer's perspective, which led into an interesting discussion about intention versus perception that, as a writer restricted to writing only what my subjects wanted me to, I found very interesting indeed.

"I guess the idea of exercising any actual *control* over what my characters do is sort of alien to me now," I confessed with a grin, leaning to top up Melody's tea.

"Well, in some ways, the best fictional characters are the same way—they spring, fully formed, from one's head and it is all you can do to chronicle their exploits on paper. I know I've certainly had times where my characters simply wouldn't do what it was they *had* to do to progress a story."

"So what did you do?"

She shrugged, looking adorably bemused. "What can you do? Change the story, see where it takes you."

At this, I could only really manage a wry smile.

Chapter Thirty-Three

THIS WENT ON for a while. My work on the first draft of the whole Isobel Dewitt story moved apace, and a few evenings a week were spent in turn either watching films, attending lectures and plays with Melody, or at dinner and then usually to bed with Isobel—strangely always at her hotel even though her home would almost certainly have been safer.

Despite how strange and potentially explosive the situation was, I can't say I wasn't enjoying myself immensely. My friendship with Melody grew stronger every time we met—our discussions were lively and heartfelt, and our mutual interests meant that there was always some new thing to do, some new event to seek out. And as for Isobel...well, the sex was great. There was no denying that she was hands down the most gorgeous woman I had ever slept with, and even as the weeks went on, there seemed to be no dimming of passion for one another when we were between the sheets.

Mary, of course, was less gung-ho about the whole affair.

"So you're telling me that you go to dinner—at which you appear nothing more than colleagues, *maybe* friends—she drinks whatever she pleases, then you go back to her hotel and..." My sponsor coloured before clearing her throat and moving on. "She's using you, Nic. Can't you see that?"

I made a face. "Using me for what, exactly? Congenial company and sex? Does it count as using if that's all you want? I don't want to *date* Isobel Dewitt, Mary—you know perfectly well that I would never get into a relationship with someone in the closet,—even *before*..."

"Yes, but...are you really telling me you feel good about the whole thing? Especially when you're still seeing Melody?"

"I'm not *seeing* Melody. We're spending time together. And we don't talk about Isobel any more."

"And if you told her what you were doing with Isobel?" Mary asked, giving me a stern look.

I frowned at this. Here, she had a point. Neither woman would be pleased to know about my relationship to the other, even though I was no longer betraying either one of them, technically.

"I should probably tell her," I murmured.

"You should probably *stop*, and then tell her."

I made a face. "I never took you for such a puritan."

"You know that's not why I'm saying that, Nic," Mary said, shaking her head. "I don't have any strong feelings about...free love one way or the other. I just think that in *your* case, forming a superficial relationship based solely on physical interaction might provide a temptation to relapse into other old habits. And I'm concerned."

"I'm not going to drink again." I injected the assertion with as much certainty as I could. In truth, it was starting to wear on me. Not so much so that I felt I was going to crack, not by a long way. But spending those nights with Isobel, who drank freely although not generally to excess, tasting wine or gin or whisky on her lips when we kissed...it was wearing.

"I know, and I believe you," Mary told me sincerely. "Right now. But who knows what might happen in the future? Why put yourself through that?"

"This isn't an arrangement for the future," I reasoned. "It's an arrangement for now. Look, I'm not expecting that this...thing...is going to last with Isobel. The friendship with Melody... Well, hopefully that will. I really like her. But Melody doesn't drink—at all."

Mary's eyebrows went up, and I could tell she had just placed another tick in the "Melody" column. "Is that why you're holding back from her? Because there's nothing to excuse away any emotional intimacy you might share?"

"What? No! I just... I told you about that, what she said."

"Yes—that she could foresee a lasting relationship with you. At which point you turned and fled. Straight into Isobel's bed."

"We'd met about four times, I think. You don't think that seemed a bit...serious?"

"Of course it's serious. But you yourself told me you felt a connection with her. And you're thick as thieves now. So, was she wrong?"

"I..." Why was there a sinking feeling in my stomach? "I can't, Mary. You know what I'm like—what I'm *really* like, not when I'm on my best behaviour. This is too much. Besides, she has her sham relationship to maintain and I already said—I won't do that."

"Have you spoken to her about that? If all you're doing is making assumptions, then you have no right to pick or choose *anything*." Frail and unassuming though she may look, Mary can be a real hard-ass sometimes. "I'm not saying you have to talk to her about any of that, not if you don't want to. But it seems just a little unfair, don't you think, making someone else's decisions for them."

But I shook my head. "I can't do that. What if she did? What if she ended her, what, twenty-*year* 'friendship' for me? I'm not exactly a good bet."

"Again, there you go, deciding what would be best for her without actually giving her a choice. You're only responsible for yourself, Nic—not Melody, not Isobel, not anybody else."

MARY'S WORDS WERE still echoing in my mind when Melody arrived that evening to pick me up. We were heading outside the city to an evening performance of a play by a one-time protégé of hers in a little up-and-coming suburban theatre. She pulled up in her little racing-green Aston Martin—the first time I saw it I had assumed it was one of Harold's until she had surprised me by revealing that it was in fact all her own, really the only luxury she had ever bought herself. She gave the horn a small toot and looked suitably shocked as it sounded far louder than she had expected. I was already waiting outside—it was one of those crisp, clear winter nights that I love, and so I was there to witness her mild embarrassment with a chuckle as I trotted over to the roadside and got in.

"Good evening," she greeted me with a smile, leaning in to give me a peck on the cheek as (I was learning) was her habit with her friends. "How was your day?"

"Oh, you know," I said with a long sigh, slumping back in my seat. "Slow day for writing, and then a lecture from my sponsor on personal responsibility. She doesn't much like some of my current recreational activities."

"Oh?" she asked, sounding mildly concerned as she pulled the car smoothly away from the building. "I'm not taking up too much of your time, am I? Is that what she's worried about?"

"Oh, no, she *likes* you. Listen..." I turned my eyes briefly onto her before training them back on the road in front of us. "It's actually something you probably deserve to know. Could we maybe...grab a coffee somewhere after the play?"

Melody frowned, her fingers tightening on the steering wheel briefly, but she nodded. "Of course."

I QUICKLY REALIZED that I should have just lied and left it until after the play to talk to her. Not that she wasn't just as lovely as ever—and the play itself was engaging and well-staged. But she was just a little... Well, I don't want to say 'distant'—I don't know how she ever came across as reclusive and withdrawn, with her warm smile and obliging manner. But she did seem a bit withdrawn, not really watching the play but instead focused internally, no doubt worrying over whatever bombshell I might be preparing to drop on her later than evening. I only hoped that it wasn't as bad as she feared, although I had a feeling it might be worse.

After we had chatted for a few minutes with the playwright and paid our compliments we extricated ourselves from the post-theatre crowd and headed back to the. Melody seemed reasonably familiar with the area and told me of a café not too far away that still ought to be open at this time of night. We exchanged a few opinions about the play but then lapsed into stilted silence, the low purr of the car motor our only accompaniment.

I could have begun to talk, of course, but I found myself using anything as an excuse not to start—the fact we were still driving, parking, taking the short walk from the parking space to the café.

Eventually, we were sitting opposite one another in a small, rather intimate booth, mugs of hot chocolate between us, and there was nothing left in my way.

I cleared my throat. Even in the half-full café, muted music playing in the background, it felt loud.

"I've been...seeing someone. Very, very casually," I said hastily before Melody had even had a chance to react. "And I haven't told you and I know that I should have."

"What? Oh, there's no reason you should have," she replied, looking flustered and surprised. "We're friends, you don't have to tell me everything. I mean, now that I know, I'm happy for you, but I don't...need to know," she finished lamely.

"No, you do," I said, feeling worse now for how nice she was being. "The someone is Isobel. We're not in a...well, in an *anything*," I added quickly. "But—"

This time she had nothing nice to say—nothing at all, in fact. Her eyes widening, her face paling, she opened her mouth several times before shutting it abruptly and biting down on her lower lip until I thought she might draw blood. I felt my stomach twist into a Gordian knot.

"You...and Isobel?" she managed weakly at last, the imprint of her teeth still visible as she spoke.

"Yes." I wasn't sure what I'd expected—I'd known it was going to be an unpleasant shock. I'd known she wasn't the type to get angry or shout. I suppose that watching this quiet implosion was harder even than I'd thought it would be. "I mean, no, not 'me and Isobel', not...like you two were. Just..." *Just sex? Sure, that would be comforting.*

"Oh." I knew, with that one syllable, that even if she didn't know all the details she knew enough. She had known Isobel far, far longer than I had and could tell, either from my expression or just past knowledge, exactly what was going on between us. It didn't seem to lessen the blow. "For how long?"

"After we stopped the interviews," I said cautiously.

"I see."

"It's not..." I frowned, unsure how to say what I felt—that this wasn't going to last, that I just wanted to enjoy it while it did, that Isobel made me feel wanted without feeling needed and that, for me, was a very heady cocktail. And I don't use the term "cocktail" lightly. "Our friendship is more important to me," I said decisively. "Please believe that. If you want me to, I'll—"

"Don't," she said with a sudden shake of her head. "There's no point. I can't do this, Nic. I'm sorry."

The inevitable was coming crashing down on me and at that point I realized what I'd known all along—that something was going to give and it was too late for it to be anyone but Melody.

My face felt hotter by the moment with my shame. "Melody, please..."

"No," came the surprisingly firm response. Her face was a mask now, pale and set. "There's nothing to say about this, Nic. You've made your choice and I understand it, but I spent the last five years extricating myself from Isobel and her grip on me. I'm not going to jeopardize that, not even for someone I care for as much as you."

"But I care about you as well," I contested, trying to keep my voice steady even as I felt my eyes filling up. "I don't have to... I'll break it off—I told you, this is more important." But Melody was already shaking her head, gathering up her things.

"If it was, we wouldn't be having this conversation." Her tone was reasoned, almost calm, as if she hadn't just been betrayed in the worst way I knew.

"Christ, Melody, it's *why* we're having this conversation!" I implored. "Isobel doesn't know that we've *met,* for God's sake."

This stopped her for a moment, though her expression wasn't what I would have expected from that revelation. "Just because you haven't told her doesn't mean she doesn't know," she said, shifting to pull her jacket on. "And if she *doesn't*—then you should tell her, Nic. It's unfair not to."

"I planned to." *But if I'm never going to see you again there doesn't seem to be much point.*

She met my eyes levelly for a long moment in which it seemed all other sounds and motions in the café had stopped, then swallowed and slid out of the booth. "Goodbye, Nic. I'm glad you told me before I made any more of a fool out of myself."

It was only a supreme amount of self-control that stopped me from breaking down in tears as I watched Melody's exit. The knotted feeling in my stomach was turning into a dull, constant pain. Eventually I felt able to speak, and called a taxi. It was time to go home.

Chapter Thirty-Four

IT WAS DONE. The one good thing to come out of my imploded friendship with Melody was that I didn't want to leave the house, talk to anybody, eat or sleep much, so I spent every waking hour I could finishing the first draft of the autobiography. Julie and Mary had both seen me in the final push to completion before, so my sudden hermitage didn't raise any warning bells, and though Isobel continued to call and invite me to dinner she didn't seem too upset by my repeated excuses and refusals.

The book itself was going very well. I finished the first draft ahead of schedule, my editor for once delighted with me as he was usually biting his fingernails at the last minute, waiting for the email that sometimes came telling him I'd be late. This, of course, meant that there wasn't much for me to do before he got back to me with his revisions, but I started on the second draft anyway, detaching myself from everything and plunging myself into rereading the book so that I could figure out what, if anything, needed to be changed.

I'd done well. I could for whole chapters at times hear Isobel's voice in my head as I read. It didn't help my mood at all, especially since it was easier for me than ever to see the spectre of Melody and her relationship with Isobel behind every story, every big event. On more than one occasion I welled up as I read it, though luckily with my over-obsessive precautions in place I never did anything so maudlin as leaving teardrops on my manuscript.

In a strange way, I'd managed to outwit even myself. Reading over it now, it was clear that the relationship behind the scenes with Melody, on again, off again—more often, I was beginning to think, than either of them had admitted—had been one where Isobel was constantly, fearfully pushing the other woman away, even though when I'd *written* it my impression had been of the opposite. How was it that my writing held truths that I hadn't known myself?

Either way, it certainly wasn't helping me not to dwell on things. I had tried calling Melody a few days after we had spoken in the café, but each call went straight to voice mail, and I never heard anything back from her. I thought darkly that one call from Melody would be preferable to a dozen from Isobel right now.

Eventually I realized I *did* have to stop moping, and though I knew it was a bad idea I also knew that Isobel was the only person who *wouldn't* ask me about Melody right now.

Seeing her number on my mobile screen one afternoon, I sighed and picked up. "Hello?"

"Nic, hello. It's been over a week since I saw you and I'm starting to worry. Please say that you'll come out with me tonight..."

I stared at the marked and highlighted manuscript in front of me for a long moment. "I'll come out with you tonight. Where?"

She named a trendy restaurant I knew it would take any normal person (including me) weeks on the waiting list to get a table. "Let's say seven? And then we'll be able to catch up and you can tell me what you've been up to all week, hiding from me." Was it my imagination, or did she sound just a little bit annoyed?

I thought about telling her about my progress on the book. Then I realized that would leave me nothing to say to her this evening. So I just exchanged another pleasantry or two, and we rang off.

Normally before my evenings with Isobel, I spent a decent amount of time getting ready, trying to make myself look if not sexy at least presentable. Tonight, I found it hard to work up much worry—Isobel seemed to want to sleep with me despite the fact that I was nowhere in her league, so what did it matter if I wore earrings or not?

ISOBEL, OF COURSE, was characteristically gorgeous, even in the reasonably modest outfit she had chosen to wear tonight. I couldn't help but notice that she already had a full glass of wine in front of her although she couldn't have arrived more than moments before I did, the bustle of the restaurant making it clear that her appearance was recent. I silently cursed Mary for bringing to my attention what I'd tried so hard for so long to ignore.

"Nic," she greeted me with a genuine enough smile. "It's nice to see you."

"You too," I said, attempting a returning smile, though I think I fell short of beaming.

Almost immediately a waiter appeared to take my drink order, looking slightly annoyed when I just asked for sparkling water and then hurrying off to fetch it. Isobel sipped her wine. "So. Where have you been keeping yourself all week?"

"I've finished the first draft. My editor is going to do a first pass and then we'll have a copy for you."

"How exciting."

I raised my eyebrows. "You remember the part where I'm your ghostwriter?" I said dryly.

"Yes, of course," she replied in an infuriatingly calm tone. "I'm sure the book will be very good."

"But you really don't care anymore?"

"It's not that I don't care, Nicola, but it's out of my hands now. This is why I only choose to work with the best—so that I don't have to spend all my time worrying about everything."

Nicola... Okay, so she was actually *trying* to piss me off? Why? "Did I do something to annoy you somehow, Isobel?"

"No, not at all," she said, shaking her head. "And besides, I could ask you the same thing."

I scowled. This was not going at all well. "Then why are you trying to annoy me? Have things become too boring for you?"

"I have no idea what you're talking about," she said, and if I hadn't been itching to accuse her the innocent expression *might* have assuaged me. "I was hoping for a pleasant evening with you, just like the ones we used to have before you disappeared for a week and avoided all my calls. Now, I'm assuming there's a reason for this, but if you don't want to tell me it's your own prerogative. Just don't accuse me of starting trouble when it's you who is stirring things up."

My hand found my napkin and began balling it slowly into my fist. When I spoke, my voice was artificially quiet. I was not about to make a scene—I wouldn't give her the satisfaction.

"I can't do this anymore," I said.

Her eyebrow winged up; she obviously hadn't been expecting this. "Why not?"

"Because I'm in love with someone. Else." I almost had a start of shock myself as I spoke. See, I'd figured this out already, but *saying* it, out loud... I actually felt slightly better. And then, seeing Isobel's expression, a little worse again.

"You can't do this because you're in love with someone else." She gave a short, sharp laugh, though I could hear the hurt ringing in it. "Is that what you were doing all week? Falling in love?"

"I told you that I was working. Please, Isobel, this..." I sighed, guilt mixing with irritation. She had no good reason to make this hard. "Don't pretend this means more to you than to me. I'm sorry about the past week, and I'm sorry that I let this go on so long in the first place. You know that I do care about you, but..."

"Not as much as you care about Melody."

Her name hit me like a bullet—or maybe a cricket bat—on its own merit, before I'd even processed what Isobel saying it meant. I sighed again, sitting back in my chair.

"I didn't plan any of this," was the only response I could manage.

"I'm not surprised—I don't think you're capable of fucking up this badly on purpose," Isobel replied, her perfect lips set in a thin line. This was an Isobel I hadn't seen before: grim, almost angry, uncaring what the public sitting around us might think.

"Listen, Isobel, I don't know how you know, but you must have realized that I wasn't trying to do you any harm—I was trying to...find you."

"So you fell in love with Melody. Did it help?" she asked mockingly.

"That's not what I...yes," I said eventually. "Yes, it helped. But it wasn't what I'd intended."

"Of course not. And how does she feel about your little getting-to-know-you scheme? As thrilled to be used as I am?"

"What? Isobel, I lied to you, and I'm sorry, but I *never* used you."

She ignored my assertion, picking up her wineglass and taking a generous sip. "So she's not happy about it either. Is that why she left?"

"What?" Now I was just confused. "Melody and I never..."

"I'm not talking about sex. But you lied to her, and used her, and I bet you haven't heard from her since she found out." For some reason, Isobel sounded even more upset about this than my breakup with her.

"Okay, just wait a minute." I furrowed my brow again. "I never used Melody, my relationship to her was always completely above board and my lies were lies of omission. And yes, she was hurt, and yes, I should have told her earlier, but I did not *use* anyone—not you, not Melody.

Furthermore," I said, the words spilling out now of their own accord, "what do *you* care? *You* let—no, *encouraged* me to believe things about her that weren't true at all. That were quite the opposite of what you implied."

"Because it was about a goddamned *private* relationship that you *insisted* on picking at, bit by bit, never mind the fact that I might be *sensitive* about it," Isobel seethed, leaning forwards over the table. "So excuse me if I misled you for the sake of not opening old wounds—I wasn't aware I was supposed to *bleed* for you!"

"Okay, if you want to write an autobiography and pick and choose what to show the world, that's fine," I said. "Good for you; that's what everyone does up to a point. If, on the other hand, you're going to cover up the most formative experience of your life and pretend it never happened, pretend it didn't leave a mark, then I don't know how you expected me to write with your voice. Say what you like about my lies, but *you* drove me to find Melody, to get *her* to help me get into your skin, because you were giving me *nothing*. Do you think that draft that's sitting right with my editor now came out of *your* interviews? The facts, sure, but the heart? The voice? *Melody* wrote as much of that book as you did, and you know what, for all her sham marriage she's a damn sight more honest than you are. At least she admits who she really is to *herself*."

I should've seen it coming. With a strangled curse, Isobel stood, upending her chair. She grabbed her wineglass and sloshed the contents straight into my face. The diners around us gasped; what had been surreptitious glances and eavesdropping turned into unabashed staring.

I think I must have frozen, mouth hanging open, for several seconds, because when I closed my lips tightly, they were already damp with the wine. I blinked. Liquid dripped from my eyebrows and eyelashes, and I could feel it trickling across my scalp from my hair. *So much for no drama.*

I stood slowly, and moved away from the table, stepping towards her. I came to a stop so close to her that she flinched, and I think she thought I was going to kiss her, perhaps as some malevolent public "outing."

I didn't, obviously, but I did speak, so quietly that I'm sure Isobel herself could barely hear me, never mind any of the onlookers. "If you want to hide who you are from the public, that's your choice. And I understand it, I do. I also think that it's slowly eroding you, and soon artifice and paranoia will be all that's left. I wish I could have known you before you let your self-imposed secrets ruin you. I'm sorry for what I did. I don't want to see you again. I'll have our agents liaise on our behalf if necessary from here on out."

"Get the hell away from me," she hissed, jerking away from me in what might've been distaste for me or the fact that I was dripping wine all over the floor. "We're done here." And with that, she stalked out, looking for all the world the same as Laura had on her dramatic flounce out of the restaurant months ago.

MY EYES STUNG now, although not from tears as they had the last time I'd been walked out on. I covered the drinks bill and found myself taking the long way home, the wine chilling my clothes, hair, and skin in the cold air so that by the time I arrived home my teeth were chattering, and huddled over a fan heater in my slow-to-warm flat, duvet around my shoulders.

This, of course, made the flat smell like stale wine, a fact which distracted me far less than the busy thoughts running through my head. I wasn't surprised with Isobel's reaction—for all her far-fetched accusations and overreactions I knew she would be upset with my feelings for Melody, especially because now I was convinced she still shared them. I *was* surprised that she had apparently already known I had been in contact with Melody, but for a person as well-connected and influential as her I suppose finding out information like that would have been child's play.

I picked up the phone, knowing that the exact last thing I should do right about now was be alone. I hesitated over Mary's speed-dial before instead choosing Julie's.

"Hey, love, are you finally ready to hang out again? Got your draft finished?"

"Jules, are you free. Now?"

Whatever it was in my voice that Julie heard, it certainly got the message across. "I'll be over in twenty. Sit tight."

I didn't sit tight, instead heading for a long, hot shower that lasted until the downstairs buzzer went. My hair and skin still damp, I hastily pulled on pyjamas as Jules grumbled her way up the three floors to my flat, and although she knocked her sense of urgency was obviously such that she didn't wait for me to answer, because as I entered the hallway I could hear her keys in the door.

We met in the doorway, Julie scanning me worriedly before reaching out to give me an awkward, one-armed hug. "You okay, love?"

I actually let out a bark of a laugh at this. "Not really. I fucked up really badly, Jules."

"C'mon, let's go sit down and you can tell me about it. I brought chocolate digestives, and you know there are no problems those can't fix."

I smiled weakly and let her lead me into the lounge. There was still the lingering smell of wine in the air, and if I hadn't felt so awful, I probably would've laughed again at Julie's stricken expression.

"Oh Nic, you didn't..."

I shook my head. "It was thrown over me."

"*Jesus*. Isobel?"

And now I nodded. "Yeah. Isobel. There are a few things I should probably tell you."

"AND THEN SHE threw her wine at me and stormed out. And I walked home, half-froze, and then...well. As you see." I sat back with a sigh. "Fucked."

Julie let out a low whistle, sitting back on the couch and regarding me with the same expression I've seen her make at one of the horrible reality TV train wrecks she loves to watch.

"Wow. No kidding. I mean, no offence, but...wow."

"Yeah. I know. So what the hell do I do?"

"God, don't ask *me*... This is way out of my league!"

"Well, you're *no* use..."

"Oh, sweetie, I'm sorry..." Julie sighed, shaking her head. "I...don't know. What do you want to happen? Do you want to reconcile with Melody? Isobel?"

"I'm in *love* with Melody. And the worst thing is that she wanted us to give things a shot—a proper shot—after the book was done. And I ran a mile."

"Well, maybe you need to run a mile in the opposite direction and get down on your knees and beg her to take you back."

"I've tried," I said, then lifted the mug of tea Julie had made me to my lips. "She won't answer her phone. She doesn't call back."

"Okay, well... I don't know, then. Be patient?"

I sighed, slumping back on the couch. "I suppose. I mean, I'm not going anywhere, am I?"

"I hope not. Some of us would miss you," she said, smiling and prodding my knee with her foot.

"Mm."

Julie stayed late that night—fell asleep on the couch, actually. Though I couldn't sleep myself, it was comforting to have somebody else there, even if it wasn't the someone I wanted.

Chapter Thirty-Five

SOMEHOW, I DIDN'T go off the rails. Well. I didn't fall off the wagon, which is basically my baseline measure of success in life. I went through the days in a daze, glad that, at least, the really creative, intense bit of my work was done for the foreseeable.

Julie kept tabs on me, as did Mary, checking in every day to make sure I was eating and *not* drinking. I appreciated it, in a numb sort of way. The only thing I did remember to do on a regular basis was call Melody's number. I didn't actually expect a response, which meant that the day that I got one I didn't know what to do.

It was a man's voice, as well, which was all the more disconcerting. "Hello?"

"I..." I stammered slightly. "I was hoping to speak to Melody Graham?"

"Ah, yes. Unfortunately, Melody's away at the moment—is it urgent?"

"No... it's all right. I'll call back."

"Oh, well, I'm not sure when she'll be back. Is there a message I could pass along perhaps?"

"Um...actually," I said, then cleared my throat. "Just tell her that Nic called." If I was trying to do this properly, then I had to be upfront with Harry (as I assumed this was), too.

"All right, I wi—wait, Nic? Nicola Booth?"

I swallowed. "That's...right."

"The infamous Nicola Booth," he said, and I could hear the sound of leather giving as he, I assumed, got comfortable in a chair. "I don't know whether to congratulate you on your moxie or berate you for your nerve."

"Mr. Whittaker..." I was *sure* it was him, now—I recognized his voice. "I've been an idiot. I'm trying to fix it. All I want to do is talk to her."

"Well, as I said, Melody's not here right now. She left about a week ago, and I'm not sure when she'll be back."

"Does she have a mobile with her? Is she checking an email? Where did she go?" I'm knew the desperate note was coming through in my voice, but I had a feeling that could only be a good thing.

"I'm not in the habit of giving out Melody's schedule or personal information to just anyone, Ms. Booth. She's a very private person."

"Mr. Whittaker, *please*. I swear that I just want to talk to her, and then I'll leave you *both* alone, if that's what she wants. Please."

There was a long pause and then an equally long sigh. "She's gone up to Scotland, to research for her play. She doesn't have a mobile or her computer on her—she said she wanted to get away from everything."

"Where does she go?"

"On location, of course. She's at Glen Coe."

GLEN COE IS a nine-hour drive from my flat. I left the next morning at half-past four and arrived in the glen at lunchtime. Of course, I drove through to the village at the west side of the glen, since it seemed likely she would be staying there. Unfortunately, there was one inn in the village and several dozen chalets, cottages, and lodges for self-catering visitors—and she could be staying in any one of them.

I parked in a handy spot near the centre of the village and wandered towards one of the streets where almost every house offers bed and breakfast—for some reason, they're always all on the same street.

I didn't really have a plan—I'd spent almost nine hours in the car, and the best I could come up with was wandering around the village until I saw her, or she saw me. Which...wasn't the best plan, but hey, I got up at three in the morning to do this.

I went into a couple of bed and breakfasts, asking in a suitably innocent fashion whether my friend had checked in yet. Having no luck, I decided to take a different track.

Addressing the elderly woman behind her reception desk in one of the bigger guest houses, I asked, "Where's the best place to get lunch around here? Good food, but...quiet. Somewhere I would have peace to write?"

"Oh, you'll want the Clachaig Inn," she told me with a wide smile that showed off her dentures. "It's a bit further up the road, just a wee drive or a brisk walk for a fit lassie such as yourself. It gets a bit busy when the tourists come in, but it's quiet right about now, if that's what you want."

I thanked her and set off, determined that I wasn't leaving until, one way or another, I'd found Melody Graham and made her tell me to my face that she never wanted to see me again. Again.

The Clachaig Inn was a charming building set near the site of the massacre—which seemed like it should make it less charming, but it still managed to look quaint and cosy. Upon entering, I discovered that there were three different dining areas…, so I would have to look through all of them to check for Melody.

A nervous-looking young man approached me as soon as I entered the first dining area. "Are you here for some lunch?" he asked me in an accent that, I swear, was more English than mine.

I smiled, about to shake my head, but then I had a thought. "I'm actually having lunch with my friend, Melody—brown hair and eyes, so tall, rosy cheeks?"

"Oh, Ms. Graham? But…she said she didn't want to be disturbed." He sounded flustered. "Are you sure she's expecting you?"

"Mm, no, I don't think she is," I confessed. "But this is important."

"Well, um, okay. She's in the back, in the Bidean Room. Do you want me to show you, or…?"

"I can find it."

"Okay. Okay. Um…someone will be in to take your order soon."

"Thank you."

THE BIDEAN ROOM had a large back window that faced out onto the glen, and, on this particular day, it was completely flooded with cold, white light. The furniture was rustic but comfortable, but despite all this the room was nearly empty—except for a table next to the crackling fire, which was occupied by a familiar figure.

Melody was pale, but for two rosy spots of pink on her cheeks. She was wearing that same dark knit jumper she'd been wearing the first time we'd met, and that alone made my heart ache. Rather than wait for her to notice me—or worse, try to sneak up on her—I cleared my throat, and it sounded impossibly loud in the room.

Her head whipped up, and she squinted in the bright light from the window, obviously expecting one of the wait staff with another pot of tea. When she saw me instead, she let out a small noise of surprise and dropped the pen she had been holding.

"Nic?"

"I'm sorry. I had to see you." I laughed at the sheer level of cliché in my words.

"How did you find me here? I didn't tell anybody..."

"I got Harold on the phone." I took a couple of tentative steps towards her. After all, she hadn't just ordered me out—yet.

Melody frowned, pushing her seat back and standing up. She wrapped her arms around herself, looking small and unsure. "He never did know when to keep his mouth shut."

"I pushed, it's not his fault. Can we...talk?"

She looked like she was about to refuse, but at my pleading look sighed and relented. "Go ahead."

I practically trotted the rest of the way across the room to stand in front of her, fighting the urge to reach for her hands and pull them from their defensive position around her. I opened my mouth, but hesitated. Where the hell did I start? Eventually, I opted for a simple, "Tell me what I can do to make things right between us."

This earned me an incredulous laugh, though I was heartened to note it seemed directed more at the circumstances than solely at me. "I don't have an answer for you, Nic. I really don't."

"Do you still care about me?" Somehow it came out quietly desperate rather than the calm, rational-but-intense tone I'd been going for.

"Yes, of course, but—"

"Then I'm yours. Completely," I said quickly, sure somehow that I only had so much time before she'd heard enough. "No lies, no one else. If you'll have me."

Melody's expression was confused, though she didn't laugh in my face as I had been dreading she might. "Nic, you have to understand... I appreciate the gesture, but there's more to this than can just be pardoned by bold statements and promises."

"Then, please, tell me what it is you need," I said, fighting the urge to move closer, already fearful that I was invading her space—which of course I was just by being in the country. "What do you need to believe that what happened...that wasn't me? That's not what I do."

"I...don't know." She sighed, biting her lip as she considered what to say next. "Time, I guess. And consistency."

I nodded slowly, although my stomach twisted a little at how unsure she sounded that even that would change her stance. "I can do that."

Something else she'd just said floated back to the surface in my head and I added, "And Melody, this isn't a gesture. I'm in love with you."

"What?" That shocked expression from when she had first seen me appear was back again.

"I love you." It was easy to say now, almost a pleasure, even knowing that there was a very good chance it would all be in vain. "It took me a while to realize because I'm an *idiot*, and you have every reason to run a mile right now just like I did with you, and I fully expect you to, but there it is."

"Nic, you...are insane," Melody told me, but I didn't mind because I saw the slightest hint of a smile tugging at the corners of her lips. "How can you possibly...?"

"Because I am." I shrugged. "I don't know; I've never done this before."

"I don't think I've ever done *this* before, either," she said disbelievingly, shaking her head.

I wasn't sure what she meant by "this" and so I just stuck to my assurances, my apologies, hoping despite knowing otherwise that maybe simple repetition would make a difference. "Melody, I am so, so sorry. For everything. But you have to believe I will do whatever it takes to fix it if I can."

She gave me a long look, and all I could think about was how beautiful she was, and how stupid I had been not to realize everything so much sooner, and how, if she would give me the chance, I would make it up to her a thousand times over. Then she cleared her throat, jarring me out of my reverie. "You could start by finding a place to stay up here for a few days," she suggested carefully. "There are plenty of nice B & Bs, and it's not high season yet."

I smiled. "I think I can do that."

Chapter Thirty-Six

WE DIDN'T HAVE lunch together, in the end. The young English waiter was slightly confused to enter the Bidean Room and find me already on my way past him out of the door. I walked back into the village and got a room from the nice old lady with the dentures. I knew there would be a delicate balance to walk now—Melody had obviously come up here to get away from things, and smothering her with desperate attention would only put her off me. On the other hand, I *had* driven all the way here for her, and I'd be damned if I'd let this opportunity go to waste.

We agreed to meet for dinner, which gave me plenty of time beforehand to wander around the tiny town and to stop into the one local convenience store to pick up some of the things I had forgotten in my early-morning haste: a hairbrush, toothpaste, socks. Then I took the opportunity to go for a very long walk through the glen, deeply regretting after a couple of hours not bringing my proper hiking boots instead of just some stout comfortable lace-ups.

BY THE TIME I'd returned to my room (which was a little overly lacy for my tastes, but comfortable enough) and had a shower it was nearly six o'clock. I got dressed and headed back up the road to the Clachaig Inn, which seemed to be one of the only places to eat in the village, never mind the best, hoping to show my keenness by getting there early.

Naturally, Melody was already there, in the same room at the same table for two in point of fact, although there were now a few other people scattered around the room. She had changed, too, into a long suede skirt and another of her chunky knit sweaters, though this one was a rich hunter green that complimented her hazel eyes. She stood up as I approached, looking nervous but also a little anticipatory, and reached out to clasp my hand in hers briefly.

"Nic. Good evening."

I couldn't help smirking at this formality, but I nodded in return. "Good to see you," I said, sounding, I'm sure, far more intense than was entirely appropriate but damn it, it *was* good to see her, particularly when at one point I thought I never would again.

We settled down in our seats, and Melody took some time unfolding her napkin and smoothing it over her knees. "Did you have a good afternoon?" she asked at last.

"I went for a walk. It was nice. Cold and wet," I added. "But nice. You?"

"I usually spend the afternoon researching at the village hall," she told me. "Or speaking with the locals. They're very obliging."

"How's it coming?"

"It's...ah, well. I haven't been as focused as I'd like. It's coming, but slowly."

I nodded. Her lack of focus had to be due to me, although I wasn't sure whether that was good or bad. Probably both. "Have you come up with your personal story, yet? Or are you concentrating on the facts for now?"

Melody gave an amused chuckle, shaking her head slowly. "The only personal story I've been able to come up with might get me sued by Shakespeare. Young lovers separated by a family feud's been done before, I'm told."

I grinned. "Although if you make it obvious enough it becomes an *homage*, you know."

"Oh, so I'd only be a laughingstock instead of a plagiarist. That's reassuring."

"I'm sure critics would be falling over themselves to excuse you," I said, "but I'm not sure you'd like that any better."

"Not particularly. Oh well." She shrugged pragmatically. "I'm sure a story will come—I just need to keep digging."

"I'm sure you'll come up with something perfect."

"We'll see." The waiter must've been waiting for a pause in the conversation, as he approached then and took our orders, including drinks—sparkling water for us both, I noted with something approaching relief.

"You...don't drink at all, do you?" I asked eventually, cutting into the silence with what I realized must be a loaded question but something I'd been itching to comment on for some time.

"Not really, no. I mean, I've had the odd glass of champagne on New Year's, but other than that..." Melody shrugged. "It's never really appealed."

I nodded. I'd never been sure whether she abstained because she didn't drink, or because of me. After some thought I decided that the former option was better, even if the latter would have been touching.

"So how is your book coming?" she asked. Her segue was less than smooth, but I appreciated that it was probably difficult enough for her to ask at all without me giving her a hard time about raising the subject.

"Quickly," I said after some thought. "Still waiting on annotations from my editor but I'm working through with my own in the meantime. Usually I'd wait for him before starting the second pass, but..."

"That's good," she said, nodding. "I'm glad."

Theorizing that, actually, this was not a topic to avoid if we wanted to sort things out and clear the air, I nodded and went on. "The sad thing, I suppose, is that it's probably one of my best works, but I can't get it out of my sight quickly enough."

I could tell Melody wanted to press further, but perhaps this wasn't the right time, or she didn't feel close enough to do so just yet. Either way, she smiled and nodded, and before long our food arrived, which at least took care of what to do with our hands. Over dinner we chatted a bit more; she filled me in on interesting bits of trivia she had turned up in her reading about Glen Coe and we talked about possible angles she could use to find her "hook." It was nice—almost like old times, except that there was still something between us that hadn't been laid to rest yet.

WE FINISHED OUR dinner and moved to one of the lounges with our coffees. I was pleased that Melody didn't seem to want to be rid of me even yet, despite some of the silences between us being tense, rather than comfortable.

"I usually go for a walk in the glen in the morning," she told me, reaching up to comb a hand through her hair. "I wouldn't mind company, if you'd like to join me."

"I...would love to," I said, trying not to sound too delighted.

"All right. Good."

And so it went. We finished our coffee and walked back down the street until we had to go our separate ways, parting with an awkward hug and a promise to meet the next morning for our walk.

That day passed much the same as the first one—with long, somewhat pregnant pauses and a sense of longing for normalcy from the both of us. After our walk, we lunched together at the Inn, and then Melody invited me to the village hall where I met the gaggle of enthusiastic locals who it seemed had been utterly charmed by her and were eager to show her old documents, historical research, and other things from their archives that she might find useful. I didn't really know what to do with myself, but eventually found myself getting drawn into conversation with one of the grey-haired men who regaled me with recitations of various poems about the area and the event. Eventually we went to dinner again, spending time discussing our findings and trying to tease out a thread of a story for her to follow. That night when we walked back to our respective B & Bs, I reached for her hand, and to my joy, she didn't pull away.

"I'm...having a nice time," I began as we reached the first of our guest houses—mine as it happened.

"So am I," she said, turning to face me, our hands still linked. "I'm glad you came here."

"Can I...kiss you goodnight? On the cheek, I mean," I added hastily. It felt strange, meeting and parting with Melody without that little gesture of affection that she had always had.

She gave a shy smile, squeezing my hand. "Of course."

Relief washed over me, and I shuffled closer, leaning in to press my cheek to hers. I had every intention of taking my time about this. Intentions which went out the window as Melody turned her head, her lips brushing over mine. I actually started slightly—I really hadn't expected that—but it took me only moments to recover and return the kiss, tentatively, lips still closed.

Melody slid her hand up my arm, letting the kiss linger for a moment before pulling away. "Goodnight, Nic," she murmured.

My pulse was racing in my ears, a flush spreading across my face that had nothing to do with the cold. I nodded dumbly.

Chapter Thirty-Seven

A FEW MORE days passed like this. We'd already confessed so much and delved so deep that it felt strange to embark on this innocent courtship, and yet here we were, walking hand in hand through the village grinning like teenagers during by day; cosied up next to roaring fires at the Clachaig Inn by night. We shared pots of tea and ever more drawn out kisses before making our reluctant way back to where we were staying and parting for the night.

If I hadn't known before that I was in love with Melody, I'd certainly have figured it out by now. Kissing her left me weak at the knees, heart pounding, tingling from top to toe. I could tell she felt the same way, and that it wasn't her lack of attraction to me that had us making our way to separate beds.

Eventually, one evening, as we walked back to our beds, I cleared my throat and began, "So here's the thing," I said, squeezing her hand as I spoke. "That stuff we still haven't talked about? I think it's probably time we maybe talked about some of it."

Melody paused, then nodded, glancing up at the window to my bedroom, which was dark. "Yours or mine?"

I shrugged. "Whichever you'd prefer. Mine has a lot of...lace."

She laughed, tugging on my hand. "We'll go to mine, then. C'mon."

MELODY'S ROOM WAS almost as lacy as mine but she did have a kettle, and that meant we had another mug of tea each as we sat down, her on her bed, me in a chair.

Eventually Melody cleared her throat, straightening her back. "Well. How about that elephant in the room?"

I smiled tightly. "Yeah. I, um... I'm not sure what to say. I feel like you probably have questions. You know I'll tell you anything."

"I'm not sure I want to know... Well, certainly not everything," she said, shaking her head slowly. "And it isn't as if I can't, well, understand."

"That doesn't excuse it."

"Yes, but..." Melody's smile faltered slightly. "I don't know if there *is* an excuse. Or, I mean, if there needs to be one. It's not like...there was no reason you shouldn't have done exactly what you wanted."

I furrowed my brow. "Melody, I didn't know *what* I wanted. That was the problem. I was scared of...us. And I'd already let Isobel so far into my head, I suppose it didn't seem like..." I made a face. This wasn't coming out right.

"Nic, you hurt me. I'll admit that. But I know you're a good person, and I also know you didn't do it maliciously. Everybody does stupid things sometimes."

"Okay, yes, stupid. It was really, really stupid. And I really want you to believe that I do know that now. Hell, I knew it back when I finally told you." I hesitated, not sure whether I should go on or not. "I...we never...again. After that afternoon. The next time I saw her, I told her we were done."

"*You* told *her*?" Melody gave an incredulous laugh. "I bet she didn't like that very much."

"She threw a glass of wine over me and stormed out of the restaurant."

"She did? Oh God, Nic, I'm so sorry..."

I shook my head, waving a hand to dismiss her concerned expression. "It's fine. It was fine. Honestly, compared to how I felt when you left that café, it was nothing."

"I'm sorry I left you there—I did worry about you getting home all right," she said, frowning.

I shrugged. "I called a taxi." I breathed in through my nose. Dare I go on? "You were right, by the way. She did know that we'd been spending time together."

Melody flinched, though she quickly shook it off, taking a long sip of her tea before speaking. "That's...charming."

"I think she was as angry at me for lying to you as she was about anything else," I said. "It was...intense. She accused me of using you. And her."

"I'm sure she thinks you were, in some way. Isobel...tends to have a very skewed view of relationships. They're as much about control as any kind of feelings that might exist."

"I know." I knew all right. I'd been inside her head, after all. "I should never have done what I did. It was always supposed to be...casual. Simple. Part of me knew it had to be anything but, under the circumstances." I had that sinking feeling again. Surely we were kidding ourselves that we could get past this? How could Melody possibly forgive me, even as a friend? "I'm such an idiot."

"At least you didn't fall in love with her," Melody said, a self-deprecating twist in her tone. "That takes true idiocy. What you did... You were afraid. And people do stupid things when they're afraid. Run the wrong way. Hide away for years. *I understand*, Nic."

I nodded, feeling a blush begin to spread across my ears in my shame, and in embarrassment at just how understanding she was being. Eventually, I spoke again. "But can you forgive me?"

At this Melody smiled, setting down her mug and patting the bed next to her. She didn't speak until I had moved to sit next to her and she had turned to look me in the eye. "If I couldn't forgive you I wouldn't have asked you to stay. And if I hadn't forgiven you I wouldn't have asked you to come up here with me."

Okay, so now really wasn't a time to burst into tears. Of all the occasions on which I'd nearly done so in the past few weeks, in theory now should be at the bottom of the list. But right then, that's exactly what I did. Melody leaned forwards immediately, gathering me into her arms, and a small part of my brain reminded me that this was the closest we had ever been.

I cried quietly for a respectable period of time. Melody ran her hands over my back, whispering quietly to me various platitudes—I don't even remember what she said—until I indicated that I was done, pulling back, wiping my face with my sleeve in a thoroughly undignified fashion.

"Sorry about that," I muttered. "Y'know," I added with a wry smile, "that was one of the good things about drinking. It was always easy to let stuff out with a good cry. It's a lot harder when you're always sober and never have that excuse."

Melody gave an appropriately sympathetic smile. Her hand was still resting on my back and I must've looked stricken when she went to remove it because she leaned into place a kiss on each of my damp cheeks and then brushed my hair away from my face. "Why don't you stay here tonight?"

Now of course I felt like an emotional blackmailer, "I'm really okay," I said, reaching for one of her hands, my primary concern still moving at the right pace even as most of me was dancing in circles, trying to say "yes."

"I'm glad you are—but I'd still like you to stay. I have an extra pair of pyjamas," she added, knitting her fingers with mine.

To this I could only manage a watery smile, and a nod, mainly because effusive joy would look strange right after a crying jag. "Okay."

It should've felt weird, sharing a bathroom, getting dressed in a pair of Melody's worn, flannel pyjamas, turning out the light and sliding into bed with her. Instead, it felt like the most natural thing in the world.

It only occurred to me *after* I'd shifted closer and slipped an arm around her waist that it was a somewhat presumptuous thing to do, but she simply gave a soft sigh and settled against me, her eyes fluttering shut in the dim light of the room. I dipped my head to kiss her shoulder, then craned my neck to touch my lips to her cheek before settling back on my own pillow and letting my own (still slightly swollen) eyes close.

"Mm, goodnight, Nic. I'm glad you're here," came the sleepy murmur.

I whispered a "me too" before reaching to turn off the light, musing that whatever I'd hoped might happened when I last-ditch chased up north after Melody Graham, this had barely made it into my wildest dreams.

Chapter Thirty-Eight

I SUPPOSE IT was a product of the fact that I'd already been in an unfamiliar bed for a few nights that I didn't feel that temporary sense of disorientation one gets sometimes when I slipped into consciousness the next morning. The curtains on the window were fairly thin, letting in plenty of white morning light, and I surmised that it was probably quite early. Not so early, however, that I didn't feel the immediate need to get up and visit the loo, and it was as I shifted that it occurred to me that the warm, soft thing wrapped around me was in fact not attached. With a slight whimper in her sleep, Melody tightened her embrace, and it was something of an effort to extricate myself without waking her.

Apparently, I wasn't as stealthy as I had thought, since when I slipped back into bed I was greeted by a warm embrace as Melody immediately snuggled up to me, her eyes opened ever so slightly. "Morning," she purred, her voice husky with sleep.

All those sensations that I'd been too tired and emotional to feel the previous night came crashing down on me now, and I actually had to stifle a slight moan. It was unclear whether Melody was aware she was causing this reaction in me as she slid her hand around my waist, her palm brushing a sliver of bare skin that had been exposed when my nightshirt rode up as I slipped back under the duvet. She nuzzled my neck, then laid a trail of slow kisses down to my collarbone.

I squirmed, but pulled back, just slightly. "Melody, I…"

"Shh," she said, slipping her hand around to press against my lower back.

After another moment's hesitation, I had little choice but to assume that Melody knew what she was doing—largely because I was completely powerless to resist—so I wrapped my arms around her in return, leaning in for a kiss. She returned it eagerly, nudging a leg between mine as her fingers continued to curl against my back.

My breath caught in my throat, a delicious tingle rolling up my spine.

Could it have been only a few days ago that I thought I might never see Melody again? It seemed impossible now, as I began my tentative exploration of her smooth, warm skin, as she parted her lips against mine and I felt her tongue graze my teeth, as her thigh pressed just closer, shifted a little more insistently.

As I insinuated my hands beneath her pyjama bottoms to cup her shapely rear, Melody...*wriggled*. There's no other word for it. Then she gave a sound that was halfway between a moan and a giggle and pulled back to grin at me, eyes sparkling, still so close our noses were touching and her face was all blurry. Though it had thrown me off my stride I found that I didn't care, laughter bubbling up in my throat, and our little room filled with the sounds of chuckling...and then a long moan moments later when Melody caught my earlobe between her teeth, in a split second sending me right back to aroused.

It couldn't have been less like sex with Isobel. Instead of glittering gowns and decadent hotel suites to roll around in, there were flannel pyjamas and lacy curtains in the window. Instead of the thrill of doing something wrong there was the overwhelming feeling of *rightness* about it. Melody was gentle without being timid, attentive but receptive. At no point did I feel as though I was part of a sex scene in a film, it was always just her, and me, reaching under clothing, fumbling with buttons, giggling at the little awkwardnesses that occur on your first time with a new lover.

Melody liked to laugh, I'd discovered early on. When her hair got in her mouth as we kissed. When I went to catch her nipple in my lips and missed, instead getting a mouthful of material. When all four of our collective legs got tangled in our pyjama bottoms and we almost went tumbling off the bed. But for every moment of hilarity there would be something that would knock the breath out of me all over again—a touch, a sound, even just a *look* that would set me trembling once more.

Melody liked to talk, too. Not *sexy* talk, or not "dirty" anyway—no elaborate fantasies or imaginative profanities. She told me how things felt. She told me how she wanted to be touched. She asked *me* what I wanted, what was working, and at first it was just as disorienting as the hilarity, but as with her easy laughter, you got used to it, and soon enough I discovered that honesty and openness could be every bit as sexy as feeling your way via the rather more approximate language of sighs and moans.

Later, feeling Melody writhe and shift against me there were no comparisons at all. Forget Isobel—forget everyone. There was nothing but Melody, her taste, her touch, the tiny gasps and moans she made in my ear and, in turn, the sound of my own helpless whimperings echoing around the sloping walls of the small bedroom, my arms wrapped tightly around her, face pressed into the crook of her neck.

"God, that was…the best wake-up call I've had in a long time," Melody murmured afterwards, grinning as she leaned in to kiss my cheek.

I shifted and groaned, tiny after-tremors still rippling through me as I moved. "I concur." I felt myself smile, and I turned my head to catch her lips with mine. "You're unbelievable," I added as we pulled apart.

Rather than reassure her, this seemed to take her aback somewhat, and she looked at me uncertainly. "This wasn't too fast, was it? You don't think we've rushed into it…"

"What, no!" I lifted a hand to stroke her hair back from her face, resting my palm against her still flushed cheek. "I mean… I don't know," I confessed. "Does it feel that way to you?"

"I don't think so," she said, shaking her head slowly. "It felt—it *feels* right."

Relief washed through me. "Me, too. I mean, to me as well." I leaned to touch my forehead to hers briefly.

"Oh good," she breathed. "Because I'd really like to do that again with you. Not immediately," she rushed to add. "But you know."

"I'm glad. And either way is fine for me," I said in a slightly teasing tone, my fingers trailing gently down her bare side. Melody squirmed and giggled girlishly, trying to capture my hands with her own.

"Breakfast is only served till half eight…"

"Do they do mushrooms here?"

"*And* the best grilled tomatoes you'll ever have."

"Fine, *fine*…" I groaned, rolling over to check the clock. By the time I had realized it was only half seven an arm had slid around my waist from behind and a pair of lips pressed against my bare shoulder. "Heeey…" I smirked, turning to look back over my shoulder. "I'm getting some mixed signals here…"

"Maybe I changed my mind!"

My smile widened and I shifted back round, snaking my hand around Melody. "I suppose that's your prerogative," I said, although there was no reluctance in my tone.

"Besides," she said, her wide smile mirroring my own, "to truly appreciate those tomatoes we need to work up a proper appetite."

NEEDLESS TO SAY, we didn't make it down for breakfast, delicious tomatoes or not. Luckily the local shop sold a surprising array of oatcakes and cheeses and we managed to put together a decent enough picnic (along with several chocolate bars) for our walk in the glen.

The weather was damp and windy, and we both wrapped up warmly, me stopping by my own bed and breakfast (and apologizing profusely for giving its proprietor "a wee scare" by not showing up the previous evening) to get my things. Then we set out—Melody wanted to follow the river up towards the waterfalls near the small loch. Buoyed by the giddiness of our morning together I felt like I could climb a mountain, and I was looking forward to spending more time alone with her, even in the wind and drizzle.

We walked in silence, hand in hand on the gentler stretches but one behind the other when the path was steep or rocky. I sifted through the events of the past few days as we walked, our increasing comfort with one another. I tried to push back the occasional twinge, the little voice observing that although I had confessed my love to Melody, she hadn't done the same.

WE HEARD THE falls before we saw them, an increasingly loud roar that made Melody glance back at me and grin. The climb became steeper and we had to scramble a bit, pausing every so often to catch our breath before continuing on.

By the time we got to the top, the knees of my jeans and the palms of my gloves were soaked through, grass-stained and grubby. Melody was just as dirty, but she didn't seem to care. "Oh, Nic, just *look* at it..."

I grinned, turning to look at the view as instructed—and she was right: it was breathtaking.

"SO I WAS thinking that we could stay a few more days and then head back down south... I should have everything I need. Oh, we don't have to drive all the way back in one fell swoop—maybe we could take it slow, stop somewhere along the way..."

I grinned, not looking over at Melody for a long moment. When I did, she was still smiling expectantly at me. "I was just realizing that we both have our cars up here. I wonder if I could pay someone to drive mine back down."

"Oh! Well... I honestly don't know." Melody laughed, slicing off another piece of smoked cheddar and popping it in her mouth. "I was just envisioning some sort of incredibly truncated convoy."

"Hm. Well, I'm sure we'll work something out," I said, slipping an arm around her waist.

"Speaking of working things out...well, I suppose there are still a few things we need to discuss." She leaned against me briefly. "I don't want to bring down the mood, but...I suppose I just need to know. Harold and I...we live together."

My smile tightened. "Right. Well, I guess that makes sense," I said.

"Not in any—I mean, just as friends. We have our own rooms. Harold has his... well, flings, usually...over all the time. So that doesn't preclude..."

"All right." I swallowed the sudden lump in my throat. I'd managed to forget all about Harold, all about the sham relationship, the fact that Melody had been living with this man for the best part of two decades. "Whatever works," I added. I... Well, I couldn't say that I liked it. But whatever suited Melody, I would make it suit me.

"Well, I mean, that works for him. I...don't know if it works for me. And if it doesn't work for *you*..." Melody frowned. "I love Harold, but if I was honest with myself it's long past time that we got on with our own lives. Separately."

There it was again—that tiny spark of hope. I finally turned to look properly at her and I know I must have looked like, I don't know, a puppy watching his owners cook a joint and hoping against hope that it's for him.

"But I don't want you to think that I'm—that I'm expecting anything from *you*, just because I feel this way about my situation. I just think it would be better for everyone involved if we approached this... on honest ground."

"Melody…" I shook my head, stepping a little closer, winding my arms around her and lacing my fingers together at the small of her back. "I love you. You could stay living with Harold forever, you can move into my poky little flat tomorrow." I chuckled slightly at this because I knew from past conversations that Melody had at least two other abodes. "I wouldn't care. I just want to be with you."

I should take a moment to observe that this was the first time I had ever felt this way about anyone. Oh, not the "in love" part—I've been in love before. But my love affairs were always chaotic, destructive—passionate, sure, but usually broken before they started. With Melody, I just wanted… us. What we'd had these past few days together—walks hand-in-hand, tea by the fire, quiet dinners, gentle (and somewhat less gentle) lovemaking. That's a term I loathe by the way but it's appropriate in this instance. All in all, for once I hadn't only fallen in love—I'd fallen in love and it felt like it was *supposed* to work, not explode in my face.

Despite the picturesque nature of the glen and the absolutely breathtaking spectacle of the falls the most beautiful thing I saw that day had to be Melody's smile as my words sunk in. She leaned in then, kissing me with an intensity that, I'll admit, made me dizzy. In the best possible way. "I love you, Nic," she whispered as she pulled back, biting her lip as if trying to keep from smiling too widely.

My own grin could've split my face. "Well, good," I said in a mock-gruff tone. "I wasn't really loving my waterfall murder-suicide option *b* very much."

Melody laughed, and we kissed some more, and then we packed up and trundled back to the B & B for hot showers and other diversions.

Chapter Thirty-Nine

THE REST OF the holiday was...well, perfect, really. We spent all day, every day together now, Melody doing less and less research and spending more and more time just walking together, or eating, or in bed. I occasionally felt slightly guilty for keeping her from her work, but mostly I just felt blissfully happy. Up here, removed from the influence of Isobel and her mind games I found it hard to believe I had ever balked at becoming more involved with Melody. I just hoped that once we returned to London things would continue to be low-key and ideal.

Unfortunately, life just doesn't tend to work that way. The way things actually happened is that I got back to an inbox full of annoying logistic emails, and was immediately plunged into the final throes of getting my book finished. Luckily, Melody was busy herself, dealing with the ins and outs of her "separation" from Harold and the inevitable complications therein. We saw each other whenever possible, though, and she was always in good spirits, even when moving her massive book collection from the manor to her new domicile in Sonning.

I helped as much as I could but understandably it was something that she had chosen to do alone, for the most part—although she and Harold had not been romantically involved they had shared their lives for a very long time and it was still going to be a rather difficult time for them both.

There was, of course, the requisite awkward dinner when Harold insisted on meeting and "vetting" me; luckily for everyone involved he seemed to approve and by the end of the night had given us his blessing with no animosity whatsoever. In turn, of course, Julie and Melody met and, I think, were each somewhat confused by the other's significance to me although they at least seemed to agree that they saw no harm in one another. Meanwhile, a couple of silly film nights with just the two of us put paid to Julie's worries that Melody would replace her role in my life altogether. With Mary, things were different—it would have been strange, somehow, for her to formally "meet" Melody or have a meal with us or what-have-you, but they did meet in passing and I think on that short meeting Mary's tacit approval was cemented.

Weeks stretched out as I worked on integrating my editor's changes to my book—which, strangely enough, by now I was able to view as clinically as anything else I had ever worked on. It was a good biography, and would sell well, but by God was I looking forward to putting it behind me.

I only saw Isobel in the flesh one more time.

MELODY AND I didn't go out a lot, preferring to spend our time either at her place or mine, reading or writing or watching films or just pottering around the place with mugs of tea and good music playing on the sound system. We did try to make it out on the town about once a week, though; a drastic increase in Melody's socializing that she assured me she had been missing for some time. It was usually to a lecture series or play that interested one or both of us, but occasionally we would simply go out for a meal for no particular reason other than to enjoy our time together.

It was on one of these evenings that I was sitting opposite Melody tucking into a delicious mushroom risotto (I really like mushroom risotto) when I spotted an all-too-familiar figure entering the restaurant. I must've made a face, since Melody raised her eyebrows and turned around to see what I was reacting to. She spotted Isobel just as quickly and turned back to me, looking about as surprised as I felt.

"We can leave if you like," I murmured quietly, raising my eyebrows at her.

"No," she replied, shaking her head firmly. "It's a big restaurant. Besides, we were here first."

Smiling tightly at her, I glanced up again briefly and then back to her. "I'm not sure whether she's seen us," I said. "She's...huh. Well, how about that..." At Melody's quizzical look I explained. "She's meeting Laura Maguire."

"Strange," Melody remarked, watching my expression. "I thought they had a falling-out."

"They did. Interesting."

We continued with our meal, but I couldn't help glancing over periodically to watch the women at the table across the room. Isobel was dressed as glamorously as ever, and Laura had certainly gone to more trouble than she ever had with me.

I at first assumed that they must have resolved their differences due to their working conditions, but when I glanced over, I began to notice signs that their relationship might not be strictly professional—a glance here, a touch there. Laura hung on Isobel's every word and the older woman soaked it up; I could tell she was on good form tonight.

I said nothing to Melody on the topic until later that evening as we were leaving the restaurant. I was sure by this point that Isobel had noticed us also, although she was careful not to let me see her looking at us.

"She's very cute," Melody murmured, arm in arm with me as we passed through the lobby. "Laura, that is."

I smirked. "I suppose," I said reluctantly. "Not really my type." I gave her arm a squeeze.

"Well, perhaps she is Isobel's." Her voice sounded slightly wistful, though when I looked over she was smiling at me. "Mind you, if she's anywhere near as dramatic as she sounded a covert *anything* will be an interesting thing to attempt. I hope she knows what she's doing."

"I'm sure she thinks she does."

"Hm. Well, I guess we'll see, won't we?"

WE DIDN'T SEE Isobel again at that restaurant, and so it was a few months later that we found out exactly how she was expecting to remain covert—she wasn't.

I don't watch much live television, but the autobiography had literally just come out and was, I was told, going to be talked about at least in passing on a late-night review show on BBC2. I tuned in, interested to hear the book being discussed.

"And now for the news everyone's been talking about," the presenter said as a screen behind him showed footage of a paparazzi-strewn event. "Isobel Dewitt made a huge splash tonight at the launch party for her just-released autobiography, *Dewitt*. Guests were hoping to see the former starlet and *it* director and hear her read from her new book, but they heard—and saw—much more than that!"

I exchanged a confused glance with Melody as we saw Isobel—Laura Maguire on her arm—appear on screen, apparently on their way into the venue, before it cut to her at the podium in front of her guests.

"Guess that must've lasted, then," I murmured.

"Guess so," Melody replied, looking properly awake now. The programme went on to show clips of Isobel's speech, which told how excited she was to be sharing not only her past with fans and friends, but also her future—with Laura.

"No one was more surprised than me—or Laura—when we found that our working relationship had naturally developed into something more significant," she was saying now, the camera cutting excitedly between her face and that of the attractive redhead in the front row, her expression showing that she'd known this was coming, "and neither of us expected things to go quite as they did. But it's become clear to us both now that our relationship is going to long outlive our working partnership, and it's recently become important to me that I cease to be one of the silent, privileged minority, keeping my private life so private that I do a disservice to all the lesbian, gay, bisexual, and transgendered people who are publicly living their own lives with pride and dignity, without any of the security and staff that I'll have on hand to keep prying eyes and unkind words away. I've decided to stand up and be counted among them."

"Wow, she's laying it on with a *trowel*, isn't she?" I said with a chuckle as the crowd broke into applause—initially somewhat hesitant in their shellshock, but quickly growing in volume, particularly once Isobel had gestured Laura up onto the podium for a kiss. "No half-arsed sort-of outing for this one."

"Well, it will certainly be good for sales..." Melody frowned then and sat up straighter, turning to look at me. "You don't think she...in the book. She wouldn't have."

I frowned. "I did pass on copies of all my notes and recordings when I was asked—it was in my contract, in point of fact. But no, I really don't. She was adamant that under no circumstances could anything about you two go into the book, specifically because of you and Harry. Oh, plus there have been advance copy reviews now," I said. "If they'd done a guerrilla edit after I passed off my final then the reviewers would've had something to say about it."

This seemed to reassure her. She nodded, sinking back into the couch with a sigh. "Good. Not that I'm not happy to have it known I'm gay," she said, shaking her head. "Just that I don't think I could deal with the media if it came out that Isobel and I were once involved."

I slipped my arm around her and turned to nuzzle her neck. "I don't think either of us will have to worry about Isobel getting under our skin ever again."

About the Author

MK Hardy is the pen name for two geeky women living and writing together in Scotland. They've been writing partners since 2005 and life partners since 2008. When they're not typing frantically at one another they like to walk the dogs, cuddle the cats, drink cocktails and play board games.

Facebook: https://www.facebook.com/mkhardywrites/

Twitter: https://twitter.com/mkhardywrites

Also Available from NineStar Press

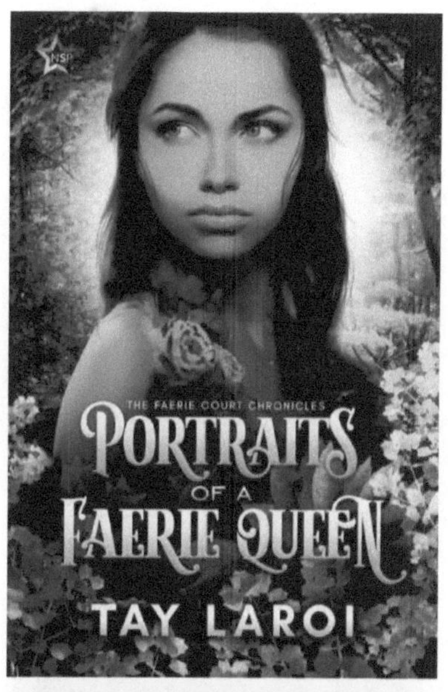

www.ninestarpress.com

www.ingramcontent.com/pod-product-compliance
Lightning Source LLC
Chambersburg PA
CBHW060544190726